"I'll give him riding lessons…"

Katie's eyes widened with surprise. "What?"

She wasn't the only one; Jake was surprised he'd offered to teach her son to ride a horse, as well.

"He's desperate to learn," he said. "So I'll give him lessons."

She shook her head. "No, you're too busy. I can't ask you to take time away from the ranch."

"You're not asking," he pointed out. And he doubted that she would have. "I'm offering."

She narrowed those pretty green eyes and stared up at him. "Why?"

He couldn't answer her; he really had no idea why he wanted to teach Caleb. Maybe it was the way the kid had asked him…with those puppy dog eyes.

Maybe it was just that Jake had missed the boy these past few days, as he'd been avoiding Caleb and his mother. He'd missed that laughter…

And he appreciated what the boy's presence had done for his nephews, how he was helping them heal. And maybe, somehow, Caleb was helping Jake heal, too…

Dear Reader,

I am so excited to be writing for the Harlequin Heartwarming line with a new series of my own: Bachelor Cowboys. *A Rancher's Promise* is the first of a four-book series that will introduce you to Ranch Haven in Wiilow Creek, Wyoming, and to the Haven family.

The Haven family has had more than their share of tragedies, but the latest one has claimed the life of one of the brothers, and his wife's as well, leaving their three little boys orphaned.

The first hero of the series, Big Jake Haven, has no problem stepping up and taking responsibility for the boys, but he's also running the ranch solo now, since his late brother was his foreman and his best friend. While he's reeling from his recent losses, he has to deal with the reappearance of his first and only love, widow Katie O'Brien-Morris, and her little boy.

Sadie Haven is the family matriarch and Jake's grandmother, and she believes that the Haven men need some good fortune and good women in their lives. She's not going to give up her matchmaking manipulations until all her family are happy.

I'm the youngest of seven siblings, so I have a big family of my own and I love writing about family dynamics and relationships. Sadie and her grandsons and great-grandsons have stolen my heart, and I hope they will steal yours, too!

Happy reading!

Lisa Childs

HEARTWARMING

A Rancher's Promise

———

Lisa Childs

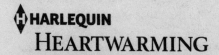

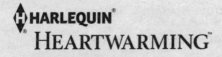

HARLEQUIN®
HEARTWARMING™

ISBN-13: 978-1-335-42656-7

A Rancher's Promise

Recycling programs
for this product may
not exist in your area.

This edition published by arrangement with Harlequin Books S.A.

For questions and comments about the quality of this book, please contact us at CustomerService@Harlequin.com.

Harlequin Enterprises ULC
22 Adelaide St. West, 40th Floor
Toronto, Ontario M5H 4E3, Canada
www.Harlequin.com

Printed in U.S.A.

Ever since **Lisa Childs** read her first romance novel (a Harlequin story, of course) at age eleven, all she wanted was to be a romance writer. With over seventy novels published with Harlequin, Lisa is living her dream. She is an award-winning, bestselling romance author. She loves to hear from readers, who can contact her on Facebook or through her website, lisachilds.com.

Books by Lisa Childs

Harlequin Romantic Suspense

Bachelor Bodyguards

His Christmas Assignment
Bodyguard Daddy
Bodyguard's Baby Surprise
Beauty and the Bodyguard
Nanny Bodyguard
Single Mom's Bodyguard
In the Bodyguard's Arms
Soldier Bodyguard
Guarding His Witness
Evidence of Attraction
Boyfriend Bodyguard
Close Quarters with the Bodyguard

Visit the Author Profile page
at Harlequin.com for more titles.

For my agent, Michelle Grajkowski, whose friendship I value and appreciate even more than her representation. Thank you, Michelle, for making sure I'm staying busy!

CHAPTER ONE

SHE CAME TO the funeral. While she hadn't spoken to him, he'd caught a glimpse of her at the back of the church—as he'd carried out his brother's casket. Her red hair had shimmered in the light streaming through the stained glass windows, and her green eyes had sparkled with a sheen of tears.

He wasn't surprised she'd shown up since it seemed like everyone in Willow Creek had attended the double funeral. Even his brother Dusty had briefly left the rodeo circuit to be here. But the rodeo star hadn't stayed. He'd cut out before the luncheon. Not that anyone had really expected him to stick around.

Was *she* staying?

Maybe. She'd already been back in town a year. But she'd been gone for eleven years before her return. In the year that she'd been back, Jake hadn't seen much of her. That hadn't exactly been an accident on his part, though.

And maybe not on hers either.

Things hadn't ended well between them. That was why he was surprised she'd shown, especially since Jake hadn't attended *his* funeral. Her husband's.

Because her parents lived in town, other people had known about his death, but Jake had always made it a point to tune out all news of Katie, like her engagement announcement and her wedding.

Jake hadn't even known she'd had a son until she returned to Willow Creek with him. With her son.

With *his* son.

The little boy looked exactly like the man Jake had seen Katie with that evening so long ago, but the child was probably only four or five, the same age as one of Jake's nephews.

Now orphans.

He needed to focus on them now. Not her.

He'd already spent too much of the past twelve years thinking about her.

Fingers snapped in front of his face. Since his grandmother's hands were arthritic from all the years she'd worked the family ranch, he was surprised she could still snap.

"What's the matter with you?" she asked, her voice strong and steady despite her age and her grief. She was steadfast despite all the tragedies she'd suffered in her eighty years of life.

He jumped up from his chair at an empty table and realized that the room had cleared out. Everyone had filed into the large community room at the church—with its white walls, tall windows and thin commercial carpeting—after the funeral. Except for Dusty, who'd left after he'd helped carry his twin's casket out of the church. How much time had passed since then?

He blinked and peered around, feeling like he was just waking from a dream. Or a nightmare.

This was definitely a nightmare: burying his younger brother, who was also his business partner at the ranch, as well as his lovely sister-in-law. Sweet Jenny. At least they were together, just as they had always been.

He needed to focus on their children now. He needed to be like his grandmother: strong and steady. For them.

Now, panic gripping him, he frantically scanned the empty room. "Where are they?" He was already failing as their guardian—since he didn't even know where they were.

"Everyone's gone," she said.

"The boys," he said, as his panic turned to fear. "Where are the boys? Who took them?"

He was the oldest—besides his grandmother—so he was the most responsible for them. Or he should have been.

Dale and Jenny had trusted him.

"Ben and Baker took them back to the ranch," she said.

Ben was the second oldest, but even though he was the mayor of Willow Creek, he wasn't as responsible as Jake was. And Baker was the baby.

Baker was also twenty-eight and a firefighter, though. His nephews were safe. They were fine. Or they would be if Jake could figure out how to help them.

First he had to figure out how to help himself. Losing Dale was more than losing his brother; it was like losing his right arm. And Jake was right-handed.

"I don't know what's wrong with me, Grandma," he admitted. "I know I need to get it together for the boys. For Miller and Ian and—" his voice cracked as emotion choked him "—Little Jake…"

The baby was named after him. After *Big* Jake.

His grandfather had always been Big Jake,

but he'd died twelve years ago. With his big, broad body and his big, boisterous laugh, Big Jake had always been larger than life, like the widow-maker heart attack that had claimed his life.

Jake hadn't become Big Jake then, not until Little Jake had been born a little over two years ago. But Jake didn't feel so big right now as burdens weighed down on him, bowing his shoulders. He hadn't been this devastated since he'd lost *Katie*.

KATIE SHOULDN'T HAVE gone to the funeral. It had been a mistake. A big one.

And not just for her but for her son too.

"Caleb, are you okay?" Katie O'Brien-Morris asked her little boy, her heart aching for his loss. A year had passed since his father's funeral, but she was worried that attending the funeral today had brought back that nightmare for him just as it had for her.

He tipped his chin back and peered at her through a lock of blond hair hanging over his eyes. And a twinge of pain struck her heart. He looked so much like Matt—so much so that his paternal grandparents had said they couldn't see him anymore because he was too painful a reminder of the beloved son they'd lost.

And so Katie had moved away from Chicago, back home to Willow Creek, Wyoming, even though it was the last place she'd wanted to be. But her parents would never leave the small town where they'd grown up and where they'd married and raised her in this pale blue Victorian on Main Street. She'd wanted her son to have more family in his life than just her, so she'd forced herself to return.

Even though she'd been back a year, she was still living with her parents. She hadn't been able to bring herself to buy or even rent a house. A house seemed too much for just her and Caleb, and too much maintenance for her to handle alone while running her accounting business. Back home in Chicago, Matt had handled all the household chores.

She and Caleb sat at the small table in the breakfast nook of the kitchen, with the only sound being the murmur of her parents' voices from the living room.

Her son had yet to answer her.

"Caleb?" she asked, with even more concern and self-recrimination that she'd brought him to the funeral.

"How come Jake doesn't talk?"

Katie gasped with shock that her son even knew the man's name. "What— Why do you ask that?" How did Caleb know about Jake Haven? What had he heard?

Did he know about *them*? Because Willow Creek was a small town, there wasn't ever much going on, so people tended to gossip about the past.

Caleb's little brow furrowed beneath that lock of blond hair. "Because he doesn't talk anymore," he said, as if she was stupid for not understanding his question.

She hadn't seen Jake speak to anyone at the funeral. Not that she'd been watching him or anything...

But anytime she had inadvertently glanced his way, the dark-haired cowboy had been sitting alone and silent. With all the mourners—the entire town turned out for the funeral—no one had approached him.

She certainly hadn't. But why had no one else? Because they'd known they would be met with silence?

How did her son know that?

"When...when did you meet Jake?" she asked. She couldn't imagine where their paths might have crossed before, and during the funeral, she'd been so worried about bringing up sad memories for Caleb that she hadn't let him out of her sight.

Caleb seemed unconcerned about the past. All his concern was for Jake. "I've known him for a while."

Jake hadn't reached out to her since she'd come back, not even to offer condolences, so she wasn't thrilled that he'd talked to her son without her knowledge. Her voice a little sharper, she asked, "Where did you meet Jake?"

"At school," he replied.

"He was at school?"

"He's not going to school yet. He just came with his mom once to drop off something for Ian."

She furrowed her brow now, with confusion. Jake's mom had been gone a long time. Not dead. Just gone...

"Jake?" she asked again. "What Jake are you talking about?"

"Jake Haven," he said with a weary sigh. Apparently he was growing tired of this conversation. But he continued, "He used to talk all the time when his mom would bring him into the classroom. Well, not really talk but like blabber and blow bubbles and stuff, but he was totally quiet in church. Like totally quiet."

The baby.

She felt a flash of guilt that she'd forgotten

the baby had been named Jake, after his uncle Jake. Dale and Jenny had been close to Dale's oldest brother and had talked about him often, too often for Katie, so she'd had to tune out some of those conversations. She would have listened raptly to them now if only that were possible. But they were gone, just like so many other people in Jake's life. She squelched the urge to pity him, knowing he would hate that.

"And Ian was acting weird," Caleb continued. "Like he kept repeating the same things over and over, kept asking me the same stuff over and over."

Ian was Caleb's age—five years old. He and Caleb were in the same kindergarten class…or they had been until the car accident had happened a couple weeks ago, just as the family had been setting off on a spring break road trip. Dale and Jenny had died instantly, while the boys had been in the hospital. All but the baby, Jake. He'd survived unscathed, or so she'd thought.

Apparently he'd stopped talking.

She knew about Ian, though. "His head got hurt in the car accident. He has what's called a concussion," she explained. "That's why he's having problems remembering things."

"He knew who I was," Caleb insisted.

"He remembers things that happened longer ago," she said. "But he forgets the things that just happened."

The oldest boy, Miller, was still in the hospital recovering from the surgeries to fix his broken bones. Katie's heart ached over the loss of Dale and Jenny and over all their poor children had endured. Even more than her son had.

Caleb must have come to the same realization because he murmured, "I guess it's even worse if you lose both your mom and dad, huh? I didn't quit talking or lose my memory when Daddy died. I just got really sad, like you did."

As she thought of how much they'd lost when Matt died, tears stung Katie's eyes. He'd been a loving, involved father, a super-supportive husband, her best friend...

Caleb's breath caught and he anxiously said, "Don't cry, Mommy. Please don't cry."

She quickly blinked away her tears and shook her head. "I'm not crying," she promised. "I'm just emotional because I'm so proud of you. I thought today might be hard for you, but you were so brave and so good." The tears threatened again, but she furiously fluttered her lashes and willed them away.

Just like his father, Caleb hated when she cried. Unfortunately she'd done too much of it over the past year. Not all the tears had been because of grief, though. Some had been because of guilt that Matt hadn't been her first and only love, like she'd been his.

That was why she'd avoided Jake Haven and why she wanted to go on avoiding Jake Haven for the rest of her life, which wasn't going to be easy now that she'd settled back in Willow Creek. Fortunately his family's ranch was far from town.

"Katie," her mother called out from the living room. "There's a vehicle pulling into the driveway."

"Must be for you," Katie called back. "I'm not expecting anyone."

"No, it's for you," her father chimed in with his deep voice.

She slid off the breakfast nook bench and headed through the archway toward the living room. "Why do you think that?" she asked.

"Because it's a vehicle from Ranch Haven."

No. It couldn't be him. It couldn't be.

He hadn't talked to her once since she'd returned to Willow Creek. He hadn't even called or sent a card to acknowledge Matt's death. Not that she'd expected anything from him. Not anymore. Not ever again.

But who else could it be?

The only other people from Ranch Haven with whom she'd had any contact had been buried today.

THIS HAS TO WORK. And not just for her sake but for his. Sadie Haven had seen her grandson suffer many tragedies in the past—too many for such a young man. Jake was only thirty-two. He'd just hit his teens when he'd lost his father—her son Michael—in a terrible ranch accident. At least Darlene, Michael's wife, hadn't died with him like Jenny had died with Dale. Yet Darlene was dead to her family all the same—because she'd walked out on her young sons right after their father's funeral. They'd managed just fine without her, but Sadie had been a younger woman back then. A stronger woman.

Then twelve years ago they had lost her beloved, Jake Sr., or Big Jake, as he'd been called. Her grandson was called that now—to differentiate him from his nephew, Little Jake.

Tears pooled in Sadie's eyes, but she blinked them away and focused on the bright purple door in front of her. She'd knocked a moment ago, after she'd climbed out of her truck, but nobody had answered it.

Vehicles were in the driveway of the pale

blue Victorian. Lights glowed through the leaded glass windows.

She raised her hand, curled her achy fingers into a fist and knocked again. This time the door opened, or maybe her fist had propelled it open because nobody stood in the doorway.

"Who are you?" a young voice asked.

She lowered her gaze to the little boy standing before her. "Oh," she murmured. "I didn't see you there." She'd only seen a couple pictures of his father. First the engagement photograph the O'Briens had run in the local paper and then later the wedding announcement, but it was clear the boy favored his father with his golden hair and bright blue eyes. "Aren't you a handsome young man!" Sadie exclaimed.

"Am I?" he asked with surprise.

She chuckled. "Oh, you'll know soon enough when you're beating off the girls with a stick."

"Mommy says I can't hit girls," he said.

"I said you shouldn't hit anyone," Katie corrected her son as she joined them at the door. She might have been standing behind it the whole time.

"But I only wanna hit girls," the little boy told his mother.

Katie's face flushed nearly as red as her hair. "Caleb," she said, the scolding evident in just the change in tone of her soft voice. She didn't need to say any more.

Just use that tone.

Just as Sadie always had.

She hadn't had to yell or threaten. Just use what the boys had termed her *scary* voice. Sadie chuckled.

Katie stepped back and pulled the door open wider. "I'm sorry to leave you standing on the porch," she said. "Please come in."

Good manners. The girl had always had them. But for just a moment she must have forgotten when she hadn't answered the first knock. Unless she'd been busy elsewhere in the house.

Sadie stepped inside now, joining Katie in the small foyer. She glanced around and realized that someone must have seen the truck pull up. Someone, or two people, must have been sitting in that front parlor that overlooked the drive. A cup of tea, steam rising yet from the surface, sat on a spindly end table next to a needlepoint project while a paper lay crumpled on the couch. If Katie's parents had been in the parlor, they must have left in a hurry, but she didn't see any sign of them now aside from the things they'd left behind.

Instead of being offended, Sadie smiled. She

wanted to have this conversation with Katie alone. But the little boy hadn't left. His mother's scolding had sent him a few steps back from her, but he peered around her, through his hair, at Sadie. He was curious about her.

"Never seen anyone as old as me?" she asked him.

He shook his head. "Mr. Lemmon is way older."

She chuckled with delight. Mr. Lemmon was the former mayor, now the deputy mayor, to her grandson Ben. "You're right. He is *way* older." Like three whole months. They'd gone to school together back when the entire K through 12 grades had been in one building. An old redbrick schoolhouse with a steeple and a bell.

Sadie emitted a soft sigh of wistfulness for the simplicity of the past. Not much had ever been simple about her life, not once she'd met Jake Haven and he'd lured her out of the comforts of town to his family ranch. Would she be able to do the same now? Would she be able to lure Katie out there?

Maybe it was better that she didn't have this conversation alone with the young woman. Maybe it was better that the little boy was present too.

Because she'd never met a child who hadn't fallen in love with the ranch—with the horses and the cattle and the barn cats and all that wide-open space to run and fight and holler. All the kids she knew loved it. Even Baker.

He claimed he didn't like it, but she knew that had nothing to do with the place and everything to do with the people. Not the people living there. The dead, and the ones who hadn't been able to stay.

Like Dusty.

But Dusty would come back. Ranch Haven was in his blood; he just needed to find that out for himself. He wasn't going to find what else he was looking for, though—what he'd left the funeral in such a hurry to find.

He wasn't going to because Sadie already had. She'd found everything her grandsons and great-grandsons needed. And she was going to make sure they got it—even if she had to do a little bit of manipulating here and there to ensure that everything worked out how she wanted it.

No.

How it was *meant* to work out.

CHAPTER TWO

KATIE'S FACE WAS HOT, still flushed with embarrassment—not over her son's innocent comments but over her own awkwardness. Something her parents obviously hadn't wanted to witness since they'd fled to other parts of the house, leaving her alone with the legendary Sadie Haven.

Even before she'd become a Haven, as a little girl, Sadie had become notorious for fistfighting boy bullies on the playground and criticizing lazy teachers. Stories about her antics had been retold over and over again. Growing up in Willow Creek, most people had believed Sadie Hawkins Day was named for her, but her maiden name was March. And that was what she'd done over every social injustice and every civil infraction she believed had been committed in town. That had started when her father was mayor and had continued through all the mayors since.

When Sadie had married Big Jake Haven, her legend had only grown—along with the family they'd started. She'd broken wild horses, killed dangerous wolves with her bare hands…

Katie had figured all those stories had been greatly exaggerated, until Jake had brought her out to the ranch that first time. Then she'd believed everything she'd ever heard about Sadie Haven.

Caleb's small hand nudged Katie forward, out of the foyer, toward the living room, where Sadie Haven stood tall yet despite her age. She had to be nearly six feet even without the heel of the black cowboy boots she wore with her long black dress. From old pictures at the ranch, Katie knew Sadie's hair had once been as black as her dress, as black as Jake's thick hair was beneath his cowboy hat. But Sadie's hair was pure white now. The older woman hadn't taken a seat as she waited for Katie.

Katie's face got even hotter with embarrassment over how completely she'd abandoned the manners her mother had ingrained in her. "I'm so sorry," she said. Again. "Please, sit down."

The woman glanced around at the antique Victorian furniture, as if gauging whether or not it would hold her weight. She shook her head. "I'm fine standing."

No. She was intimidating standing, especially to Katie, who was nearly a foot shorter than the older woman.

"Would you like something to drink?" she asked. "Tea? Coffee?" Whiskey straight. Her father probably had some hidden somewhere in the house. But she would wait until Sadie asked for it, just as she'd wait to ask why Sadie was here.

Why she'd come to her. Because Katie knew, without asking, that she wasn't going to like the answer.

"I'm fine," Sadie said again. "I don't have much time. I need to get back to the ranch."

"Of course," Katie said. "The boys…"

Those poor little boys had lost both parents so tragically. So unexpectedly—just like Matt had been taken from her and Caleb in a car accident. Tears stung her eyes again as she thought of the senseless tragedies.

Sadie nodded. "Yes, nearly all of my boys are at the ranch right now. Miller will be home tomorrow from the hospital. And Dusty, well, Dusty just left again."

A smile curved Katie's lips as she remembered the teenage boy who'd spouted his big dreams every time she'd seen him growing up. "He really did it. He joined the rodeo." From what she'd heard, he hadn't just joined it; he'd excelled at it, earning titles over and over.

"He'll be moving back to the ranch soon," Sadie said, as if she knew something nobody else did. She probably knew a lot of things that nobody else knew.

"That's good. I'm sure you'll need help with Dale and Jenny's boys." Jenny had told Katie that she'd struggled to keep up with the three of them. That was why she'd started falling behind on her job as ranch bookkeeper—a role she'd taken over after she and Dale had discovered the previous bookkeeper had been embezzling from Ranch Haven. Raising one boy was a lot of work for Katie; she couldn't imagine raising three. "That's why I'm here," Sadie said.

Katie furrowed her brow. "I don't understand…" She was an accountant, a certified public accountant, not a nanny. "I'd be happy to help, but I don't see how I would be of much use."

"Good," Sadie said—in a tone that suggested everything was settled.

"I… I don't understand," Katie murmured again. "I barely know the children."

"I've got help for the children," Sadie said. "I hired a teacher away from the school that will serve as a tutor to the older boys and as a nanny to Little Jake. I brought on a cook, since there's going to be too many people for me to feed. I'm not much of a cook anyhow. And a physical therapist will be arriving tomorrow with Miller to help him get back on his feet."

"That's great," Katie said. "It sounds like you have everything under control." Like always…

No matter what happened, Sadie Haven managed.

Jake wouldn't have had to quit college when his grandfather died. Sadie had told him not to quit school—she had officially forbidden him to do it. But he'd done it anyway. So maybe the legendary Sadie Haven didn't always have everything under control, at least not her oldest grandson.

"Jake," Sadie said.

Katie gasped; it was as if the woman had read her mind.

"Jake's the one who needs your help," Sadie said. "With the ranch."

A laugh sputtered out of Katie. Better that than the snort she'd nearly uttered, though. "Oh, no, Jake doesn't need my help." He'd taught her to ride—back in high school—but it hadn't come easily and it had never been pretty or painless.

Katie liked animals that were more like her—small and approachable. Not like the Haven family—big and intimidating.

"You were helping Dale and Jenny with the ranch," Sadie said.

"With the books," Katie said. "I just did their quarterly taxes while they handled the payroll and accounts payable and receivable." Many of the clients of her accounting business only had her file their taxes while they contended with the day-to-day bookkeeping records.

"Yes," Sadie said. "That's what you need to do for Jake. He doesn't know how."

She'd just filed the quarterly taxes for the ranch before the accident. "He's smart. I'm sure he could figure it out." She'd been two years behind him in school, and he had helped her with the subjects she'd struggled in. Jake had never struggled with anything. Not even with breaking up with her.

Sadie shook her head. "He doesn't have time—not with all the new calves. He's got to be with the stock. It's just been two weeks with Dale and Jenny gone and things are a mess. You have to come out *now*."

A pang of guilt struck Katie that she hadn't

thought about the void Dale and Jenny's passing left everywhere. She was still just coming to terms, a year later, with the gaping void Matt's passing had left.

"I forgot all about the books and the payroll..." she murmured. Since the accident, she'd been too upset over the sudden loss of the young couple who'd been her friends since high school to even think about who'd taken over the day-to-day record keeping for them. Helping out was the right thing to do. It was what Willow Creek always did, just like the entire town had turned out for the funeral.

They looked after each other.

Many of the townspeople—Dale and Jenny included—had even traveled to Chicago for Matt's funeral. And if they hadn't made it in person, they'd sent flowers and sympathy cards. Except for Jake...

He'd been silent.

Maybe he'd forgotten all about her. It had been twelve years, after all. Twelve years since that day beside the campus fountain when he'd told her he was quitting school and didn't want her to follow him back home like she'd followed him to college, that she'd been smothering him. She hadn't forgotten the heartbreak and humiliation, which was why she'd been avoiding him since she'd returned to Willow Creek. Why she'd always made Dale and Jenny bring the books to her, so she wouldn't bump into him at the ranch.

"So pack up your stuff, and I'll drive you out to the ranch," Sadie said.

Katie shook her head so vehemently that her hair fell across her eyes. She had to push it back to focus on Sadie. "I'll be able to do that work from my office." Which she'd closed for the day, as most of the town had closed down for the double funeral.

"No, you can't. The books are too much of a mess, made even worse by Jake trying to figure out Jenny and Dale's system."

Dale and Jenny had worked together on the books. But with their only knowledge coming from online accounting courses, they'd struggled to replace the former ranch accountant whom Sadie had forced to retire a few years ago or face prosecution for embezzlement.

"They did have an interesting system." It had taken Katie nearly a year to figure it out and fix it for them. Jake couldn't have undone all her work within two weeks.

"You can do your work for your other clients out of Dale and Jenny's office at the ranch," Sadie said. "And you and the boy can stay in the house. Your son will love it out there, with the horses and the rest of the stock."

"Horses?"

Katie whirled back around; she'd thought Caleb had grown bored of the adult conversation and had left them to play. He'd been so quiet, and unlike Little Jake Haven, Caleb was never silent. Another trait he shared with his father, who'd always been singing or sharing funny stories.

"Big horses? Or little ones?" Caleb asked the older woman. Clearly he'd stayed because she fascinated him for some reason. But then Sadie Haven fascinated everyone.

"There are some foals now," Sadie replied.

"Foals?"

"Young horses. We breed horses as well as cattle. There are a lot more calves, though, and some dogs and cats and goats running around the place too."

"Goats running around?" His blue eyes widened with shock.

She nodded. "You'll love it there, and the teacher that's teaching Ian can teach you too. In fact, I think she's your teacher right now— Miss Emily Trent. She's moving into the ranch today."

"Miss Trent is going to live there too?" Caleb asked.

Sadie nodded. "She's going to teach the older boys and take care of Little Jake."

"You hired Miss Trent away from the school?" Katie asked with alarm. Caleb was so attached to his teacher that it wouldn't be good for him to lose her. He'd already lost too much when they'd lost Matt and moved away from the only home he'd known, along with his preschool and his friends, in Chicago.

"I love Miss Trent," Caleb said softly.

Apparently Katie's little boy had developed his first crush on the beautiful blonde teacher. Losing her would hurt him, and Caleb had already endured too much pain.

"Couldn't she help your grandsons after school?" Katie asked. "And still remain at the public school?"

Sadie shook her head. "She can't drag Little Jake with her every day, and I haven't been able to persuade a nanny—even from one of those services—to move out to the ranch."

It was remote. Miles outside of town, with the house in the middle of the thousands of acres the ranch encompassed. There were other buildings. Several barns for the stock and houses for the employees.

"You're not going to persuade me either," Katie warned her. "I can do the books remotely."

Sadie shook her head. "It's going to take a while to sort out all the day-to-day and get caught up from the past couple of weeks. And your boy would love it. He'd get to live with his teacher and his friend." She turned toward Caleb. "You and Ian are friends, right?"

Caleb nodded. "Best friends. I miss him not being at school."

Katie knew they were close. He talked about Ian constantly, but she usually tried to tune it out because he always shared his friend's stories about the ranch. And she didn't want to hear about the ranch because it made her think of Jake. Guilt churned her stomach, making her feel sick about how often she'd thought of him over the past twelve years.

Too many times.

Matt had deserved better; he'd deserved *everything*.

And so did his son.

"Mommy, I wanna live at the ranch. I wanna live with Miss Trent and Ian."

"But Grandma and Grandpa O will miss you too much," she said.

He shook his head and lowered his voice to

a whisper. "Grandma O won't have to worry about me being loud or breaking her stuff anymore."

A pang struck Katie's heart. Moving here, staying with her parents, hadn't been as good for her son as she had hoped it would be. She should have moved out, found them a place of their own, because her mother was quite protective and nervous about all her antiques. And she often had headaches, probably more since they'd moved in, that required everyone being as quiet as possible.

Katie's stomach churned even more now, with that guilt and several other emotions. "I can't. I can't..." She did not want Jake thinking that she was chasing after him again.

"You can," Sadie said. "The house is huge. It's even bigger than last time you were there. I had a couple wings built onto it. Dale and Jenny had their own."

"And Jake?" she asked.

Sadie snorted. "He moved into the foreman's cottage years ago—when Jenny and Dale started having babies."

"Doesn't he like kids?" she asked. He'd once claimed that he wanted a bunch of them, but then he'd also once claimed that he loved her.

Sadie chuckled. "He just likes his sleep a little bit more. That's why he doesn't have time to mess with the books. Without Dale, there's no foreman and Jake's too busy with the ranching operations. So you'll have the office all to yourself. Don't worry about Jake getting in your way. Just worry about your boy."

"I do…" she murmured. And she'd been put into a precarious position. Caleb's happiness meant everything to her, just as it had to Matt. He was already missing his dad and now his friend. He couldn't lose his favorite teacher too.

Unless…

Unless Katie moved them out to the ranch. There were only five weeks left of school. And if they moved to the ranch, Caleb could finish out the year with his favorite teacher and his friend.

But she wasn't sure she could be that close to Jake again, that she *should*, even for Caleb. Unless Sadie was right. Unless she wouldn't see him at all.

TOO MUCH. It was all too much. The day. The double funeral.

Jake's day hadn't ended when the funeral had concluded this afternoon. Once he'd returned to the ranch, he'd taken off his black suit and switched to jeans and a work shirt to head out to the barns. He had several ranch hands, men and women he trusted, but they'd also had the day off for the funeral.

Jake couldn't take a day off. Sometimes he felt as if he couldn't take a minute away from the ranch. After he saddled up Buck, his buckskin quarter horse, and checked on the stock, his day still wasn't over even as the sun slipped away, leaving the sky dark and starless.

Buck knew his way back, though, and Jake let him have the lead across the land. But as they neared the lights from the ranch, the horse slowed as if he was as reluctant to return as Jake was. Jake gently nudged him with his knee, and Buck continued toward the barn, stopping only at the entrance.

Jake swung his leg over the saddle and dismounted. When he led Buck to his stall, he found fresh hay awaited him. One of the grooms must have reported to work despite Jake telling them not to come back after the funeral. Or maybe one of his brothers had cleaned out Buck's stall for him.

Jake pulled off the saddle and brushed down Buck's silky coat before leaving him to his water and feed. The saddle weighing heavily on his shoulder, Jake pulled shut the stall door, stopped in the tack room to store the saddle and walked out of the barn. He glanced toward the house, but he didn't see any sign of Ben's Lincoln SUV or Baker's old pickup. They must have already left for the night. Despite Grandma pleading with them, they hadn't moved back to the ranch. Yet.

He expected she'd eventually get her way. As she usually did. Except with him.

That exasperated the heck out of the old lady, but she only ever shook her head and remarked that he was the right one to have been named after his stubborn grandfather. But the original Big Jake had usually conceded to her, except for sneaking his cigars and sweets even after she'd banned them from the house.

Jake had easily found his grandfather's stash in the tack room, and he suspected his grandmother had known all along that it was there—just like she always knew everything else.

If only she had a head for numbers...

But she refused to help him with the books. So, as the overall ranch manager, he would have to tackle them on his own. He forced himself to walk away from the barn toward another building, an old brick building with a steeple and a bell. When the town had been about to tear down the old schoolhouse, Grandma had protested and bought it from them, then had it moved to the ranch.

The old redbrick building served as the business office. He and Dale and Jenny—and even his grandmother—each had a desk in it, since they'd removed the walls for the individual classrooms and made it one open space. Jake usually spent as little time as possible at his desk. He'd rather be in the barn or the saddle.

But he had to tackle the books. He'd put them off long enough. Paychecks and expenses had to get paid, or he'd lose his workers and the ranch.

He'd already lost more than he could handle.

And today, the funeral, had reminded him of *everything* as well as *everyone* he'd lost. He'd lost the life he'd once planned for himself and Katie.

He'd lost himself. He wasn't the man he used to be—the man he'd wanted to be.

When the two of them had talked about getting married, they'd planned to have a big family. At least five kids—like his mom and dad had had. But they'd wanted to wait to start their family until after they'd traveled the world, until after they'd achieved all those dreams they'd shared.

The life they'd planned. The life she'd lived with someone else…

It didn't matter. He would make do, like he always had, because he was a Haven. What didn't break a Haven only made them stronger.

Like Grandma.

Where had she gone after the funeral? He hadn't seen her at the ranch when he'd come back to change. After the accident, she'd talked him into staying in the big house to help with the boys. She'd recently hired some women. They were supposed to move in after the funeral, so he would be able to return to his place—the foreman's cottage. It had been too small for Dale and his family, but it was perfect for Jake, and quiet.

The ranch was not—even before all the people had moved in. The kids had filled it with loud voices and laughter. The laughter had stopped now. Ian barely spoke at all anymore and Little Jake not at all, not even the giggling and gibberish that used to bubble out of him nonstop.

Maybe that would change when Miller came home tomorrow with the physical therapist. Not that life would ever get back to normal. At least not the old normal. They would have to find a new one, just like they had when

Grandpa Jake died twelve years ago. When he'd had to quit college and come back here.

He'd found his new normal without Katie. So he would be able to find it again. Yet all the people he'd lost had left a hole behind—at the ranch and in his heart.

He released a ragged sigh, but he held back the sob clawing up the back of his throat. He never gave in to tears—not anymore. Tears hadn't brought back his dad or kept his mom from leaving them. There was no point to shedding them.

Dale and Jenny were gone. And he had to learn how to carry on without them. For their boys.

For the ranch.

And for himself.

Dale would have wanted that for him. Dale had wanted Jake to be as happy as he'd been with his sweet Jenny. At least there was that. Jake took comfort in knowing his brother had been happier than anybody Jake had ever known. Jenny had been too.

They were that high school couple that had lasted, whose love for each other had never wavered and only grown deeper. They hadn't been like him and Katie.

Jake drew in a deep breath and used it to

push down that threatening sob and all his emotions. He had to focus on the books now.

As he approached the old schoolhouse, he noticed the glow of light coming from under the double doors. He'd probably left a light on whenever he'd been in the building last. But he couldn't remember when that had been since he'd been actively avoiding the place, avoiding the memories it brought of Dale and Jenny sitting at their desks, laughing and smiling even as they'd worked.

He hadn't noticed that light earlier when he'd passed the building on his way to the barn. Maybe Grandma had taken pity on him after all and was taking a look at the books. Her truck was back now, parked near the steps of the porch that stretched the entire length of the front of the big house.

His lips curving up into a slight grin, he pushed open one of the doors and stepped inside the big open room. And his grin slipped away when he saw *her*.

She was the last person he'd expected to see at the ranch. The last person he wanted to see.

But he couldn't pull his gaze away from her, where she sat at Jenny's desk. She'd changed into blue jeans and a white sweater from the black dress she'd worn to the funeral. Black used to be her least favorite color, so he doubted she had many clothes in it. Was that the dress she'd worn for her husband's funeral?

She must have lost weight after it, because that black dress had hung on her small frame, making it look more like a hand-me-down from an older sister than something she'd bought for herself. But Katie was an only child, just like her son was now. She used to say that she didn't wish that on anyone else, that she wanted a lot of kids.

But she'd had just one. Because her husband had died.

Jake didn't even know how. But that wasn't what he wanted to ask her. He had just one question for her. "What are you doing here?"

CHAPTER THREE

"So you can speak..." Katie murmured, but she could barely hear her own voice over the mad pounding of her heart. He'd been standing there so long, just staring at her, that she'd wondered if Little Jake wasn't the only one who'd stopped speaking but Big Jake, as well.

He was big. Bigger even than she'd remembered.

Earlier, at the church, carrying the casket with his other brothers, he hadn't seemed as big—since they were all as tall or nearly as tall as he was at over six feet. But he wasn't just tall; he was broad too. Heavily muscled from all the years of hard work. His brothers weren't as broad as he was, and they were friendly and not at all intimidating like Jake was now.

The way he'd just stood there, staring at her with those dark, unfathomable eyes, had unnerved her so much that her fingers trembled slightly. She pulled them from the top of the white pine desk and tucked them into her lap.

"What about you?" Jake asked. "Can you speak?"

Heat rushed to her face as she realized she hadn't answered his question. "What am I doing here?" she repeated. "What are you doing here?"

His grandmother had assured her that she'd have little to no contact with Big Jake.

His hat, a dusty tan Stetson, moved as if he was wrinkling his forehead beneath it. "Last I checked this is Ranch Haven, and I'm a Haven." Then he repeated his question. "What are you doing here?"

Because she was not a Haven.

Because he'd broken his promise to her—the one he'd made in high school when he'd gifted her with the little opal ring. She glanced down at her hands in her lap, at the diamond band that glittered on her left hand. Matt had kept his promise to her. So Jake had actually done her a favor all those years ago. If only he hadn't been so cruel…

But because he had been, she was quick to explain, "The only reason I'm here is because your grandmother summoned me." She wanted it to be clear that she wasn't chasing after him. "She wants me to take care of the payroll and taxes and clean up the mess she says you've made of the books."

Despite the shadow the brim of his hat cast over his face, he seemed to turn red with embarrassment. "I did not make a mess of them," he said, but then he added in a mutter, "because I haven't touched them." A ragged sigh slipped through his lips. "Dale and Jenny took care of them."

She bit her lip as emotion overwhelmed her. Dale and Jenny had been just a year behind her in school, so she'd always been close to them. Even after Jake had dumped her, they'd stayed in touch. And when she'd returned to Willow Creek a year ago, they had been her first and favorite clients. More importantly, they had been supportive friends when she'd needed them most. Now, even though they were gone, they needed her to be supportive of their survivors. Even Jake…

She cleared her throat and said, "I'd been working with Dale and Jenny on the ranch accounts. I should have offered my help before now." But she hadn't wanted to be around Jake for so many reasons.

He shrugged his broad shoulders. "Why? Dale was the one who hired you. Not me."

She flinched as if he'd slapped her. He was making it clear that he hadn't wanted her involvement in ranch business, in his life. And obviously that hadn't changed with Dale's and Jenny's deaths.

His rejection wasn't going to destroy her this time like it had the last. She'd lost far more in her life since she'd lost him. She lifted her chin and met his stare with an unflinching one of her own. "And now your grandmother has hired me."

Sadie Haven had done more than that, however. She'd basically taken Katie and her son hostage, but pride kept Katie from admitting how easily the old lady had manipulated her. Jake was the only one who'd ever really been able to stand up to his fierce grandmother, so she doubted that he would understand how malleable she'd been to the older woman's manipulations.

But she'd had her own reasons for agreeing. Caleb was the first one. He wanted to be here with his favorite teacher and his best friend. Katie couldn't give him the thing he wanted most, and the thing she wanted more—his father back. But she could give him this. Some time at the ranch.

When she'd helped him pack up his stuff, while Sadie had waited for them downstairs, she'd told him that this was only temporary. Ian would get better and return to school and his teacher would too. Or worst-case scenario, they would stay here until school was over for the year. She'd been very clear that five weeks was the longest they would stay, and in that five weeks, Katie would make sure that someone else was hired to take over the books.

With as big an operation as the ranch was, it was no surprise that Jenny had struggled—even with Dale's help—to keep up with the finances, especially since they'd been raising not just one kid but three. She'd been such an amazing woman and friend. She and Dale and their kids were the other reason Katie had agreed to stay at the ranch. She wanted to help out however she could. Tears stung Katie's eyes, but she blinked them away and focused on the computer monitor.

"I need to get back to work," she told him. "Your employees and creditors deserve to get paid." Then she drew in a breath and held it as she waited for either his protest or the sound of him leaving.

Finally the door opened and then it closed again. Not with a slam but with a soft click. He didn't seem to want her here, but he hadn't thrown her off the ranch. Despite wanting to help Dale and Jenny, she wished he would have fired her before she and Caleb had even had a chance to unpack.

Sadie had dropped her at the office, so she could get started right away, before driving off with Caleb. Katie's stomach had dropped then with a sense of loss and a totally unfounded fear that the older woman was going to keep her son. Nobody was going to take Caleb away from her. They were really all each other had now.

But, despite how clingy he sometimes was with Katie and how leery he often was of strangers, he hadn't protested about being alone with Sadie. He'd been eager to see Miss Trent and Ian. And the horses and the goats and the dogs...

Sadie had told him the other animals would have to wait until the morning but that her dog was at the house. Then she'd whisked him away.

Katie had let herself into the office and gone right to work, eager to finish up quickly and get back to her son. She'd nearly been done when Jake had interrupted her.

But now her fingers hesitated over the keyboard. She wasn't in a hurry to finish up now if Jake had gone to the house, to his grandmother, to demand to know why she'd hired Katie. That confrontation, between two such strong and stubborn people, could be ugly. She didn't want Caleb witnessing any ugliness. So instead of finishing the work, she jumped up from the desk and rushed out into the night.

But she caught no glimpse of Jake. Had he already made it into the house? Even with his long legs, he couldn't have walked all the way there and across the porch. And she hadn't heard the rumble of an engine, so it wasn't as if he'd started up a vehicle to drive off.

She peered in the other direction from the house, wondering where he'd gone. To the barn? Back to his cottage?

At that thought, the tension eased from her.

But now she was worried about herself, about how coming here might have exposed her to more heartbreak. Would Jake hurt her like he had all those years ago? No. She wasn't going to let him get that close to her again. She wasn't going to let anyone else matter as much as Matt should have mattered to her—as she'd mattered to him. He'd loved her even when she'd thought she could never love again. It had taken years of his friendship and patience to heal the heart Jake had broken.

HOLDING HIS BREATH, Jake stood in the shadows, which held the scent of Katie, who stood so close to him. She smelled like she always had, subtly of flowers. Nothing overpowering, but something that made him want to breathe deeper, get closer, to figure out what flower it was that she smelled like.

It wasn't a rose.

Maybe gardenias?

Or something sweeter...

Honeysuckle?

He'd spent years wondering what that smell was, but he had never asked her—even back when they'd been dating. He'd liked the mystery of trying to figure it out.

He couldn't figure her out now, though. Why was she willing to help him after the way he'd treated her all those years ago, and even recently, when he hadn't reached out like the rest of the town undoubtedly had after her husband's death?

Guilt churned in his stomach over not at least offering his condolences. But even then he'd been so busy with the ranch, and he'd figured she wouldn't have wanted to hear from him again, not with the way he'd ended things between them. So she wasn't here to help him. She was helping out his family. Working for his family...

Dale and Jenny had hired her the minute she'd opened her business. They'd claimed they needed her help, but he suspected it was because she'd needed clients to support herself and her son. In the year she'd been back, her business had grown, so she didn't need the ranch work now. His grandmother could have hired another accountant, just as she'd hired a teacher and a physical therapist and a cook.

Why Katie?

What was Sadie's true intent?

Finally Katie stepped back inside the office and closed the door. And Jake released the breath he'd held. And with it the scent of her.

She could finish up the payroll and taxes tonight. Jake wasn't too stubborn to refuse her help. But he needed to make it clear to his grandmother that she had to hire someone else. Anyone else.

He couldn't have Katie here now, not when he was already reeling from losing Dale and Jenny. He had to focus on their orphaned sons and the ranch, and Katie was entirely too distracting.

He moved away from the shadows at the side of the former schoolhouse and headed toward the main house, intent on setting old Sadie straight.

Barking started up behind the front door the minute his boots hit the front porch. Too bad

Grandma's little pooch hadn't gotten as quiet as his nephews suddenly had. He drew in another breath before he pulled open the door and stepped inside. As usual, the long-haired Chihuahua attacked the bottom of his jeans, tearing at the denim with her tiny teeth.

Grandma had rescued the thing a couple of years ago. Not from a shelter but from the front seat of the Cadillac the dog's previous owner had locked it inside without the window cracked or the air on despite it being a hot summer day. Grandma had broken the window of the passenger door and when the people had rushed out of the restaurant in protest, she'd threatened to use the crowbar on them for nearly killing the tiny thing.

They—and the local sheriff—hadn't pressed any charges against her and hadn't argued about her taking the dog with her either. Jake had known better than to argue with her about her keeping the yappy little pet, but he was going to argue with her now.

"Grandma!" he yelled, which only made the dog bark louder. The kids' rooms were in the new wing of the house, so hopefully he hadn't disturbed them. They should have been asleep by now. It must have been a long, exhausting day for them. It had been for him.

But a short shadow fell across the hardwood floor of the foyer. That definitely wasn't his grandmother's shadow. Jake turned toward the child and tensed with shock. Katie's boy. She'd brought him with her to the ranch?

Why hadn't he stayed with her parents while she was here?

"Is Feisty biting you?" the little boy asked, his blue eyes wide with horror as he stared at the dog tugging on Jake's jeans, growling deep in her throat.

"Feisty doesn't bite," Jake assured him. If she did, his grandmother wouldn't have trusted her around her precious great-grandsons. "This is just a game we play."

The dog was trying to get him to do what she wanted him to do, just as his grandmother did. No wonder the two of them had bonded so tightly; they were very much alike. He reached down and picked up the four pounds of black fluff. As soon as he did, the growling stopped and the little dog lapped at Jake's chin, showering his face with bacon-treat-scented kisses.

The little boy giggled, and Jake's face heated with embarrassment. Having a dog like this was a disgrace on a ranch. It couldn't herd or protect cattle. But...

She herded and protected her people. Fiercely.

And the little people in the house especially had become Feisty's people. She wriggled in Jake's grasp, so he bent over and released her. The minute he did, she jumped into the little boy's arms and planted kisses all over his face.

The boy's giggles increased to deep belly laughs. And Jake's heart contracted. That was what had been missing in this house for the past two weeks. He'd thought it might be a lot longer before he heard it again. He had even worried that he might never hear it again.

A child's laughter.

He had never appreciated it more—so much that he had to close his eyes for a moment as emotion overwhelmed him. When he opened them, he found his grandmother staring at him as she stood behind the boy and her dog. Her hand, gnarled with arthritis, rested protectively on the little boy's shoulder.

That was how she was with her great-grandsons. Protective. But this child wasn't hers.

The suspicion that had propelled him here returned. He tensed and stared back at her, his eyes narrowed in a glare. "What are you up to?" he asked.

"About five-eleven-and-a-half," she said, "if I believe Doc Brewer's claims that I'm shrinking in my old age." She sniffed in dismissal of the young MD's assessment.

The little boy peered up at her through the blond bangs hanging over his eyes. "You used to be taller?" he asked with awe. "I didn't know people could shrink…"

She shrugged. "Shrink and shrivel—that's what my doctor thinks I'm doing. But what do doctors know?"

"Mommy says they're really smart," the boy said. "That they know all kinds of stuff, like why we have to get shots." His little body shuddered in revulsion.

And a chuckle threatened to slip through Jake's lips.

"I think they stick you more when you get older," Sadie warned him.

Jake shook his head. "Grandma, you might not want to scare the kid too much before he goes home."

The little boy turned back toward him. "I'm not going home," he said.

Jake sucked in a breath, realizing the kid probably thought he was talking about Chicago—about the place where he'd lived with his mom and dad. Jake, being thirteen when he'd lost his dad, had struggled; he couldn't imagine how hard it had to have been on the little guy to lose his dad when he must have been only four or five.

About the same age Ian was. And Miller was just a little older than Ian. And poor Little Jake... He probably wouldn't even remember his parents. Maybe that would be easier, though. He wouldn't know what he was missing.

This kid did. "What's your name?" Jake asked him. Someone had probably mentioned it before, but he'd made a habit of ignoring any talk about Katie and her kid since she'd moved back to Willow Creek. It was too painful to remember what he'd given up.

"Caleb," he said. The little boy let Feisty wriggle down, then he reached out his small hand toward Jake.

Jake sucked in another breath before he closed his big hand gently around that little one and shook it. "I'm Jake."

Caleb's eyes widened, and he murmured, "You're *Big* Jake..." Then he nodded as if it somehow made sense to him.

Had Katie mentioned him to her son?

No. She wouldn't have called him Big Jake. People had only started doing that when Little Jake was born. Maybe his nephews had talked about him.

"You run the ranch," Caleb said.

A smile twitched at Jake's lips and he glanced over Caleb's head at his grandmother. "I'm glad you know that. Somebody else seems to keep forgetting…"

"Ian remembers," Caleb assured him.

"I'm glad he does, but I wasn't talking about Ian," Jake said. He released Caleb's hand and straightened up. "Doc Brewer mention another *s* during your last appointment?" he asked Grandma. "Like senility?"

Sadie snorted. "You want me to sic Feisty on you again?" The little Chihuahua was sitting calmly on Grandma's slipper now; her romping around must have worn her out. He doubted she would rally enough to be sicced on him.

So he snorted back at Grandma and said, "No, I want you to tell me what's going on here."

"She hired Miss Trent," Caleb answered for her, which was something few people dared to do for his grandmother. "And Miss Cooper. She makes really good cookies." He rose up on tiptoe and whispered to Jake, "You should get some before Ian eats 'em all. He remembers he likes cookies."

Jake's lips twitched again. There was something about this kid, something so sweet and pure. Jake had to blink to see his little face clearly. "You seem to know Ian pretty well." To know that he was having issues with his memory.

"He's my very best friend," Caleb said. "And Miss Trent is my teacher too. I'm going to be staying here now, so she can teach us both and so that Mommy can work with you on the ranch." His brow furrowed beneath those blond bangs. "I don't even think she knows how to ride a horse, though."

Jake was stunned, so stunned that he was surprised that he could speak at all, but somehow the words slipped out of him, "She knows. I taught her."

Now the little boy was the one who was stunned. His mouth fell open with a little gasp of shock. "You taught my mommy how to ride a horse?" he asked with awe, as if the task seemed somehow impossible to him.

"Well, it wasn't easy," Jake admitted. Just convincing her to get up on even their gentlest horse had taken a lot of persuasion and kisses.

His stomach clenched as the memory overtook him. He shook his head, trying to shake off the thoughts of her as he'd had to do so many times over the past twelve years.

"Will you teach me too?" Caleb asked. "I wanna help you on the ranch."

A door snapped shut, a door Jake hadn't even heard open. The front door. For once Feisty hadn't barked when someone walked across the porch. But Katie was so small that she probably hadn't made a sound. Feisty didn't either, as if with a quick sniff of Katie's jeans, she'd automatically approved of the stranger.

"Mr. Haven won't have time to teach you," Katie answered for him. "And you won't have time for horseback riding," she continued. "You'll be busy with school. Miss Trent might be starting those lessons in the morning, so you should have been in bed an hour ago, buddy."

"He wanted to wait for you," Sadie said, her voice warm with compassion.

This little boy had had a lot of changes in his life in a short while. Losing his father. Moving away from his home and friends.

And now Grandma had actually moved him to the ranch. Him and Katie...

Why in the world would Katie have agreed to that? Why would she upend the little guy's life once again?

Back when they were kids, he'd always thought she'd be a great mother. But now he wondered if maybe her grief over losing her husband had affected her judgment.

"I'm here now," Katie assured her son, and she stepped around Jake to close her arms protectively around the little boy—as if the kid needed protecting from him. "So we need to get you to bed."

"I'll show you where your rooms are," Sadie said.

"I know where they are," Caleb said. "I'll show Mommy, but first she needs to have one of Miss Cooper's cookies."

"Mommy needs one?" Katie asked. "You're not hoping to sneak one for yourself?" Her lips curved into a smile that lit up her whole face.

Jake hadn't seen her smile since she'd been back—not that he'd seen much of her. Her smile rolled back the years, made her look like a kid again.

Made him feel like a kid again as his pulse raced and his heart pounded hard in his chest. Her smile had always affected him that way.

"Miss Cooper said it's up to you if I can have any more," Caleb admitted, before he pushed back his bangs and stared up at her with wide eyes.

She chuckled. "Don't give me those puppy dog eyes…"

"Please, Mommy, just one more," he implored her as he took her hand and tugged her down the hall toward the kitchen.

The two of them left without sparing him another glance, which was fine with him. He didn't have any time to spare, but it was going to be hard to avoid them if they were really going to stay on the ranch. He turned his attention from the now-empty hallway to where his grandmother stood in the foyer, and he stared hard at her.

"Those aren't puppy dog eyes," she told him with an amused smile.

"That's because I know better than to try to manipulate you," he said. "There's no manipulating the master."

"What are you talking about?" she asked with obviously feigned innocence.

"I know you've cooked up some scheme," he said. "I know you too well." Which was why he'd quit college and come home even when she'd insisted she could handle the ranch and his younger brothers on her own. He'd known that she'd been reeling from losing his grandfather and that she'd needed him no matter what she'd claimed.

"You don't like doing the books, so I found

you someone to do the books." She shrugged. "Simple as that."

"Nothing is ever simple with you," he said. "She's not the only accountant in Willow Creek. You could have found someone else." Anyone else.

"She's the one who's been helping Dale and Jenny," she said. "It would have been stupid to hire anyone else." And nobody had ever accused his grandmother of being stupid. Usually she was much too smart, especially for the people around her.

He sighed. "But why did you have to move them into the ranch?"

She shrugged again. "Just making things easier."

Not for him. He already had more than he could handle with his grief over losing his brother and sister-in-law. He didn't need the reminder of what else he'd lost in his life.

CHAPTER FOUR

KATIE'S LEGS TREMBLED slightly as she let her son tug her down the hall toward the kitchen. Jake hadn't gone back to the foreman's cottage. He'd come to the house instead, obviously to confront his grandmother. And just as she'd feared, her son had been present for that confrontation. Not that Caleb seemed any the worse for wear because of it. Just as he'd taken to Sadie Haven, he'd taken to *Big* Jake Haven. He'd been in awe of the man.

Katie was the one who was uneasy with Jake, with Sadie, with the whole situation. How had she let this happen?

"Mommy! Mommy!" Caleb called out in excitement. "Look at this kitchen!"

She realized he'd tugged her through a doorway at the end of the hall that opened onto a room with a lofted ceiling, tall windows and rows of cabinets and countertops. With its commercial-size stainless appliances and island, it looked more like a restaurant kitchen than anything that would fit inside a house. It was bigger than the entire brownstone that they'd lived in in Chicago.

"Isn't it ginormous?" Caleb asked.

It was. But with its wide pine flooring, green cabinets and brick backsplash, it was also warm and inviting—especially with a fire burning in the hearth at the end of a long, farmhouse-style table. This was not the kitchen Katie remembered from her visits to the ranch. But that had been over a dozen years ago and the house had been expanded since then; the kitchen apparently had been too. The ranch must have been doing well under Jake's management.

"Wow," Katie murmured.

"That was my first thought," a woman remarked as she pushed open a swinging door and stepped out of a pantry that was the size of Katie's bedroom. "I think I would have paid Mrs. Haven for the opportunity to cook in this place instead of the other way around."

"You're Miss Cooper of the famous cookies?" Katie asked.

"I don't know about famous," she said. "But yes, and it's only Miss Cooper to the whippersnappers." She smiled at Caleb before turning back toward Katie. "You can call me Taye."

Katie had expected someone older, but this woman—in her worn jeans and oversize T-shirt—looked like she was barely out of her teens. Her face was round and full, as was her tall body. She was probably nearly as tall as Sadie Haven. Her hair was a rich, dark blond and bound back in a thick braid, and her eyes were a startling pale shade of blue.

"I'm Katie Morris," she replied. "This whippersnapper's mother." Though she didn't feel as though she was doing a great job of mothering him right now. Why in the world had she agreed to move him—move them—out to Ranch Haven?

"Are you okay?" Taye asked softly, and those pale eyes were sharp with a wisdom beyond her years.

"I think she needs a cookie," Caleb said.

Taye chuckled. "Is that so? Just your mama needs one?"

He pushed back his bangs and stared up—way up—at Miss Cooper. "Maybe I can have another one too?"

"Ask your mama, not me," Taye told him.

He turned those eyes on Katie, making her smile. "Just one," she said. "Then we need to get you to…" Her voice cracked. She didn't even know where they were sleeping.

Taye lifted a wooden cover off a blue crockery jar and held out the jar toward Caleb. "Just one," she reminded him as he reached inside.

He pulled out a big, thick cookie with chunks of chocolate in it, but instead of biting into it himself, he handed it to Katie. "Here, Mommy, try it. It's so good."

Touched by his generosity, she obligingly took a bite and nearly moaned with ecstasy as the flavors of rich chocolate and vanilla exploded in her mouth. The texture was soft and moist, as well. She swallowed and said, "This is so good."

"Not flat and hard like yours, Mommy," he said.

Instead of being offended, she laughed and admitted, "I'm not much of a baker."

Taye shrugged. "Chocolate chip cookies can be tricky. Took me a while to perfect this recipe."

"They are definitely perfect," Katie praised her. Before she could finish the cookie, Caleb popped the rest of it in his mouth, making his little cheeks swell.

"You didn't answer my question," Taye reminded her. "Are you okay?"

Tears stung Katie's eyes, but she nodded. "Yes, fine. It's just…"

Taye smiled with understanding. "A little overwhelming?"

She nodded again.

"I'm feeling that way myself," Taye admitted.

"Aren't we all?" another voice remarked.

Caleb choked on his cookie before managing to murmur, "Miss Trent…"

The blonde appeared at the bottom of the stairwell next to the pantry door. She arched a perfect brow and asked, "And what are you doing up, young man?"

Katie's face heated with embarrassment that she wasn't enforcing his bedtime. "I was working late and—"

"He knows where his bedroom is—right next to Ian's," Miss Trent said. "And you better brush well after all those cookies you had."

"Yes, ma'am," he said, his blue eyes wide. "I will." And he headed toward the stairwell.

Miss Trent touched his hair as he passed her. "You're a good boy," she praised him.

He grinned wide and ran up the steps, not even sparing Katie a backward glance.

"Wow…" Katie murmured in awe. Bedtime had become a battle of wills between them lately.

"I know," Taye remarked. "Emily Trent is

like the kid whisperer. How'd you peel that other one off you?"

"Little Jake finally fell asleep," Emily said with a soft sigh. Then she turned toward Katie and said, "I'm sorry. I didn't mean to over-step with Caleb. I'm just in bossy-teacher mode after getting Ian to bed too."

"I appreciate it," Katie assured her. She was too tired to fight with her son over brushing his teeth right now. But she needed to make sure he did it thoroughly. So she started toward the stairs to follow him.

Taye caught her arm and stopped her. "Take a minute," she advised. "And another cookie. You look a little shell-shocked." She held out the jar toward Katie and then toward Emily. "Looks like you could use another one too."

Emily Trent was nearly as petite as Katie was. And she was stunningly beautiful with long silky blond hair and deep blue eyes. She was as tough as she was beautiful, after grow-ing up in a series of foster homes until finally finding a permanent home with one of their teachers. She'd been just a few years behind Katie in school, so Katie knew her story from that and because everybody in Willow Creek knew everything about everyone else.

She didn't remember Taye Cooper, but she

had probably been more than a few grades behind Katie in school.

"You're going to need to make more of these," Emily said as she grabbed a couple.

"Caleb loves them," Katie said.

"I love them," Emily said. "And I need chocolate. Not sure what I got myself into…"

A surge of relief rushed through Katie. "So I'm not the only one wondering how I wound up here…"

"Sadie Haven," Emily said around a mouthful of cookie. "That's how I wound up here. Can't believe I let her talk me into taking a leave from school and coming out here. How'd she rope you into it?"

"You were part of it," Katie admitted. "Caleb didn't want to lose you as a teacher."

Emily sighed and shook her head. "I'm sorry. I know that would have been hard for him. He's gotten attached to me."

"Kid whisperer," Taye murmured around a mouthful of one of her own cookies.

"And I was the one helping Dale and Jenny with the books before…" Before the terrible accident that had taken them too soon. Much too soon.

Tears stung her eyes, and Taye reached out for her arm, gently squeezing it. "I'm sorry. I didn't know them that well," Taye said. "But I would see Jenny when she came into the bakery where I worked in town to buy cookies for the kids. She was super sweet, and I hear her husband was, as well."

"They were," Katie confirmed.

"So how'd Sadie talk you into moving here?" Emily asked Taye.

The younger woman smiled. "I was happy to help out."

With a surge of shame, Katie remembered the real reason she was here. Because Dale and Jenny were gone.

They had helped her out when she'd first moved back to Willow Creek. She needed to return the favor they'd done when they'd become one of her first clients and closest friends. She wasn't sure she could be happy about it, though—especially when Jake didn't seem very happy about her and her son moving onto the ranch.

Why would it bother him? He was the one who'd broken up with her and broken her heart all those years ago.

JAKE NEEDED TO pack up his stuff and move back to the foreman's cottage. Now. There was no way he was staying here—not with Katie and her son. Not with that living reminder of the life he could have had…

Had Grandpa Jake not died…

Had he not been the oldest and had to take over the ranch… But he hadn't been about to run away like his mother had, leaving his grandmother to handle all the responsibility alone. He'd already felt so much guilt over Big Jake's death. Maybe if he'd been at the ranch instead of at college, his grandfather wouldn't have had that heart attack. After that, he hadn't been willing to risk losing his grandmother. He couldn't have left her alone with all the responsibility and her grief. He couldn't have done that to her.

So how could she do this to him?

She had to know how hard it would be for him to be around Katie day in and day out. And the boy…

A smile tugged at his lips as that child's laughter echoed inside his head. He'd needed that, needed so badly to hear that sound again.

If only…

His nephews had to recover. They just had to.

He couldn't let Dale and Jenny down; they'd been such incredible, loving, generous people.

But he couldn't stay at the house—not even for them.

He headed upstairs to the room he'd taken in Dale and Jenny's wing. It was close to the boys, so that he could get up in the middle of the night instead of Sadie. She was strong, but she needed her sleep more than he did.

And the boys had yet to sleep through the night.

Maybe that was why he was so incredibly tired. So tired that he felt more Grandma's age than his own. Or maybe that was just because it felt like this day would never end. If he took the time to pack up and move back to his cottage, he was going to lose even more sleep than he usually did.

Maybe tonight would be different—with the others in the house. Not that he'd been entirely alone with Grandma and the boys before the women had moved in.

Dusty had been here the past two weeks. And for Dusty, he'd helped out quite a bit. But his presence—looking so much like his identical twin—might have confused Ian and Little Jake even more. It was like their dad was here but wasn't…

It had also been hard on Jake.

His heart ached with missing Dale and

Jenny. His heart ached for his nephews too. At least Miller would be home tomorrow, so they wouldn't need to keep making trips back and forth to the children's hospital that was a couple hours' drive from Willow Creek. Grandma had hired a physical therapist to help out with the seven-year-old's recovery, and she'd been at his bedside the past week while they'd dealt with the younger kids and the ranch and the funeral arrangements.

He'd talked to Miller about that, asked if he'd wanted them to wait to have the funeral until his hospital release. But he'd shaken his head and said he didn't want to be there.

Jake hadn't wanted to be there either. But he'd had to…

He'd had to do so many things over the past several years that he hadn't wanted to do. Like break up with Katie…

But that had been for her own good. Just as Grandma was trying to claim having her here—helping out—was for *his* own good. He sighed and pulled off his hat to run a hand through his hair.

He would stay in the main house tonight. Just for tonight…

Tomorrow Miller would be here—with that physical therapist. So there would be plenty of people to help Grandma with the boys. People who were much better at dealing with heartbroken kids than he was.

He showered in the bathroom off the guest bedroom, put on an old, soft T-shirt and his pajama bottoms and crawled into the king-size bed. A sigh escaped his lips over the comfort of the mattress.

Maybe he would be able to sleep—even with Katie in the house. And her boy…

His eyes were already gritty with exhaustion, his lids heavy with it. He closed his eyes and let sleep claim him. But he must have been out only a few moments when a scream had him jerking upright in bed. He tossed back the covers and jumped up.

He couldn't wait for someone else to answer that cry. He rushed out into the wide hall and ran toward the nursery. The toddler didn't speak anymore. He made no sounds at all during the day. But at night…

He usually awoke like this—with a bloodcurdling scream that chilled Jake's skin more than the Wyoming night air in early spring. He pushed open the door to the nursery and rushed toward the crib. Little Jake stood up in it, clutching the railing as he screamed. Even as Jake tried to lift him, he clung to those narrow slats.

"I've got you, little guy," Jake said. "I'm here. You're safe. Come to me."

With a hiccup, the toddler released the railing and reached for Jake, clutching at his T-shirt as he'd clutched those slats. He fisted the soft material in his hands, and his little body trembled in the aftermath of his nightmare.

Jake wasn't even sure the boy was awake yet. His eyes were closed tight, tears streaming from between his long lashes. Pain clenched Jake's heart, which ached for the poor little guy. "You're okay. You're okay…"

He'd been the only one who'd escaped the accident unscathed. Or so they'd thought…

But these nightmares persisted while he remained so very quiet otherwise. "Poor little guy…" Jake murmured as his arms tightened around his nephew. His namesake…

"Uncle Jake…"

The voice came from behind him and he turned to find Ian standing in the open doorway, blearily blinking at him. He wasn't alone. Other people had gathered behind him.

"I've got him," Jake said—to everybody. "You can go back to bed."

But the toddler kept crying.

"Why are you here, Uncle Jake?" Ian asked. "He wants Mommy. Where's Mommy and Daddy?"

Jake's stomach pitched with the dread that filled it whenever Ian asked that question—which had been at least a few times a day since the accident. When would his memory return?

When would they have to stop answering that question and devastating the poor child every time that they did?

"She's not here," Jake said. "Neither is Daddy. They've gone away."

"On vacation?" Ian asked. "Are they on vacation without us? I thought we were all going on spring break together."

They had been leaving for their road trip to Florida early on the first morning of spring break when the SUV Dale had been driving hit black ice and rolled several times. The school had scheduled the break later this year, so that the weather would be better. But even that late in April, snowstorms were possible in Wyoming.

Ian glanced around at the women standing in the hall behind him. "Is that why everybody's here? Because Mommy and Daddy are on vacation? Miss Trent?"

"Yes, Ian, I'm here," the teacher said as she joined the little boy in the doorway. "I'm here."

"Why?"

"Because Mommy and Daddy are gone," Jake repeated. "They've gone to Heaven, Ian."

Ian shook his head. "No. No, they're not. You're teasing, Uncle Jake, and that's not funny. It's not funny!" He launched himself at Jake then, swinging his arms to pummel Jake with his small fists.

Jake lifted the screaming toddler higher, so that his brother wouldn't accidentally hit him. *Big* Jake could take the blows. *Little* Jake could not. The toddler stopped screaming, as if his brother's upset had calmed his own. Or at least fully awakened him from his nightmare.

Jake didn't think he would ever awaken from his.

CHAPTER FIVE

KATIE FELT THE blows of those small fists as if the distraught child was striking her instead of Jake. She felt the pain—Jake's pain. The kids' pain.

Tears welled in her eyes, threatening to spill over, but a small hand gripped hers. And a voice urgently whispered, "Mommy, what's wrong with Ian? Why's he hitting Big Jake like that?"

"He's confused," she said. "He's forgotten…" *He's forgotten that his parents are dead.* Her voice cracked as she trailed off before speaking those words. She couldn't say it, couldn't imagine the cruelty of having to tell the child over and over again what he'd lost.

Miss Trent had gone inside the nursery with Jake, and she gently tugged Ian off him now. She turned the little boy toward her and held him tightly. "I've got you," she said. "You're going to be all right…"

He stopped yelling, stopped striking and

threw his arms around her waist to cling to her. And over Ian's head, Little Jake reached out toward her.

Someone emitted a shaky sigh, and Katie turned to find Taye standing next to her. "We've got the easy jobs," the cook told Katie.

She nodded in agreement. But their responsibilities were just jobs to them. This was Jake's family. Jake's pain. His loss as much as it was the boys'. She saw it in the tension in his big body, in the lines in his handsome face, in the couple of stray silver hairs in the temples of his mussed hair, and in his eyes when he turned and met her gaze. And something shifted inside her heart. She felt sympathy instead of resentment toward him.

Emily took the little guy from Jake's arms as Ian continued to cling to her side. "I've got this," she told him. "Go back to bed."

Jake wore pajama bottoms and a wrinkled T-shirt, but he didn't look as if he'd had much—if any—sleep. Dark circles rimmed his dark eyes. He looked away from Katie toward his nephews.

And the pain…

The helplessness…

She understood it only too well. "Caleb, you need to go back to bed," she told him. And he must have been tired enough that he didn't protest. He just turned back toward the open door of his room, which was next to his friend's.

"I'll tuck you in," Taye offered, and she followed him into the room, closing the door behind them. Which, when Jake stepped out of the nursery and closed that door, left them alone together in the hall. Panic pressed on Katie's heart, making her want to turn and flee. But that look on his face…

His nephew's blows couldn't have hurt him physically. But emotionally…

He was clearly devastated. So devastated that she couldn't leave him. Not without saying something.

"I'm so sorry," she said. "I can't imagine how horrible this must be for all of you."

"Can't you?" he asked, his eyes narrowing slightly as he stared down at her.

She tensed at the question, as if he was questioning whether or not she'd mourned her husband. Of course she'd mourned Matt…was still mourning Matt…might always mourn Matt. He had been the most loving, supportive husband and a wonderful father.

"I meant that Ian's memory… Having to keep telling him…" She shuddered. "It was hard enough to tell Caleb once." She couldn't imagine having to go through that over and over again. Having to put a child through that over and over again.

"I'm sorry too," he said.

And she tensed again, wondering for what he was apologizing. The past? For breaking her heart. That had happened a lifetime ago. Or for Matt…whose life had been cut so tragically short.

"No kid should have to lose a parent so young," he said.

"No, no kid should," she agreed, her heart aching for Caleb's loss and hers. She understood the Haven children's loss too well. "How's Miller doing?" She'd expected to see him today, at the funeral.

"He'll be home tomorrow," he said. "He's done with surgeries—hopefully forever. Hopefully the physical therapist can help him recover fully."

"And Ian?"

"The doctor says that he's young and that the brain has a way of healing itself, that eventually his memory should return." He sighed again. "I don't know if that's a good thing or not. I'm not sure what he'll remember, of the accident…" His voice cracked with emotion.

And Katie's heart cracked. The town had

been rife with gossip about the crash, about how bad it had been, how the boys had been trapped inside…

She shuddered and reached out to touch his arm, like Taye had done for her. Her fingertips tingled from the heat of his skin and the softness of the dark hair on it, but his muscles tensed. And he jerked away, as if unable to stand her touch.

She moved her hand, which was trembling now as well as tingling, to the tie of her robe, cinching it even tighter.

Did he think she was besotted with him? That she'd followed him here to the ranch like he'd accused her of following him to college, of smothering him?

"I didn't know you were staying in the main house," she said. "Sadie told me that you live in the foreman's cottage." Had the old woman lied to her?

"She also told me that you don't want anything to do with the books and that you never go into the office. So don't worry that I'm chasing after you again. I got over the crush I had on you years ago." That wasn't completely true. But she was no longer the lovesick teenager whose heart he'd broken so callously next to that campus fountain where they'd once tossed in coins with all their wishes for the future. She'd been devastated when he'd dumped her, because her feelings for Jake had been much more than a crush. But Matt had healed her broken heart with his humor and his optimism and his love. If only he was here now...

The funny stories or the silly games he'd played with Caleb and his friends would have cheered up the boys. Theirs had always been the house where everyone wanted to come for playdates. He'd made everything light and fun—even her heartbreak all those years ago. But now her heart was breaking with missing him.

"I know you're not here for me," Jake said. "You're here for the same reason I'm staying in the house. For Dale and Jenny. For the boys. Won't this be hard on your son, though? More upheaval after moving back from Chicago?"

She bristled with defensiveness. Was he questioning her parenting? She didn't need anyone else doing that. She questioned it enough herself. "I'm here for Caleb too. Your grandmother hired his teacher away from the school, and it would have been very hard for him to lose her, especially since he was already missing Ian."

"And his father," Jake added.

Her heart ached with her son's pain. "Very much…"

"I am sorry," Jake said. "About your husband."

Tears rushed up, choking her. She could only nod in acknowledgment of his belated condolences. Not wanting to cry in front of him, she turned away and headed back to her room. Once inside, she closed the door and leaned against the cool wood, and she let the tears slide down her face. She missed Matt, but most of all, she missed that she would never be able to make it up to him that she hadn't loved him as completely as he'd loved her. That no matter how hard she'd tried, she'd never been able to forget about Jake Haven.

JAKE HAD HAD to clench his hands at his sides so that he wouldn't reach for Katie. So that he wouldn't stop her from walking away from him. So that he wouldn't set her straight about the past. There was no point in rehashing it when he had less to offer her now than he'd had back then.

So he let her walk away from him just as he'd walked away from her a dozen years ago.

That was the hardest thing he'd ever had to do until now. Until he had to keep telling Ian over and over again that his parents were gone. That was what he needed to focus on now: helping his nephews heal. That and the ranch.

Not the past...

But when he returned to his room and crawled back into the now-cold sheets, he couldn't sleep. He couldn't think of anything but that day twelve years ago.

He'd made his decision. He'd known what he'd needed to do. After he and Katie had returned to college after his grandfather's funeral, he'd had her meet him at the fountain in the park on campus. Since he'd started college two years earlier than she had, they'd spent a lot of time at the fountain during her visits and in the couple of months since she'd graduated high school and joined him on campus.

So it was somehow fitting that he do it here. He'd seen her reflection in the water when she'd joined him, her hand wrapping around his arm as it had just a few moments ago in the hallway. When she'd touched him...

The years had rolled back like they had when she'd smiled. And he'd reacted the way he always had to her touch. His skin had tingled while his heart had hammered away in his chest. How had the attraction never faded?

Maybe it was because she was even more

beautiful now than she'd been back then. And he hadn't believed that would have been possible.

He'd had to close his eyes that day when he'd told her. "Katie, I'm leaving college. I need to help Grandma run the ranch."

"I know," she'd said with total understanding and acceptance. "I'll go back with you. I'll help you."

Just as she was trying to help out now...

"No," he'd said. And then he'd forced himself to be cruel—for her sake. The wishes he'd made on those pennies they'd thrown into the fountain weren't going to come true now, but hers could. He just wouldn't be part of them anymore.

"You need to stop following me around like some lovesick calf," he told her, forcing disgust into his voice. "It was cute when we were kids. But I have to grow up now and so do you."

"Jake?" She'd called his name as if she was calling out to someone else, someone lost inside him.

And he had been then.

Lost.

"We don't have a future together, Katie," he'd said. "We never did. We don't want the same things out of life."

"What?" she'd said. "I don't understand…"

And he hadn't wanted her to…

If she'd figured out what he was really doing, she never would have accepted the breakup. She would have followed him back to Willow Creek like he'd secretly and selfishly wanted her to.

But that wouldn't have been fair to her. She was just a kid herself. She had no business trying to help him raise his younger brothers, trying to help him with an operation the size of the ranch.

She'd wanted to travel. Wanted to see the world, live in a big city for at least a little while before returning to Willow Creek to raise that big family she'd wanted.

He couldn't do any of those things now. But she still could.

Without him…

So he'd forced himself to say the cruelest thing of all. "I don't love you," he said. "It was just easy being together in high school. I was going to break up with you when I graduated but you were so clingy. Then you followed me here, and you're smothering me, Katie. I can't take it anymore. Just leave me alone."

Then he'd turned and walked away from her, leaving her crumpled beside that fountain, sobbing over his cruelty. He'd felt so badly for what he'd done—even though he'd known it was best for her.

He'd mourned the loss of her every bit as much as he'd mourned Grandpa Jake. And when the suffering had seemed insurmountable he'd come back for her. He'd wanted to apologize for making her cry; he'd wanted to assure her that he loved her just as much as she loved him. Two months had passed, but he'd found her at the fountain. She hadn't been alone, though, and she hadn't been suffering. She'd been laughing with some blond guy her age who'd been juggling coins. And Jake had turned and walked away from her then, knowing he'd done the right thing for her. He had figured it was better to never tell her the truth and apologize, so that she could continue to move on and appreciate her life without him. Hard as he was working on the struggling ranch with his teenage brothers, he wouldn't have had the energy to make her laugh or to spend any time with her at all.

Even after his brothers had grown up and the ranch had started prospering, he'd stayed so busy that the relationships he'd tried to have hadn't lasted. The women had always resented the ranch, had called it his first love. Maybe it had been—even more so than Katie.

But now he had even more to deal with than he'd had twelve years ago. He no longer had Dale to help him with the ranch, and he had to find some way to help his nephews heal. Just like twelve years ago, Katie deserved more—especially now that she was grieving. She deserved someone who could give her and her son all the time and attention they deserved.

CHAPTER SIX

CALEB MORRIS HADN'T lied when he'd told Jake that Miss Cooper baked really good cookies. She'd made even more for Miller's homecoming. And she and the teacher and Katie had blown up balloons that they'd anchored to the table with little bags of candy.

They'd made Miller's homecoming a party.

Jake wouldn't have thought of that. His brothers hadn't either. They'd been as stunned to see the decorated kitchen as he'd been.

Even Grandma wouldn't have thought of it, and she usually thought of everything. But she wasn't the sentimental type, never had been. She looked smug as she stared at them from the head of the long table.

And, despite the warmth of the fireplace at his back, Jake's blood chilled in his veins. "She's up to something," he warned his brothers, who sat on either side of him at the other end of the long table from her. The women and children sat between them, Miller in a wheelchair at his great-grandmother's side. The physical therapist, a pretty young woman with thick brown hair and warm brown eyes, sat next to her patient. Across from them, on the long bench, the teacher bounced Little Jake on her lap while Katie's boy sat on one side of her next to Ian, who actually laughed at something his friend said to him. Katie was at the sink with the cook, helping her with the dishes.

Despite all the women in the house now, his brothers obviously knew who Jake was talking about, because Ben snorted and murmured, "When isn't Grandma up to something?"

Baker shrugged and said, "Maybe she's just happy everybody's here to welcome Miller home." Despite his years in the army and as a paramedic, the baby of the Haven brothers was still a bit naive—at least when it came to women.

Of course he hadn't had his heart broken like Jake had. And he hadn't broken any hearts like Ben had. Ben couldn't help himself. Women fell hard for his good looks and his charm. Or maybe it was just his charm since he looked the most like Jake with black hair and dark eyes.

No woman other than Katie had ever fallen for Jake. Although last night she'd claimed that it was just a crush, which made it sound like nothing more than what her son was obviously feeling for his beautiful teacher.

"No, Grandma's not happy," Jake said, rejecting Baker's observation.

"Maybe that's because not everybody is here," Ben remarked. "I can't believe Dusty left right after the funeral."

Jake could. Dusty was a heartbreaker, too, and the most like their mother—who'd broken all their hearts. So, Jake supposed, Baker had had his heart broken; maybe he'd just been too young to remember.

"Did you really expect him to stay?" Jake asked. Because he hadn't.

With light brown hair and hazel eyes, Dusty was only like his twin in appearance. Dale hadn't really shared his dream of joining the rodeo; he'd confessed that even if he hadn't fallen for Jenny, he wouldn't have left the ranch. He'd loved it like Jake had.

Like Jake still did.

Even though he'd once had dreams to travel and live somewhere else for a while, he'd always known he'd come back here to live—to work. He was a Haven, and this was Ranch Haven. It was where he belonged.

Yet not everyone felt the same. Neither his

mother nor Dusty had. Would these women stay? Grandma claimed she'd brought them here just to help with her great-grandsons. But did she have something else in mind, something more permanent?

"Look at them…" Jake murmured. And he turned to look at Katie, who smiled at something the cook said as they washed the dishes together.

She'd formed a fast friendship with the younger woman. There was something about Taye Cooper…something that reminded him vaguely and unsettlingly of his grandmother.

She was tall like Sadie and strong and smart. She looked at a person like she could see inside them. She didn't need that ability to see Katie's pain, though. The widow was obviously still reeling from her loss and her son's.

"That kid is good for Ian," Baker remarked, his voice gruff as he stared at his nephew talking to Caleb. Baker had dark hair like Jake and Ben, but his eyes were light, more topaz than brown. "He's making him laugh."

That obviously affected Baker the way it had Jake, to hear a child's laugh again. Maybe his grandmother had been right to bring Katie and her son here.

For the boys.

It wasn't right for Jake; it just tortured him with *what-ifs* and *could'ves* when he needed to focus on the present. And Katie... He had never been the right man for her. She'd always deserved more than he could offer her.

"Haven't you noticed that these women Grandma hired are all young and pretty? I think she has a plan." One that Jake had no intention of falling into...

Ben laughed now. "Think she watched *Seven Brides for Seven Brothers* or something? You think Sadie Haven is playing matchmaker?"

"Manipulator," Jake corrected him.

"You think that because she brought Katie here," Ben said.

"You don't think that?"

Ben shrugged now. "Katie was helping Dale and Jenny with the books. It makes sense that she would continue in their...absence..."

Jake focused on his brother now. Was he like Ian? Trying to pretend that they were just on vacation? But Ian wasn't pretending. He really couldn't remember, while Ben could—he obviously just didn't want to. Jake couldn't really blame him. "You need to talk to her."

"Katie?" Ben asked, and he chuckled again. "You used to threaten me so that I wouldn't talk to her when we were in school together."

Ben had been in Katie's class, two grades below Jake. And he'd always teased Jake that he was going to make a play for her, as he had every other girl in his class and the ones below him and the ones above him and probably a few of the younger teachers, as well.

Jake hadn't really been worried about losing her to his brother. He'd believed then that she'd loved him too much to ever fall for anyone else.

"I'm talking about Grandma," he said. "You're the most like her. You can figure out what she's up to."

"Me?" Ben laughed again. "You are. You probably should have been named Sadie instead of Jake."

Baker finally laughed then—just a short, quick chuckle before the brief smile slid away from his mouth. He wasn't trying to forget that Dale and Jenny were gone. Like Jake, it was obviously always on his mind.

The physical therapist, Melanie Shepard, stood up then and reached for the handles on the back of Miller's wheelchair. "This was a lovely homecoming for him, but he should probably get some rest now," she said. "Where is his bedroom?"

Jake inwardly groaned as he realized they

hadn't thought about Miller needing a room on the first floor. They could set up one, but they would need to bring down a bed. When they'd arrived at the ranch, the physical therapist had read them the list of the doctor's strict instructions. Miller could put no weight on his leg for the next six weeks.

"It's upstairs," Miller answered for himself. Sitting in the wheelchair, he looked even smaller than seven years old—more like Caleb and Ian's five. But he sounded older and so very tired.

"We'll set up a room down here for you," Jake said, and he stood up and walked toward his oldest nephew.

Miller shook his head. He looked so much like his dad with his dark blond hair and hazel eyes. "I wanna sleep in my own bed, Uncle Jake."

"We can bring down your bed," Jake assured him.

"I want to sleep in my own room."

He'd spent the past two weeks in a hospital. Of course he wanted to be in his own space. "Okay then," Jake said. And he turned his back and crouched down in front of the wheelchair. "Then climb aboard this horse and I'll give you a ride to your room."

"Horse?" Ben teased. He stood in front of Jake now with Baker next to him. "More like jack—"

"Benjamin," Grandma warned him before he could even finish the word.

Ben ignored her and focused on their nephew. "Hey, Mill," he said. "Great to have you home. I gotta get back to work, but I'll be by later."

"You're leaving?" Sadie asked, and she sounded horrified. Maybe more so that her plan wasn't going to work. Whatever that plan was...

"I have a city to run, Grandma," he said, and he leaned down to kiss her cheek.

"I'm leaving too," Baker said. "My shift starts soon." He reached out toward Miller, who'd looped his arms around Jake's neck. But he pulled his hand back before his fingers did much more than brush the boy's hair—almost as if he was afraid to touch him.

Was the little boy more fragile than Jake had thought? He turned toward the physical therapist. "It's okay to give him a piggyback ride, right?"

Melanie nodded. "Yes. With the rod and pins holding his femur in place, you're not going to hurt anything. He just can't put weight on it for a while, but we'll start transitioning to crutches soon so he can get around easier on his own."

Some of the pressure on Jake's chest eased slightly. "So he'll be running around again in no time?"

She smiled. "It's going to be a while before he'll be running, but he's going to be fine physically."

Emotionally? Was he as messed up as his little brothers were? Jake couldn't ask her that in front of the kids. And as a physical therapist, she probably could only address Miller's physical recovery—not his emotional one.

"Hang on tight, but don't use your spurs," Jake teased as he straightened up and headed toward the stairs.

"I'm not wearing spurs, Uncle Jake," Miller said. "I'm not even wearing my boots."

"You're wearing some kind of boot," Jake said as the hard cast bumped against his side. "I'll draw some spurs on it when we get upstairs."

A small hand tugged on his sleeve. "Can we have a ride next?" Caleb asked. Ian stood beside him, and he was smiling.

Jake's heart lurched with hope that the boys were improving. Thanks to Katie's little boy.

"Hold on tight," he told Miller again. Then

he reached down and snagged a boy with each arm. Holding them like footballs, he carried all three up the stairs. He staggered and groaned, acting as if their slight weight was too much. But they must have known he was acting, or they just didn't care, because all three of them giggled. And his heart lurched again with love—for all of them.

PANIC OVERWHELMED KATIE as she watched Jake carrying her son up the stairs, carrying him away from her. She wasn't afraid that he was going to drop Caleb. She was afraid that her son was going to fall for him. Or worse yet, that she might again. This was the Jake she remembered, the one playing with the boys.

"Wow," Taye murmured. "That's a pretty amazing guy there…"

Katie shook her head, unwilling to believe it. She'd known an amazing man. She'd been married to him, and Matt Morris had been nothing like Jake. He would have died rather than ever make her cry.

And it had taken his death for her to shed tears over him. But that was only because he had never let her down. He'd never broken any promises to her, and he'd always made her laugh.

She tore her gaze from Jake and the boys and looked down at her hand. In the sunlight pouring in through the tall windows, her diamond sparkled, almost as if it winked at her, like Matt often had. And the gold band gleamed. She'd vowed the day that she'd buried him that she would never take it off. She would give him in death the unwavering love and devotion that he had deserved to have from her in life.

She had loved him. But it had never felt like enough.

It had never been as much as he'd loved her—because there had been a part of her that had always still loved Jake. How? After the way he'd treated her? After how he'd rejected her?

She shook her head. She was such a fool.

"You don't think Jake's amazing?" Taye asked, her pale blue eyes narrowed.

"You don't know about them?" Emily asked as she joined them at the counter.

"You lost an appendage," Taye said with a smile. "Where's the little guy?"

"Crawling up the stairs after the big guy and his brothers with Sadie and that little dog right behind him." She smiled, probably grateful for the slight reprieve.

"So what about Katie and Jake?" Taye asked.

"They were a thing in high school," Emily said. "Like Dale and Jenny were. Everybody thought they'd get married."

"Everybody but Jake," Katie murmured.

"That's not what I heard," Emily said.

Katie shook her head. "It's ancient history now." And thinking about all of it made her feel ancient. "We weren't meant to be." She sighed. "And I'm not meant to be here. I shouldn't have brought Caleb here."

What if he forgot they were leaving in five weeks? What if he got attached not just to his teacher and his friend but to the rest of the Havens and also to the ranch, and he wanted to stay?

"He's been so good for the boys," Emily said. "He's already done so much for them just by being here." She glanced toward the hall. "Unlike our mayor, who couldn't wait to get out of here." She huffed with disgust.

"Baker took off too," Taye pointed out.

"But he has a shift starting," Emily said. "He had a real reason to leave."

For some reason—maybe because she'd once thought of them all as her brothers when she'd spent so much time with them as a teenager—Katie felt compelled to defend Ben.

"The mayor, no doubt, had a real reason for leaving, as well."

Emily smirked. "Yeah, probably a woman."

She couldn't defend Ben from his reputation, so Katie chuckled. "Growing up and becoming mayor hasn't changed Ben much?"

Emily shook her head. "I guess Dusty hasn't changed either. He didn't even bother to show up."

Melanie gasped. "He didn't come home for his brother's funeral?"

"He was here for about a hot minute," Emily replied. "Guess that's about the most you can expect from Dusty. But he's never pretended to be anything other than he is—unlike Ben, who fooled more than half of this town into thinking he's responsible enough that they voted for him. They fell for all his empty political promises."

Just as Katie had once fallen for all Jake's empty promises. She wouldn't make that mistake again, not that she expected him to make any promises to her. Not that she wanted him to...

All she wanted was to help fill some of the mammoth void Dale and Jenny had left. She wanted to help them like they'd helped her. She hoped that helping them didn't hurt her son, though. That he didn't get attached to a place where they couldn't stay...

CHAPTER SEVEN

A FEW DAYS had passed since Miller's home-coming. Sadie had been so hopeful that day, as she'd sat at the head of the table with all her family present. All her family but Dusty.

She was willing to wait for him. Once he wasn't able to find what he was looking for, he would come home. And he'd find it—*her*—waiting for him.

If she stayed…

She was skittish. Sadie saw that in her. Melanie had figured everything out now. But she hadn't taken off. She'd stayed to help with Miller. She'd obviously already fallen for the little boy. And it hadn't taken the other boys long to get to her, too, just as they had to Miss Trent and Taye and Katie.

The women had come together to plan the perfect little party for Miller. Sadie hadn't thought of that, but she wouldn't have to think about those kinds of things now. She had help. And she was determined to keep it.

So her plan needed to speed up.

Sadie Haven had never been a patient woman. And the older she got, the less patience she had. She could wait for Dusty to come around. Since Jake was the oldest, she would focus on him first.

She just needed some help. So, with Feisty prancing along beside her, she walked into the kitchen in search of Taye, who'd proved to be the kindred spirit Sadie had thought she'd be. But instead of finding the young woman, she found a little boy. He had a chair pushed against the counter, and he stood on it, reaching for that crockery jar that was usually full of cookies. The chair teetered as his weight shifted forward, and two legs lifted from the floor. As it toppled over, Sadie reached out and caught the boy. Unlike Jake, who'd lifted him with one arm, she'd had to use both. And her shoulders strained with the effort of catching Caleb midfall.

He gasped. His blue eyes wide with shock, he stared up at her.

"Busted," she teased him. "Did you ask your mama or Miss Cooper if you could have a cookie this close to lunch?"

"I ate my lunch already," he said. "All of it."

She swung him back and forth a little in her

arms before releasing him to stand on his own. "Yeah, you feel like you got a bellyful. You sure you have room for a cookie?"

"I always have room for Miss Cooper's cookies," he said.

"What about your mama?" she asked.

"She always has room for Miss Cooper's cookies too," he replied.

Sadie chuckled. This boy was quite the little character. "I meant did you ask her if you could have one?"

"She's busy with the picnic."

"What picnic?" Sadie glanced through the patio doors on the deck. Patches of snow, left from that freak late-April spring storm, clung to the cedar in places where the sun had yet to melt it all away. "Kind of cold for a picnic."

"It's upstairs," he replied. "In Miller's room."

"If it's upstairs, what are you doing down here?" she asked.

"I ate all my lunch, but everybody else was finishing up," he explained.

"Oh…" she murmured. "So your mama said you could have a cookie?"

"Well…" His face flushed pink. "I ate all my lunch."

"And you think that deserves a reward?"

He nodded. "Yes, it does."

He was a reward—a bright spot in so much sadness lately. Moving him and his mama here had been one of Sadie's smartest moves. Now she had to make sure that they stayed.

She'd lost Katie as family once. She wasn't losing her again, or her little boy. He already felt like one of Sadie's own. She was keeping them both.

WHAT WAS KEEPING CALEB? It was taking him a long time to wash his hands. But when Katie popped her head into the bathroom adjoining Miller's room, she found it empty. The door to the hall stood open. She had an inkling of where he'd gone. So she headed down the back stairwell to the kitchen.

She heard them before she saw them. Her little boy's easy chatter. The rumble of a deep laugh that was distinctively Sadie Haven's.

She was tough and unnerving. But with the kids, she showed a soft side that Katie wouldn't have believed existed. She was gentle and loving with them as if they were injured animals she was rescuing.

They were injured. Her great-grandsons. And Caleb.

But Katie's son wasn't Sadie's great-grandson. The older woman treated him like he was, though. He sat atop the stainless steel island against which the old woman leaned. And he leaned against her, dropping cookie crumbs into her pure white hair as he nibbled on a giant snickerdoodle. Sadie either didn't notice or didn't care. She had a cookie shoved in her mouth, as well.

"See," she murmured around a big bite. "These are the best."

Caleb shook his head. "Chocolate chip..." And he rained more crumbs into Sadie's white hair and onto the counter and the floor.

That would've made Katie's mother flip out. The crumbs everywhere, the boy sitting on the counter, the chair toppled over on the floor.

"What happened?" she asked with alarm. "Are you all right?"

"I startled him when I caught him with his hand literally in the cookie jar," Sadie answered for him. "But he didn't hit the ground."

Katie's alarm eased, and she expelled a shaky breath. "That's good."

"Not as good as chocolate chip," Caleb said with a little giggle. He was teasing the old woman.

She shook her head and crumbs tumbled from her white tresses. "Snickerdoodle's way better!" She said it sternly, but Caleb laughed.

Despite having met her just a short while ago, he was so comfortable with the old woman—so much more than he'd ever been with her parents. Katie had moved him to Willow Creek with the hopes that her parents would replace the grandparents who'd no longer been able to bear looking at him. She understood why it was hard for them, but she hated how hard it had been on Caleb and her to lose them too. Caleb hadn't bonded with her parents like he had Matt's. Unlike Grandpa and Grandma Morris, who he used to ask about often, he hadn't mentioned her parents once this past week. Maybe he'd just been too busy with the other boys and all the women and Feisty to miss them. Even if that was the case, she knew she needed to find them another place to live when they left the ranch. A place where he felt comfortable being a kid, one who was allowed to scatter crumbs and dirt and leave toys lying around and to be loud from time to time.

"What do you think, Mommy?" Caleb asked.

She was startled now. Had he guessed what she'd been thinking? "About what?"

"Chocolate chip or snickerdoodle?"

She shook her head. "I'm not getting in the middle of this."

"Chicken," Sadie said.

Katie didn't think the woman was teasing her like she'd teased her son. She almost seemed to be goading her. What did Sadie think she was afraid of? Her? Or Jake?

Or just being at the ranch?

It was a toss-up for Katie. She wasn't as comfortable here as her son was. She felt as if she had to keep up her guard—to protect herself and Caleb from getting hurt.

Katie smiled. "No. I really can't decide," she said. "I love them both."

Sadie nodded. "That's true. You can love more than one."

And Katie wondered if they were still talking about cookies. Or did the older woman know…?

She shivered slightly. It didn't matter what Sadie Haven thought. Katie's heart belonged only to one man now, the only one who'd deserved it.

"We should go help the others clean up the picnic," Katie said, and she reached for Caleb, lifting him down from the countertop. She groaned slightly. "You're getting heavy. Must be all those cookies."

He wriggled from her arms and stood on tiptoe next to her. "I am getting big, Mommy.

You're not going to be able to lift me pretty soon, not like Big Jake can and Miss Sadie."

A pang struck her heart. He was right. She wouldn't be able to lift him much longer. It was sometimes a struggle now.

"I can help clean up from the picnic," Sadie offered. "You should take him outside. Show him the ranch."

"I... I can't do that," Katie said with a sudden surge of panic. "For one you shouldn't clean up after us..." Especially when they hadn't invited her to the picnic.

Taye had looked for her to include her, but Sadie must have not been in the house, or at least not where Taye had checked. Katie and Emily and Melanie hadn't offered to help look for her. Sadie Haven unsettled the teacher and the therapist even more than she unsettled Katie.

"And for another, I don't know where anything is on the ranch," she continued.

"Sure, you do," Sadie insisted.

"You do, Mommy?" Caleb asked—a bit awed or maybe just skeptical.

Sadie nodded. "Your mama used to come out here a lot when she was a teenager."

Caleb stared at her, and it was definitely awe in his wide eyes. "Is that when Mr. Big Jake taught you how to ride a horse? Can you teach me, Mommy?"

Her stomach plummeted and she shook her head. "I barely remember how myself," she said, mostly because she'd tried blocking out all memories of then, of Jake. Unfortunately she hadn't been entirely successful. "And did you forget that I told you about having to focus on school?"

"But, Mommy, it's Saturday!"

The past week had been such a blur that Taye and Emily had had to remind her that morning that the workweek had ended. But she'd still gone into the office in the old school-house for a little while this morning, just to make sure she wasn't falling behind with her other clients while she caught up with ranch business.

But the only part of the ranch that was her business were the books. Not the barns. Not the animals. And certainly not Jake.

"We don't want to get in the way of the ranch work," she said.

Sadie shook her head. "You won't be in the way. Jake and the hands will be out in the pastures feeding the cattle and checking the calves, making sure they're starting on the grain."

So he wouldn't be in the barn.

She could show Caleb around a little bit. He had been stuck inside all week with his friend and the other Haven boys. He deserved to get out, to explore a bit. And she wanted this time with him—just the two of them.

"Okay," she said. "But we have to dress up in warm clothes and put on some boots."

Caleb threw his arms around her and hugged her tightly. "Thank you, Mommy!"

Guilt flashed through her over his exuberant response and his gratitude. She should have taken him out to the barns earlier in the week. But she'd been busy with work, and he'd seemed happy with his teacher and the other boys. And the cookies.

Especially the cookies.

He'd forgotten about them now as he rushed up the stairs to his bedroom to grab the warmer clothes and boots they'd packed.

Katie turned to follow him, but Sadie stopped her with just her voice. "He's a good boy," the older woman said. "A real special kid."

Tears stung Katie's eyes. "He is." She knew that, but she was especially touched that Sadie Haven had noticed, as well.

"He's wrong about the chocolate chip, though," she continued. "Snickerdoodle's best."

Katie chuckled and headed up the stairs after her son. Maybe Sadie wasn't so intimidating after all.

Now Jake...

She was grateful that he was out tending to the cattle. She had no desire to run into him in the barn or anywhere else. They'd done a pretty good job of avoiding each other after Miller's homecoming. Hopefully they would be able to continue avoiding each other for the rest of her and Caleb's stay on the ranch.

JAKE SLUMPED IN the saddle, exhausted from the long days he'd spent tending cattle in the pastures, as far from the main house as it was possible to be, as far from Katie as it was possible for him to be. He could have taken the trucks like the hands did when they delivered the hay and grain. But Jake preferred to ride; it was easier to check the fences, easier to find any head that might have strayed too far from the hay drops. He didn't want any of them starving while snow continued to linger on the ground even this late into spring. The snow was just one more painful reminder of the storm that had taken Jenny and Dale.

At least Jake wasn't feeling the cold. He'd been riding long enough and working hard enough that sweat had beaded under the rim of his Stetson and trickled down his back beneath his sheepskin jacket. He could have stayed out in the pastures, but he had other things to deal with—like that horse Dusty was having delivered. Jake wouldn't have even known about it if he hadn't happened into an area of cell reception that morning. Then he'd had to ride Buck hard to get back in time for delivery.

Dusty hadn't stayed after the funeral to help out, but he had no problem sending Jake something else to take care of…as if he had the time. Dusty had promised, though, that the horse was going to benefit the ranch. That breeding it would create rodeo horses they could sell for even more than they sold the quarter horses they bred.

Since taking over the ranch from Grandpa Jake, Jake and, later, Dale had worked on ways to expand the operation beyond cattle. At first it had been risky, but their risks had paid off as the ranch prospered. While Dale and Jenny wouldn't benefit from that now, Jake would make certain that their kids did—that they owned as much of the ranch as he and his brothers did.

So hopefully Dusty was right and that horse was worth the trouble it was already causing

Jake, having to ride back at a breakneck speed. As they neared the barns, he reached down to pat Buck's neck; his hair was damp, like Jake's back. For all their effort, they'd just made it. An unfamiliar truck had already backed a trailer close to the barn. He'd told Dusty to make them wait for him before they let the thing out.

Dusty had won the horse in some kind of side bet with its owner. If he could ride the bronco that no one else had ever ridden, it would become his. While that was a source of pride for the rodeo rider, it was a source of concern for Jake. That meant the bronco was difficult and unpredictable—the last thing he needed around his family and his workers.

And now there were those other women and Katie and her son. But he hadn't seen them around the barns yet. Hopefully he never would. Katie and Caleb had already invaded enough of his life—his home, his work, his dreams. He'd once loved her so much—so much that he'd let her go. But he hadn't let her go completely; some part of him had always held on to her. But it wouldn't be fair for him to do that now, to try to include Katie and Caleb any more than they already were in his crazy life.

At least Little Jake hadn't had a nightmare since that first night Katie had arrived. Jake suspected that was because of Caleb; the toddler was so enthralled with him that he spent his days trailing him around and tiring himself out. Ian was better, too, with Caleb around to constantly remind him of all the things he forgot. Jake often heard the boys giggling in Ian's room after they were supposed to be sleeping. He hadn't ratted them out because he loved hearing the laughter again. Sometimes Miller had hopped in on his crutches to join them.

But it wasn't easy for Miller to get around with that heavy cast, which was why Jake hadn't moved back to the foreman's cottage yet. Miller didn't want the girls helping him shower. So it landed on Jake.

Just like this dang horse Dusty had sent him.

His knees pressing against Buck's sides, he urged the quarter horse to hurry down the drive toward the trailer. Two men stood near the back of it, pulling down the ramp. He recognized one as the barn manager; the other must have been the driver. But the men weren't the only ones standing too close to the doors of the trailer.

A red-haired woman and a little blond boy stood near the end of the ramp.

"No!" Jake shouted. "Stop!"

But the men were already drawing open the doors. Jake and Buck closed the distance between them and the barn—just as the horse burst from the back of the trailer. His black coat was wet, not just damp like Buck's. And he frothed at the mouth, horrible cries coming from it. He kicked at the air, kicked at the men, then turned and started down the ramp— toward the little boy and the woman, who stood frozen with fear, just watching as the bronco charged at them.

CHAPTER EIGHT

KATIE WOULD HAVE SCREAMED—like the horse seemed to be doing as he thrashed and reared up. But she didn't have time. Not to scream and not to move before that thing, hooves banging against the metal ramp, charged toward her and Caleb.

Caleb! She couldn't lose her son or let him get hurt. She reached for him, but she was too late.

A horse brushed against them, knocking them back from that metal ramp. It wasn't the black horse but a tan one, with a rider on it. As Jake and his horse moved between them and the wild horse, he caught the bridle dangling around the open mouth of the beast. He pulled the bronco up short while he strained against him.

The other men rushed forward then, catching hold of the bronco and moving him away from the middle of the barn toward an open stall. The bronco reared up, his front legs paw-ing at the air. He didn't want to go inside that stall. He didn't want to be here.

Katie could relate. The ranch was the last place she wanted to be, especially now. This proved to her that it was too dangerous for Caleb and way too dangerous for her. Her heart pounded hard with fear.

"Are you okay?" she asked her son.

His blue eyes wide, he nodded. "Yeah, that was cool!"

Jake swung out of the saddle and helped the other two men get the black horse into the stall.

"Mr. Big Jake is so cool," Caleb murmured, and he started away from her, toward where Jake's horse stood, reins dangling in the sawdust on the barn floor. Before her son could reach for them, Katie grabbed his shoulder and pulled him back against her. While her body trembled with fear, his seemed to tremble with excitement. "That horse is so pretty..."

He wasn't looking at the docile tan one who stood calmly beside them. He was staring instead at the black one who reared yet in the stall, his nostrils flaring as he fairly foamed at the mouth.

She shook her head. "No, no, it's not. We need to get out of here," she said. They were in the way—they'd nearly gotten trampled because of it.

She tugged on Caleb's shoulder, trying to pull him back from the horses. But he resisted, shaking off her hand to rush over to Jake just as the tall cowboy closed the door on the stall and that crazed horse.

Her breath escaped in a sigh of relief. The horse wouldn't hurt Caleb. But then Jake turned, his face red with fury, and she worried that he was the greater danger. Maybe not to Caleb but to her.

He looked up, over her son's head, and focused on her, his gaze hard. "You have to be careful around the horses," he said. Then he glanced down at Caleb. "They're so much bigger than you and your mama and could easily hurt you even if they don't mean to."

Katie shuddered. He hadn't had to remind her of that. She'd always been uneasy with the horses—probably because her mother had constantly warned her about how dangerous they were, how easily they could hurt someone. She'd certainly been right in this case. But Caleb had been so curious about the horse trailer, especially when they'd overheard the men saying that the delivery was some notorious bucking bronc.

"I think that one means to hurt people," she said. "And Mr. Jake is right, Caleb. We need to get away from the horses. You're too little to be around animals this big." So was she.

"But Miss Sadie said you were born in the saddle, Mr. Big Jake, so you would've been super little when you started riding," he said.

And Katie had thought the only thing her son and the older lady had been talking about was cookies. Apparently they'd been talking about Jake, as well.

Some of the tension eased from Jake's body when he chuckled. "I was. My mama was a rodeo rider. Pretty much all of my brothers and I were born in the saddle."

"Wow…" Caleb murmured in awe. "I wish—"

"It's too late for you to be born in the saddle," Katie informed him.

"It's not too late for me to learn to ride a horse," Caleb persisted. And turning his puppy dog eyes on Jake, he implored him, "Will you teach me, please, Mr. Big Jake, please…"

Before he could answer, Katie did. "Mr. Jake is much too busy to give you lessons, Caleb. And you have other lessons you need to—"

"It's Saturday, Mommy, and kindergarten is easy. I don't have to work hard at my numbers and letters. I already know them. I need to learn how to be around the big horses," he said. "So I don't get hurt."

Her son had been spending too much time with Sadie Haven. He was beginning to get as manipulative as she was. But the old woman was as intuitive as she was manipulative. She chose that moment to arrive in the barn.

"So where's this notorious bucking bronco Dusty had delivered here?" she asked as she sauntered into the barn.

She wasn't alone. She'd brought the other kids with her. The trek from the house to the barn must have been too far for Miller to attempt on crutches because Melanie pushed him in his wheelchair while Emily carried Little Jake and Ian rode Taye's strong shoulders.

"It's in there," Caleb answered his new best friend. "It nearly jumped on me and Mommy but Mr. Big Jake saved us."

He had.

Once again Katie realized how close a call she and her son had had with that dangerous bronco, and she started trembling again in reaction. "We…we need to go back to the house," she insisted.

Caleb shook his head. "Everybody just got here. I wanna stay in the barn. I never got to be outside at Grandma and Grandpa O's."

She flinched.

Taye swung Ian down from her shoulders and stepped closer to Katie. Pitching her voice low, she said, "We'll all keep an eye on him—if you need to get out of here for a while." Taye was always so perceptive, but in this instance, probably everyone could tell how upset Katie was over their close call with the bronco.

"Thank you," she murmured. She had to get out of here—before she fell apart.

"You can stay," Katie told Caleb, and her voice stern, added, "but be very careful." Then she headed for those open doors to the barn. She couldn't escape the place fast enough. But she never made it through the doors before a big hand closed around her arm, stopping her. Trapping her in the barn with all her emotions. And fears…

THE MINUTE HE touched her, Jake knew he'd made a mistake. But he was too shaken over her and Caleb's near miss with that crazy horse to let her just walk away. He had to make sure that she and her son were more careful in the future. Because he was too busy to keep an eye on them, too busy to protect them all the time.

That was why it was best he kept his distance from them. Yet he didn't loosen his grasp on her arm. He used his free hand to pull open the door of the tack room, and then he tugged her inside with him. Usually he only smelled the leather from the saddles and the hay that tracked everywhere when he was in that room. But now he smelled Katie, the sweetness of that soft floral scent she wore.

Memories of long ago rushed over him, of hiding inside the tack room with her so that he could kiss her without his younger brothers watching and jeering at them. Despite how hopeless a future with her was, he wanted to kiss her again.

But he knew she wouldn't welcome that since she acted like she could barely stand his touch, jerking her arm free of his grasp. "What are you doing?"

"What are you doing?" he repeated the question to her, his voice vibrating with the emotion coursing through him. It wasn't even anger; it was something rawer than that—something close to despair. He couldn't lose anyone else.

Not that Katie and her son were his to lose. And this incident proved they could never be. If he hadn't headed back to the barn when he had...

If he hadn't gotten Buck between them and that bronco...

He shuddered and said, "We just had a double funeral a week ago. Did you want us to hold another one for you and that boy?"

She gasped. "That's a horrible thing to say. And of course not. I had no idea that *thing* was in the trailer. Your other horses don't act like that."

No. They didn't, or he wouldn't have kept them around. But Dusty wasn't here for him to lash out at, so he'd taken his anger out on her. It wasn't fair, and he knew it.

But before he could apologize, she continued, "And you wouldn't be holding funerals for us anyway, Jake. We're nothing to you."

He flinched at that. That might have been how she saw it, but it wasn't how he felt. They mattered to him. Katie always had, and her son...

There was something pretty special about that kid. He had a natural charm that enchanted everyone around him.

"I just don't want to see anyone get hurt," he said. That was why he'd wanted to keep his distance from Katie and her kid. He didn't want to fall for them when he knew he had nothing to offer them. As if to remind himself, he added, "I think your son has been through enough in his young life."

Her body still tense with defensiveness, she said, "I know what he's been through—losing his father who doted on him, who was the most amazing man..." Her voice cracked as tears welled in her green eyes.

She'd really loved her husband.

She blinked away those tears and cleared her voice before continuing, "He also lost his grandparents who refuse to see him anymore."

He furrowed his brow with confusion. "Your parents wouldn't do that."

She shook her head. "No, they wouldn't. Matt's did. They couldn't bear to see Caleb or even talk to him anymore. He reminded them too much of what they'd lost, of what we'd all lost."

"Do you feel like that?" Jake asked. "The kid doesn't look like you, so he must look like his dad." He knew that for certain because he'd seen the man who'd been making her laugh in the spot where just a couple of months earlier Jake had made her cry so hard.

She was smiling now albeit with a wistfulness. "He does look exactly like his father," she said. "He acts just like him too."

"So is he too painful a reminder of his father for you?" He felt a little like that, and he hadn't actually ever met the man. No. Caleb didn't really remind Jake of Matt Morris but of the life Jake had given up all those years ago when he'd given Katie up. It had been for the best, though—for all of them.

"Caleb is the best representation of Matt," she said. "He's all the good. The kindness, the sweetness, the love…"

He heard it in her voice. She still loved her late husband. Jake couldn't compete with him—even now that he was gone. Especially not now. Jake couldn't give them anywhere close to the time and attention that Matt Morris had. They deserved more than Jake could give them. He could barely take care of all his other responsibilities at the ranch and with his nephews, and now this darn bronco Dusty had sent him.

He certainly didn't need the distraction or the responsibility of caring for Katie and her son. But he couldn't blame the boy for any of that, especially not the child's fascination with the ranch. And because Caleb was so fascinated, he had to learn to be more cautious, so the boy didn't get hurt.

"I'll give him riding lessons," Jake offered.

Her green eyes widened with surprise. "What?"

Jake was just as surprised as she was that

he'd made the offer. "He's desperate to learn to ride," he said. "So I'll give him lessons."

She shook her head. "No, you're too busy. I can't ask you to take time away from the ranch."

"You're not asking," he pointed out, doubting that she would have. "I'm offering."

She narrowed those pretty green eyes and stared up at him. "Why?"

He couldn't answer her. He really had no idea why he wanted to teach him. Maybe it was the way the kid had asked him…with those puppy dog eyes.

Maybe it was just that Jake had missed Caleb these past few days that he'd been avoiding him and his mother. He'd missed that laughter…

And he appreciated what the boy's presence had done for his nephews, how he was helping them heal. And maybe, somehow, he was also helping Jake heal.

Jake shrugged. "He's been good for Ian and Miller and Little Jake…" And for him. "And he asked."

"He doesn't realize what he's getting into," she murmured with a slight shudder.

"You don't like how I taught you?" he asked and once again those memories rushed over him, the memories of kissing her soft lips as he'd lifted her into the saddle…

The way he'd held her hand…around the reins, his thumb brushing across her knuckles. Did her skin still feel like silk like it had all those years ago?

Were her lips still that soft?

God help him, he wanted to find out. He wanted to kiss her. And he wondered if she wanted it too because she was staring up at him as if those same memories were playing through her mind. Her lips parted slightly, her breathing as shallow as his. Were her lungs aching for breath too?

Was she breathing in only to smell him like he smelled her?

Her body was tense, but it seemed to lean toward his, into his just as she had when they were young. And every time she'd leaned into him like that, he'd leaned down to her.

He'd just started to lower his head when the door creaked open behind him. Had he not shut it tightly?

He whirled around to her son standing in the open doorway. Caleb stared up at them with wide eyes. He wasn't the only one watching them. The others had gathered behind him in the doorway.

"Are you kissing my mommy?" Caleb asked.

Katie gasped.

And Jake felt as guilty as he had when her father had caught them making out on the swing on the porch of their blue Victorian in town.

"No, of course not!" he exclaimed, as if his body was not aching with the desire to do just that.

"I heard Miss Sadie telling Miss Cooper that that's what you used to do in here," Caleb shared.

Jake's grandmother stood close behind the boy, so Jake raised his gaze to glare at her. She should have been more careful so that the boy wouldn't have overheard her. Fortunately Caleb didn't sound upset about it, just curious.

"Miss Sadie is getting senile," Jake replied with a pointed glance at his grandmother. "So don't listen to her."

"What were you doing, then?" Caleb asked as he continued to study the two of them.

"We were just talking about me giving you riding lessons," Jake replied.

"You will?" Caleb asked, his voice quavering with excitement.

Jake nodded.

And Caleb vaulted himself at Jake, wrapping his arms around his legs in a tight embrace. And Jake found himself reaching down to skim his hand over the soft blond hair to the little boy's back. He patted him—probably awkwardly—but then this wasn't his son.

He had to remind himself of that.

That Katie had lived their life—the one they'd planned together—with another man.

A man she still loved. She wasn't ready to move on with anyone, let alone Jake.

That was good. He already had more responsibilities than he could handle. He had to focus on his family, the one Dale and Jenny had left behind. He couldn't start a family of his own now. Or maybe ever...because the ranch and his nephews were always going to take priority with him.

CHAPTER NINE

THE LAST THING Katie wanted was Jake spending more time with her son. No. The last thing she wanted was Jake spending any more time with her. Was he about to kiss her in the tack room just moments ago, before Caleb had interrupted them?

Was she about to let him?

No. She must have just imagined that moment, imagined that attraction sparking between them. Even more than it had when they were younger.

Because if she hadn't been imagining it, if she had been feeling all those feelings, that was like betraying Matt all over again, just as she had every time she'd thought of Jake over the years.

And if she let her son fall for Jake, that would be another betrayal. The only person Matt had loved more than her was Caleb.

Now his son already idolized Big Jake. If Caleb spent any more time with him...

Maybe that idolization would dissolve with familiarity. And maybe the reality of horseback riding and ranch life wouldn't appeal to her son any more than it had to Katie. Born and raised in town, in that Victorian house with all the antiques and her worrywart mother, teenage Katie hadn't been comfortable at all when she'd visited the ranch. But she'd known how much Jake had loved it, so she'd tried to love it too. She'd even agreed that when they were done traveling and living in a big city, they would settle down on the ranch and raise their kids here. But Katie hadn't intended to be the kind of ranching wife that Sadie Haven had been. She wasn't going to ride the range with him and help him brand cattle or anything like that.

She'd intended just to handle the finances, like she did now. And Jake had understood and appreciated that; he'd said then that they complemented each other. That they completed each other.

Her breath escaped in a shaky sigh. Taye, standing beside her at the fence surrounding the outside riding arena, gripped her arm. "Are you all right?"

No. She wasn't. She couldn't lie to Taye, so she shook her head.

The others must have thought it was the riding lesson that concerned her—because Caleb had begged for Jake to start them right away. He'd already waited a whole week to learn and hadn't wanted to wait another moment longer.

"I was younger than him when I learned to ride," Ian assured her.

"He'll be fine," Sadie told her as they watched Jake lift Caleb onto the back of a small horse. "That's the gelding he used when he taught Miller and Ian how to ride. It's even more docile than Buck."

Fortunately it was smaller, as well. But it wasn't the size of the horse that unsettled Katie so much as the size of the man. He was so big, so much larger than life, just like his grandmother. But he was also gentle and patient. She'd seen him with the boys, how sweet he was with them.

He was sweet with Caleb, too, making sure to always include him like he had the day of Miller's homecoming when he'd picked up her son and Ian.

"I want to go riding too," Ian said.

"You can't," Sadie told him.

"Why not? I always go riding."

"You can't until your brain heals," Sadie said.

"What's wrong with my brain?"

Pain clutched Katie's heart. He'd forgotten again what had happened to him and his parents. Usually he only forgot in the morning or the middle of the night. She'd thought he was getting better, especially since Miller had returned and the cast on the seven-year-old's leg served as a visual reminder of the accident.

Miller arched up from his wheelchair and thumped his cast against a fence rung. "Your brain got hurt when my leg got hurt," Miller said. "You know that."

Ian stared at his brother's cast, but his dark eyes were clouded with confusion.

Not wanting to remind him of everything else that had happened, Katie caught his hand in hers and drew his attention. "Maybe Uncle Jake will let you help teach Caleb how to ride," Katie suggested, "since you've been doing it so long."

The confusion left his gaze, and he climbed the rungs of the fence to shout out to his uncle. "Remember how you taught me, Uncle Jake."

Everybody smiled at Ian's having to prod someone's memory. Even Miller...

Miller was the most impatient with his younger brother's forgetfulness. But then she supposed he hadn't been around as much as

Jake and Sadie had been since the accident. He'd been in the hospital for two weeks.

Miller had been quiet when he'd first come home. Not as quiet as Little Jake. But he hadn't acted like a young boy—like Caleb—did. He'd seemed withdrawn and uninterested in what was going on around him. Now he called out directions to his uncle, as well.

"Hey, peanut gallery. Get your butts in here and help me," Jake said with an exasperated-sounding sigh. Then he headed toward the fence, leading Caleb and the horse behind him. Caleb gasped and clutched at the saddle horn.

Katie gasped, too, and clutched at the top railing of the fence. She was tempted to vault over it and grab her son off that horse. He'd already had a close brush with getting hurt—or worse—just a short while ago. Starting the lessons today was a bad idea.

But Jake turned back and steadied him with his hand on his shoulder. "Hold on with your knees," he told him. "Squeeze your legs together. You won't fall off."

Caleb let out a shaky breath and nodded. "Okay, okay…"

"You got this," Jake assured him.

Caleb's chin tilted up and his shoulders

squared with pride. With those few words Jake had given the little boy confidence in himself.

That was a gift.

She mouthed the words *Thank you* to him. She should have thanked him earlier—in the tack room—when he'd offered to teach him. She knew that he was busy, that he didn't have time. But he'd agreed to do this for Caleb.

And he'd agreed to start the lessons right away instead of making the impatient little boy wait any longer. He had that new horse to deal with, his nephews, the ranch…

But he'd taken the time to give her son lessons and something even more important than that: confidence. Tears stung her eyes, so she looked away, not wanting Caleb to see them. Or Jake…

She blinked them back and focused. Caleb and Jake might not have noticed that emotion was overwhelming her. But someone else had.

Sadie.

The older woman was staring at her, and a smile of satisfaction curved her lips.

"What is it?" Katie asked, wondering why Sadie seemed so pleased with herself.

The older woman either hadn't heard her or was ignoring her, as she helped Ian over the fence to join his uncle. Then she took the wheelchair from Melanie and said, "I'll bring Miller through the gate."

"That's why she seems so happy." Taye answered the question Sadie had ignored. The younger woman gestured inside the fence, at Sadie helping Jake with the boys. "She's taking care of her family."

Emily snorted, which surprised the others into laughing at her. She was so pretty it seemed too unladylike for her to do. But as pretty as she was, she was also tough.

Katie wished she was stronger. That she hadn't needed anyone's help after Matt died, but she'd felt so alone after losing her best friend that she'd had to come home to Willow Creek.

"I think she's up to something," Emily continued as she shifted Little Jake from one hip to the other. He watched the boys inside the fence and seemed entirely uninterested in their conversation. Not that he would repeat it even if he was listening. "It's too much of a coincidence that she hired only single women—or manipulated them into coming here—that either have a history with her grandsons, like you, Katie, or that are about their ages like the rest of us."

Taye laughed off Emily's concern. "She's not trying to set me up with anyone."

"Or me," Melanie chimed in.

"Not yet," Emily said.

Melanie shook her head, which sent her thick chocolate brown curls tumbling around her shoulders. "She can't. I'm already married."

Emily glanced at her hand. "You don't wear a ring."

"I, uh…" she murmured, and tears pooled in her dark eyes.

Katie reached out and touched her arm. "A lot of people don't like wearing rings." She doubted that was Melanie's reason, though. There was something else going on with the young physical therapist. But it wasn't their business.

"And then there's you, Katie," Emily continued. "You're still wearing your rings."

She glanced down at her own hand, at those rings that winked back at her. "I still feel married."

"Are you divorced?" Melanie asked. She was new to Willow Creek. She didn't know.

Katie hadn't had to tell anyone for a while what had happened. "My husband, Matt, died in a car accident a year ago."

"Like how the boys lost their parents," Emily said. "I didn't know that was how he'd died too. No wonder Sadie was able to coerce you into moving out here to help with them."

"I did it as much for Caleb as for them," Katie admitted. "He loves his teacher and his best friend, and he's already lost so much."

"He's not the only one," Melanie murmured. "Sounds like you lost a lot too."

"A wonderful man," she said, as memories of Matt flooded her mind. He'd been her friend a long time before he'd become her husband. When Jake had broken her heart, he'd picked up the pieces and patiently put them back together again with his friendship and his humor. "He was so sweet. So loving…"

It wasn't fair that he'd been taken so young, just as it wasn't fair that Dale and Jenny had been, as well. Tears pooled in her eyes, and before she could blink them away, one trailed down her cheek. She missed them all so much, but Matt most of all.

A CRY OF dismay slipped through the little boy's lips, so Jake slowed the horse's trot. "I'm sorry if I scared you," Jake said. "I shouldn't have had him going so fast. But you're doing so well."

He really was—the kid was a natural in the saddle.

"I'm okay," Caleb said, but his voice cracked. "I'm not scared."

"Then what's wrong?"

The kid's bottom lip looked like it was quivering, like he was about to cry. "I think Mommy's crying…" And there was a quaver of panic in his voice now.

Jake glanced over the fence, at where the women stood together talking. Katie reached up and brushed a hand across her cheek. Had she been crying?

About what?

Was she that nervous that her son was going to get hurt riding? Or that he was going to get hurt spending time with Jake? Jake didn't have much time to spend with him; he'd offered the lessons but had warned the boy that it would probably be only a couple of times a week.

"Your mother looks fine," Jake assured Katie's son. But he wondered…

Obviously so did Caleb because he stared so intently at her that he began to slide out of the saddle. Jake caught him around the waist and held him in place.

"Sometimes people cry happy tears," Jake told him. "Maybe she's just really proud of how well you're riding already."

Caleb glanced at him. "Do you think?"

Jake nodded. "Yes, you're doing really well. Maybe you were born in the saddle too."

Caleb let out a little chuckle. "Mommy is not a rodeo rider. She doesn't even like to ride the horses on the carousel. She sits on the sled instead."

"Maybe I didn't do a very good job of teaching her then," Jake said. Or maybe she hadn't wanted to do anything that reminded her of him. A pang of regret struck him that he hadn't handled the breakup better, that he hadn't been gentler with her. He'd just been so afraid that she would insist on quitting college, too, and coming back to Willow Creek with him. And he hadn't wanted her to make the sacrifices he'd had to make.

"You're a good teacher, Mr. Big Jake," Caleb complimented him.

"See then, your mama is just proud of you," he said.

The little boy's breath hitched. "I don't know.

Mommy doesn't cry happy tears. She smiles or laughs when she's happy. She only cries sad tears."

Katie's son was very observant—because Jake realized he was right. Jake had never seen her cry when she was happy. Instead she smiled that smile that lit up her face and had once lit up his whole world.

"She's cried a lot since Daddy died," Caleb shared. "And he's not here to cheer her up. He used to make her laugh so much that she wasn't ever sad. Not like she is now." Tears welled now in the little boy's eyes.

And Jake's heart ached for the loss he'd experienced. "You make your mommy very happy too," he assured him.

Caleb released a shaky sigh. "Not like Daddy did…"

Jake had already suspected he didn't have a chance with Katie. Not that he wanted one. It wasn't as if he had the time for a relationship with anyone, least of all a woman with a young child. But now he knew for certain that she wasn't over her husband. And suddenly he felt like crying himself.

He hadn't done that in years, though—not since he'd realized tears didn't change a thing. They didn't make people come back from the dead or even come back home after they'd left you.

Katie was physically back in Willow Creek. But not emotionally. Emotionally she was still with another man.

CHAPTER TEN

FOR THE PAST couple of weeks, Katie had been able to manage her other clients over the phone and the spotty internet connection. But she'd known that wouldn't satisfy everyone for very long. While most of her clients had understood and appreciated that she was helping the Haven family deal with Jenny and Dale's loss, there were a few that were not as appreciative. Mr. Herrema, who owned a small printing shop in town, insisted on meeting with her at her office.

She hadn't realized until then that she should have driven her own vehicle to the ranch instead of riding with Sadie.

Even though Katie was happy to be able to help fill some of the void Jenny and Dale's deaths had left with their sons and with the business, she was beginning to feel a bit like a hostage. Trapped...

Not just physically but emotionally, as well.

She was trapped in the past, in those memories of when she'd loved Jake. Every time she watched him give a riding lesson to Caleb, she remembered that he'd been just as patient and kind with her. Maybe even more so since she'd been so afraid, while her son was fearless. Jake had distracted her from her fears with his kisses and his sweet encouragement. She'd loved him so much, and she'd thought he'd loved her just as much. But she'd been wrong. Twelve years ago, he'd told her how wrong she'd been to ever believe they would have a future together. Nothing—and everything—had changed since then, only further ensuring that they had no future together. She couldn't betray Matt by going back to Jake, not after he'd worked so hard mending the heart Jake had broken. Not that Jake was at all interested in her or in anything but the ranch.

Katie couldn't stay at the ranch. No matter how much Caleb loved it, it wasn't their home. They'd only been staying there to help and because he would have missed Ian and Emily too much. But once the school year ended, she would leave. That was only three more weeks.

If she could make it that long…

She had to make sure that when she left, she had someplace to go and some way to finance it. She was glad that she'd been able to get the ranch books up to date, but she couldn't lose any of her other clients. Establishing her accounting practice in town had taken too long.

At breakfast that morning at the long table in the kitchen, she asked if anyone had a vehicle she could borrow to run to town.

"Jake can take you," Sadie offered. Even though he wasn't there, she seemed to think he would be willing—or could be coerced—into driving Katie.

At the thought of being alone with him again, like she'd been in the tack room, panic surged through Katie, pressing on her lungs—making it hard for her to draw a deep breath. She'd been doing her best to ignore him, except when he was giving Caleb riding lessons. Then she forced herself to watch him—to make sure the horse didn't hurt Caleb. But despite her best efforts, those memories of her riding lessons kept creeping into her mind, and she was worried that watching Jake be so sweet and patient with her son was going to allow him to creep back into her heart.

If she and Jake were stuck in a vehicle together, like they'd been stuck in the tack room for those short moments last Saturday, she was worried about what might happen. What she might want to happen...

Heat suffused her face, and she shook her head. "He's much too busy with the ranch."

And he was. He was always gone before anyone woke up in the morning and came back at night after everyone else had already eaten. The only time he was around was for those afternoon lessons with Caleb. He included the other boys in those too. He'd even offered to teach Katie again, but she'd declined. She didn't want him helping her into the saddle, holding her hands over the reins...

Making her pulse quicken in anticipation of his kiss...

A kiss that hadn't come. A kiss that could not come.

"And I don't know how long the appointment will take." Mr. Herrema liked to drone on and on about his financial plans—ones his business didn't have enough income to support.

Sadie didn't offer her the use of one of the ranch vehicles. Instead she stood up from the head of the table and headed out of the room— probably with the intention of tracking down Jake.

"Take my car," Emily offered. "The boys and I have school all day anyway."

That was true. Caleb would be with her. And

surely, Katie would be back before his riding lesson that afternoon. But even if she missed it, she was sure that he would be fine. Unlike her, he was a natural in the saddle.

He'd even announced that he was going to be a cowboy, too, like Mr. Big Jake. So much for familiarity with Jake dissipating Caleb's hero worship of the man. If anything, her son was only growing more and more attached to Jake.

She stared at him across the table where he chattered with Ian and Miller and made faces at Little Jake to try to get him laughing. Once in a while the toddler's lips parted on a sweet smile and occasionally a giggle slipped out. But not often. Not often enough.

"Caleb will be fine," Taye said as she plopped the last blueberry pancake onto Katie's plate. "The kid whisperer can handle all of them with no problem, like she always does."

Emily wasn't the only kid whisperer, though. Melanie was amazing with Miller; he rarely used his wheelchair now. And Taye kept everyone happy with her cooking and especially her baking.

The clothes that had been loose on Katie since Matt's death now fit her again, some a little too snuggly. But she poured syrup onto a pancake and ate it anyway; it was too fluffy and fruity to resist.

Emily placed a set of keys next to her plate. "Take your time in town. I won't be going anywhere for a while." She uttered a weary sigh as she slid off the bench. Little Jake immediately scrambled out of his booster seat, reaching for her. She and Melanie herded the boys upstairs to the playroom she'd turned into her makeshift classroom.

"I think Emily needs a break," Taye remarked to Katie, who nodded in agreement.

"Yes, we need to make that happen this weekend for her," Katie said. "And for Melanie." The physical therapist had been looking especially tired and pale lately. Since she and Melanie shared the bathroom between their two bedrooms, Katie knew why.

Taye nodded and swept her empty plate off the table. "Now you need to go enjoy your time off."

Usually she would have helped Taye clean up before she headed to the ranch office, but the younger woman rushed her out the door. Despite Taye's prodding, Katie was a little late getting to town. She'd forgotten how far Ranch Haven was from Willow Creek and from her little office on Main Street.

She drove past her parents' Victorian with its purple door, where the yard had come alive with flowers. The windows sparkled in the sunshine; everything was so pristine. She couldn't bring Caleb back there—it would be like caging him after his freedom at the ranch.

She would have to find them another place. One with a yard that Caleb could actually play in without being scolded not to trample the flowers or the grass. How had she thought moving back home was a good idea for her son?

Or for her?

She had been in so much shock after Matt's unexpected death and his parents' rejection of Caleb that she hadn't taken the time to think about her actions. Just as she hadn't taken the time to think before she'd let Sadie Haven whisk her and Caleb off to the ranch.

She'd expected that driving away from it, watching it get smaller and smaller in the rearview mirror, would give her a sense of freedom. But she'd only felt a sickness in her stomach; maybe it was from eating too many pancakes that morning. Or maybe it was because she'd left Caleb behind, and she was worried that he would never want to leave the ranch or Mr. Big Jake.

Maybe Katie was worried that she'd started feeling the same. Watching Jake with her son reminded her of the plans they'd made, the big family they'd wanted. She also had to remember that he'd broken her heart and another man had healed it with his kindness and his patience and his humor. In the beginning when she'd been so sad that she'd just wanted to stay in bed and cry, Matt had insisted on her coming out of the dorm for fresh air and sunshine and trips to the comedy clubs he'd loved. He'd kept her spirits up and made her smile and laugh again. He'd healed her with his love and had made her able to love again. She owed him her loyalty.

She also owed her clients, who'd taken a chance on her when she'd returned a year ago and started her own business. Her assistant, Robert, was supposed to have opened the office today for this meeting. But as she parallel parked at the curb down the street, she saw Mr. Herrema, sunlight gleaming on his bald head, pacing back and forth in front of the building. Maybe he'd refused to go inside with Robert.

Or maybe Robert had forgotten that a client was coming into the office. Since she'd moved to the ranch, he had been working from his home, and from the texts and emails that came through from him, it was apparent that he kept odd hours. She'd have to talk to him…

But first she needed to speak to Mr. Herrema. She turned off the engine and stepped out into the street. Someone tooted and waved as they passed her. They hadn't forgotten her in the twelve years she'd been gone; they were unlikely to forget her in the few short weeks she was spending at the ranch.

Maybe that was why she'd returned to Willow Creek. She'd felt so alone and lost in Chicago without Matt and his parents. So she'd moved home to her family and to the friends she still had in town. Unfortunately she'd lost the closest two of them much too soon.

Dale and Jenny. They were why she was staying at the ranch. She closed her eyes against the sting of tears, drew in a deep breath and joined Mr. Herrema on the curb.

"Where have you been?" he demanded. "You're late, and I don't have time to wait around for you to show up!"

Yet he'd done just that.

"I'd forgotten how far from town Ranch Haven is," she admitted honestly.

The bald man's face flushed a bright red. "That's not my fault," he said. "I can't believe you've moved out there to chase after your old boyfriend."

Instead of flushing with fury like his face had, her skin chilled, like she'd been doused with ice water. "That's insulting and uncalled-for. I'm only temporarily staying at the ranch to help with the books after Dale and Jenny's deaths."

He snorted. "Jake Haven runs that ranch now. You're there for him and everybody knows it. I took a chance on you because I thought you were a professional, Katie. That you'd grown up during your time away from Willow Creek, but it's clear you're still acting like the teenage girl you once were, mooning over Jake Haven."

Pain jabbed her heart as his words reminded her too much of what Jake had told her that day by the fountain when he'd dumped her. That she'd been chasing after him. Clearly he wasn't the only one who'd felt that way then. And apparently even now.

"You're wrong about me, Mr. Herrema," she said as she glared at him. "You're the one who's not behaving professionally. I think it's best that you find another accountant for your business needs."

He sucked in a breath. "I came here to fire you!" Or at least that was what he wanted her to believe now. "I'll find someone who's serious about their business. And you'll find that you're going to lose a lot more clients than me, Katie, if you focus only on the Havens. They don't run this town."

Instead of feeling threatened, she was amused. "Actually they do," she pointed out, as a smile twitched at her lips. "Ben Haven is the mayor." And if Mr. Herrema was so lacking in compassion that he couldn't understand why she'd had to go out to the ranch to help after the devastating loss of Dale and Jenny, then she truly didn't want him as a client.

Mr. Herrema sputtered out something unintelligible as his face got redder yet; then he stomped off down the sidewalk.

She didn't spare him a backward glance before reaching for the knob of her office door, which turned easily without her having to unlock it. Robert had come in to meet Mr. Herrema, just as she'd requested.

When she stepped inside, he was there, pushing a cup of coffee into her hand. "Are you okay?" he asked. "Mr. Herrema was losing it while he waited for you. He was way early, and then you were late. I imagine he just let you have it."

"I gave as good as I got," she admitted. Perhaps she was as unprofessional as she'd accused him of being. But what he'd said had made her defensive, and not just of herself. She'd been defensive of the Havens too. How could someone not feel compassion over all the losses they'd suffered?

"His business is tanking, and he knows it," Robert said. The accounting major had been handling Mr. Herrema's books, under Katie's supervision, so he knew the state of the man's finances. "He just wants to blame someone else for it."

She knew that, and that was why she wasn't particularly upset about losing his business. She couldn't afford to lose anyone else's, though, and she certainly didn't want the rest of the town thinking the same thing he did—that she was chasing after Jake Haven again.

"GET HIM TO the ER," Jake urged the barn foreman as he helped load the groom into the passenger side of the ranch pickup.

"I'm fine, Mr. Haven," the young man insisted. But blood trickled beneath the towel he held against the side of his head.

"You took a hard blow," Jake said. "You need to get checked out. Make sure you don't have a concussion."

Like Ian.

Now Jake knew how dangerous a concussion could be, even a mild one. He closed the passenger door and tapped the roof. "Go."

As the pickup started down the driveway, he pulled out his cell and punched in Dusty's contact.

"Hey, Jake, I don't have time to talk—"

"I don't have time to deal with this beast you sent us," Jake said. "You either need to have him moved somewhere else, or you gotta come back to deal with him yourself. He nearly knocked out a groom this morning when he tried to clean his stall. He's too dangerous."

The black bronco wasn't the only dangerous thing at Ranch Haven right now. Katie was, or at least his feelings for Katie were. Jake glanced toward the schoolhouse, but he knew she was gone. Grandma had called and tried to get him to bring her to town earlier, but he'd already been out checking the calves, making sure they were starting to eat the grain. He had a million other things to check on, as well. He didn't have time to go to town himself, let alone drive someone else. He barely had time to sleep.

Caleb and Ian raced toward the barn now, their little boots kicking up dust as they crossed the driveway. He muted his cell and asked them, "Where are you going?"

It was too early for a riding lesson now. Not that the boy really needed any more. He had mastered all the basics.

Ian stopped and glanced at his friend. "Where are we going?" he asked.

"Just to the barn," Caleb replied patiently. His friend was about the only thing the blond boy was patient with, but then he grabbed Ian's arm and tugged him through the double doors. "We only have a few minutes left of recess."

Recess...

The ranch had become a school and a rehab facility with food that tasted like it came from a five-star restaurant and first-class bakery. Grandma had gone all out to help her great-grandsons recover.

If only the rest of Jake's family would step up, as well...

When Grandpa had died, Jake's brothers had still been teenagers. He hadn't expected them to help, but Dale had. He'd helped before and after school and then full-time once he and Jenny had graduated. But Jake hadn't seen Baker or Ben since the morning Miller had come home from the hospital.

Dusty had taken off even before that and

then sent this bronco for him to handle. Instead of agreeing to deal with him, Dusty was just defending the horse. "Midnight's just restless without the rodeo…"

Jake unmuted his cell. "Like you would know," he said. "You're never without the rodeo."

Dusty had barely been able to stay away from it for two weeks to deal with the immediate aftermath of his twin's death. Not that Dusty had dealt with anything. That was probably why he'd left right after the funeral, just as their mom had left after their dad's, so she wouldn't have to deal with her grief. Or maybe she just hadn't wanted to deal with theirs. Was that why Dusty was staying away? Because it was too hard to see their nephews in so much pain?

Jake's stomach knotted at the thought of it, of how hard it was to deal with Little Jake's nightmares and Ian's memory lapses…

"I'm not riding now, Jake," Dusty said. "Well, not since I rode Midnight in that exhibition show, and that was just so I could win him for the ranch."

"If you're so concerned about the ranch, then come home!" Jake didn't wait for another excuse, just clicked off the phone. He drew in a deep breath of crisp spring air before turning to head back inside the barn. Until Dusty got back—if Dusty came home—Jake would have to take care of the bronco himself. He didn't want it hurting anyone else.

But as he walked down the wide aisle of the barn, he glimpsed someone else near the stall—two someones. They'd pulled a bucket close to the door. Caleb stood on top of it, reaching for the clasp that held that door shut.

"No!" Jake yelled.

His shout startled Caleb, who toppled off the bucket. But he'd released the clasp before he fell. The stall door creaked open, so that nothing stood between the wild horse and the freedom the bronco craved.

Nothing but the little boy who lay sprawled on the ground.

"No!" Jake yelled again, and he ran forward, hoping that he could reach the boy before the horse's flailing hooves struck him.

But the horse was so much closer and so much faster…

CHAPTER ELEVEN

KATIE HAD EXPECTED to feel good being back at her desk, back in her office and not at the ranch. Instead she felt uneasy. Maybe that was just because she'd left Caleb there—so far away from her.

Not that anything would happen to him. He was safe with Emily and Taye and Melanie.

And once she'd checked on a couple more things, she would return to the ranch. But not for long. Just until school was done.

While she wanted to help Dale and Jenny's sons, she didn't need to live with them to do that. She and Caleb could visit them and, once they found a home of their own, have the boys come to them for playdates and sleepovers. At the ranch, they had so many people who cared for and about them. And despite Sadie's protests, Katie could handle the ranch books until they could find a bookkeeper for the payroll and daily business of accounts receivable and payable. She would keep doing the tax filings for them, as she'd done for Dale and Jenny.

But she needed to focus on her and Caleb now, on finding them a place of their own in Willow Creek. When she'd first moved home, she wouldn't have been able to qualify for a mortgage or probably even a lease, not when she was just launching her business. But she could qualify now, as long as she didn't lose any more clients.

"Are other people complaining that I'm not here?" she asked Robert, who'd sprawled in a chair in front of her desk.

He hesitated, and that in itself was an answer. "You know Willow Creek," he said. "People here like to do business the old-fashioned way. Face-to-face."

"Assure them I'll be in the office soon," she said. Summer was coming. The school year ended in three weeks. That wasn't soon enough for Katie, but it would probably seem too soon to Caleb. It was too soon for her to buy a house, so she'd have to see what was available to lease on short notice.

"Good," her assistant replied. "I've missed you. It's been super weird not having you here."

"I miss you too," she said. But she hadn't missed the office as much as she'd thought she would have. Maybe that was because the only space she'd been able to afford on Main Street was cramped and smelled faintly of smoke from the cigar shop it had once been, mixed in with a musty smell from the damp basement beneath it. "I'll be back full-time as soon as I can."

"The ranch business is big," Robert said. He'd helped her out with it too. "They really need a full-time bookkeeper on staff."

She sighed. They did. "You interested?" she asked him hopefully.

The younger man shuddered. "Too far from the comforts of town for me."

She laughed. "The ranch is very comfortable," she assured him. "The house is beautiful. The food is amazing—"

"I can tell," Robert interjected. "You finally look like a strong gust won't blow you down Main Street."

She narrowed her eyes in a mock glare. "You're not supposed to comment on someone's weight."

"You look healthy," he said. "Maybe you should stay at the ranch."

"I can't." For so many reasons…

He nodded. "I know. You'd risk losing more clients like Mr. Herrema."

"Exactly." Her cell vibrated then, against the desktop. And she tensed with concern that it might be another irate client. But the number was for Ranch Haven. The one client she hadn't been neglecting. Sadie was probably summoning her back already. She smothered a sigh and picked up with a forced-cheerful voice. "Yes?"

"Katie." Unexpectedly, it was Jake's voice on the other end, sounding lower and more serious than usual.

She shivered as her pulse quickened. "Yes." Why was Jake calling her?

"Katie, there's been an accident…"

Alarm shot through her and she jumped up. "Is it Caleb? Is he all right?"

"He's going to be fine—"

"Going to be? So he's not? How badly is he hurt?" Her pulse raced with panic.

"He has a couple bumps and bruises. That's my fault, and I'm sorry—"

"What do you mean? Did you hurt my son?" she asked, her heart breaking that she'd trusted him with her little boy. With Matt's little boy…

Caleb must have been hurt during their riding lesson. But it was too early for that. Caleb should have still been in school with Ian and Miller.

"Katie—"

"I want to talk to him!" She had to make sure that he was all right. But she wouldn't believe it even then—not until she saw him for herself. She grabbed her briefcase bag and headed toward the door, which Robert was already holding open for her.

"Do you want me to drive you?" her assistant asked.

She shook her head.

"I'm sorry, Mommy…" Caleb's voice replaced Jake's deep one, but his was raspy as if he'd been crying.

"Don't be sorry," she said. "All I care about is if you're all right. Are you okay, sweetheart?"

"Ye-yes…" But he didn't sound certain.

"I'm on my way back," she assured him. "Mommy will be there soon. Let me talk to Miss Melanie now."

"Not Mr. Big Jake?"

"No. I need to talk to Melanie." The physical therapist would tell her how badly her son had been hurt.

"He's okay," Melanie told her before she could even ask. "He's lucky."

No. He wasn't. Or he wouldn't have been hurt at all. And he wouldn't have lost his father already. No. Caleb wasn't lucky. But he was everything else—*everything* in the whole world—to Katie.

"He doesn't need to go to the ER?" she asked, her hand shaking so badly she could barely get the key into the ignition of Emily's car.

"Not at all," Melanie assured her. "He's really fine. Just got the wind knocked out of him. He's a little shaken, but that's probably a good thing."

"A good thing?" Katie asked, shocked that the physical therapist could suggest that.

"You'll understand when you get here," Melanie assured her. "Then Caleb will tell you what he did."

So apparently her son had a reason to apologize to her. But Jake had, too, claiming it was his fault...

He'd taken responsibility. For what?

"I'm on my way," Katie said. Finally she got the car started and turned toward Ranch Haven and her son. But she nearly sideswiped a car parked on the other side of the street as she did it.

Maybe she should have had Robert drive her. Or maybe she should have gone to her parents and had one of them follow her back with her vehicle. But she didn't want to take an extra minute to get to Caleb. While Melanie had assured her he was all right, Katie couldn't get over that he could've been hurt even worse— that she might have lost him like she'd lost his father. Another reason she needed to stay loyal to Matt's memory. She couldn't be distracted while raising their son; she had to keep him safe. And she had to keep her heart safe from being broken by another loss.

THE HORSE HADN'T hurt the boy. Jake had.

When he'd yelled and Caleb had tumbled off the bucket, the little boy had struck his face and his shoulder against the stall door. Then Jake had nearly crushed him when he'd thrown himself across the small kid lying limply on the ground. Jake had braced himself for Midnight's hooves to stomp on his body.

The horse had whinnied and reared up. But the hooves hadn't struck Jake like one had struck the groom. Midnight hadn't tried to escape. He'd given Jake time to scoop up Caleb and Ian and close the stall door.

Jake stared at the bronco now over that stall door. "What's your deal?" he asked the beast.

Midnight's nostrils flared.

It was almost as if the bucking bronco had

somehow known that the little boys had already been through too much, so he'd spared them any more pain. Jake was the one who'd inflicted it.

Maybe if he hadn't overreacted, Caleb wouldn't have fallen. If he'd spoken more calmly… No, he should have watched the little boys the minute they'd walked into the barn, but he'd been distracted with his call to Dusty. With everything he had going on, he was always distracted. That was why he had no time for relationships, especially not with someone who had a child—a child who would get hurt because Jake couldn't watch him for even a few moments. His stomach lurched as he felt sick at the thought of what could have happened to Caleb. How badly he could have been harmed because of Jake's inattention and because of that horse.

He needed to call Dusty again. Needed to make sure that he was on his way back to the ranch. Or that he was at the very least sending someone to pick up this beast.

Katie was no doubt on her way back. A pang of alarm struck his heart that she might be so upset over her son that she would crash. Like Dale and Jenny had with the boys in the SUV…

Instead of calling her, Jake should have driven to town to pick her up and explain what had happened. But Melanie had assured him that the little boy was fine and that there was no reason for Katie to rush back. If only Jake could have assured the boy's mother of that...

But Katie hadn't given him the chance.

Of course she'd wanted to talk to her son herself. Jake couldn't blame her. He couldn't even blame her if she blamed him, since he blamed himself.

He intended to wait in the barn until she got back, to make sure she made it safely. While he waited, he finished cleaning out the stallion's stall. Midnight didn't try to kick him, just eyed him warily.

"You don't have to worry about me," Jake assured him. "I'm not going to try to ride you." He'd never been tempted to become a rodeo rider like Dusty. He'd never felt the need to prove himself that way. Was that what the little boys had been trying to do?

Jake had been so scared that he'd hurt Caleb that he hadn't taken the time to ask what they'd been up to. He should have known they'd been up to something. He'd been a boy himself once, but that seemed like a hundred years ago now.

When his dad had died and his mom had taken off, he'd grown up fast.

But he'd been older than Caleb was when all that had happened to him. Katie's son was too young to have lost his father. Just as Jake's nephews were too young to have lost their parents.

Jake didn't want them to have to grow up fast. He wanted them to stay young and innocent. But safe. He'd already failed to ensure their safety, though. That was why he had to focus on the ranch and leave the children for the others to take care of. So he'd carried Caleb back to the house for Melanie to check him out.

He wished he could do more for the boys; he didn't want to let down Dale and Jenny. They'd always been there for him, helping him more with the ranch than anyone else had. Now that they were gone, it was even easier to see how much they'd done and how many people it had taken to replace them. But nobody would ever really replace them.

Just as no one would ever replace Matt Morris for his still-grieving wife and son. Not that Jake wanted to replace him. He'd spent so much of his life taking on other people's responsibilities that he didn't want any of his own. He had to focus on his nephews now and the ranch and even this stupid bronco until Dusty returned.

If Dusty returned...

The horse let out something that sounded like a snort. He probably doubted his master's concern just as much as Jake did. The horse pawed at the ground and whinnied.

Jake had obviously shared his space long enough. He backed out of the stall and closed the door. When he turned around, he saw what the horse had already seen—that they weren't alone.

Katie had made it back to the ranch. He didn't expect her to stay, though. He braced himself, waiting for her to hurl accusations or anger at him. She'd probably already packed up Caleb and was ready to return to town and leave Jake and the ranch behind her—just as he'd once encouraged her to do.

He was actually surprised she'd stuck around as long as she had—these past two weeks. But she'd done that for Dale and Jenny and the boys.

He knew that. She'd made it clear to him from the start that she wasn't here for him, that she'd gotten over her crush on him years ago.

Yet instead of the reaction he expected, she hurled herself at him. Wrapping her arms around him, she hugged him tightly.

CHAPTER TWELVE

Jake's body had felt hard with tension when Katie had thrown her arms around him. Now he tensed even more and using stiff arms, he eased her away from him. Then he stared down at her with dark eyes full of concern, as if he thought she'd lost her mind.

Katie had been out of her mind with concern the entire drive back to the ranch. But once she'd seen Caleb and was comforted that he was okay...

She'd learned the truth.

Her son had told her the truth. That he'd been opening the stall of that scary stallion when Jake had stopped him. Jake hadn't hurt him like he'd said on the phone. Jake had actually saved him.

Hearing the thing now, rearing up in that stall...

She shuddered over the thought of what it could have done to Caleb. He had a slight scrape on one chubby cheek, and his shoulder was a bit sore and starting to bruise, but as Jake and then Melanie had assured her, he was going to be fine. Katie was not.

And not just because of her son's near miss. But because she'd hugged Jake. From his reaction, he was probably afraid that she was going to try to suffocate him again.

"I'm sorry," she said. "I should have given you a chance to explain on the phone. Caleb told me what happened. And instead of yelling at you, I should have been thanking you that he didn't get seriously injured." At the thought of how seriously he could have been harmed, she shuddered again.

Jake shook his head, and the brim of his hat slid lower over his face, leaving his eyes in the shadow of it. "I understand why you were upset," he assured her. "I should have watched them from the minute they walked into the barn."

"I'm surprised you were in the barn then," she said. But she was so grateful that he had been. If he hadn't stopped Caleb...

"I came in from the pastures because a groom got hurt earlier," he explained. "That horse hurt a groom."

She shuddered again over the realization that Caleb had nearly been next. "That's terrible. Is the groom okay?"

Jake released a shaky breath and nodded. "Fortunately, yes. He and the barn manager returned a little while ago. He'll be fine. He's just going to rest today and tomorrow."

She wondered if those were the doctor's orders or Jake's. "Well, thank you," she said again. "For making sure my son didn't get hurt too." She wanted to hug him again, almost needed to hug him, and not just to express her gratitude but because she couldn't stop shaking over the thought of what could have happened to Caleb.

"I'm just glad I was here," Jake said. "I didn't realize they came down to the barn on their recess."

She shook her head. "They snuck out of the classroom while Emily was busy with Little Jake and Miller," she said. Caleb had confessed to that, as well. "Emily didn't give them recess. Caleb did."

Jake's lips twitched as if he was fighting a smile.

She didn't see the humor in the situation. She couldn't. She could only see what might have happened. And when she did, her eyes filled with tears. She couldn't lose him like she had his father. She couldn't lose anyone else she loved.

"Katie, he's okay," Jake said. He stepped forward and as if he sensed that she was the one needing the hug, he closed his strong arms around her. "Shh… He's okay…"

"I know," she said, but she was still trying to convince herself of that. "He's gotten more scraped up riding his bike."

Jake blew out a breath then, one that feathered through her hair and brushed across her cheek. Some of that tension eased from his body. "I was worried that I'd hurt him," he admitted. "I yelled and startled him and he fell…" He shuddered now.

Realizing he needed comforting, as well, Katie didn't pull out of his embrace like she should have. Instead she tightened her arms around him in another hug. "He's fine. Just a little mad that I canceled your riding lesson for the day."

He tensed again. "You did?"

"Yes, to punish him for sneaking out and bringing Ian with him." She pulled back and looked up at him then. "I'm sorry that he could have gotten your nephew hurt and you too." Jake had thrown himself across Caleb. Caleb had told her that—how Mr. Big Jake had saved him.

Tears stung her eyes again; she was upset at

the thought of how both Caleb and Jake could have been hurt. Despite how he'd hurt her in the past, Jake was a good man—a protective man. He'd saved her son, and that lessened her old resentment of him…almost too much.

"It's okay," he said. He reached out and ran his fingertips along her jaw in a light caress. "Everybody's okay…"

She wasn't. She wasn't okay at all. She was shaken and not just from what had nearly happened but because of what she *wanted* to happen. She didn't want to keep thinking about what could have happened to Caleb, didn't want to worry about her business or when she'd have to leave the ranch. She just wanted to feel as young and carefree as she'd been when they were teenagers. She wanted Jake to kiss her like he used to.

She wanted it so much that she found herself leaning toward him, raising her face to his.

And Jake leaned down, just as he used to, and finally his lips brushed softly across hers. Her skin tingled and her pulse quickened, and her breath escaped in a gasp at the jolt of emotion—of longing—that surged through her.

That longing was stronger than anything she'd felt for Matt. With that realization came a pang of guilt that kicked her hard as the horse could have kicked her son. She jerked back from the force of it.

"I'm sorry," Jake said. "I thought—"

"I'm sorry," she said. But she wasn't apologizing just to him but to Matt, as well. Even more to Matt—because he'd loved her so much, so completely. "I'm sorry I gave you the wrong idea." But she was lying. She'd wanted his kiss, so badly, and not just for comfort.

"Katie—"

"No, that was a mistake." She shook her head. She couldn't let him think that she was interested in him again or in a future with him. "And it won't happen again."

She could not let it happen again. She couldn't betray Matt, and she couldn't trust Jake with her heart—not after how he'd broken it. Overcome with guilt, she turned away from Jake and hurried out of the barn before she gave in to temptation again. Jake wasn't the only temptation, though. Staying was too. And she couldn't stay—not now. Not with the risk of Caleb getting hurt again.

And of her getting hurt again.

JAKE WAS TEMPTED to run after her, to explain to her why he'd broken up with her all those years ago and to beg for another chance. He'd had that same notion two months after he'd broken up with her, after he'd received the opal promise ring back from her in the mail. She'd included a note that he'd broken his promise, and she didn't want the ring. He'd returned to college to put that ring back on her finger, to keep his promise, but when he'd found her at the fountain laughing with Matt Morris, he'd realized he'd done the right thing. The unselfish thing. So he hadn't apologized to her like he'd wanted. He hadn't begged for another chance because he'd known she would be happier without him. Nothing had changed. In fact, life was only more complicated for him and for her. He had more responsibilities with the ranch and even less time for relationships.

So there was no point in dredging up the past any more than that kiss already had. Her lips had been just as soft as he'd remembered, her breath just as warm, and all those old familiar feelings had rushed through him. But now they'd been even more intense. So intense that Jake's legs felt a bit shaky. He leaned against that stall door.

Katie must not have felt the same, though—not with the way she'd jerked away from him. Her green eyes had been wide with shock as if she'd been appalled that he'd kissed her. She was never going to give him—or probably any other man—another chance. She was clearly still in love with her late husband. Matt Morris must have been quite a man, and he'd definitely been a better husband and father than Jake would ever be able to be. He just had too many priorities to take on anything more—even love.

Midnight must have sensed Jake's pain because he uttered something that sounded like a wistful sigh of his own. A sigh of commiseration. Then he stuck his head over the stall door and nudged Jake, knocking his hat onto the barn floor.

"Are you trying to tell me not to lose my head again?" he wondered. Jake wasn't worried as much about his head as he was something else.

He was worried about losing his heart again.

MAYBE THAT YOUNG doctor was right. Maybe Sadie was starting to age. In addition to shrinking and shriveling, she was slowing down. She hadn't been able to move fast enough to get away from the barn before Katie came running out and caught her.

The young woman was so upset, she didn't seem to realize that Sadie knew exactly why she was distressed. Sadie had been eaves-dropping.

Finally—things were starting to fall into place. But then Katie said, "Caleb and I need to leave."

Sadie didn't stop walking, but she did turn toward the petite woman who fairly trotted beside her. "Why?"

"How can you ask me that after what could have happened to my son today?" she asked.

Sadie shrugged. "Could have. Didn't. Jake saved him. He didn't come to any harm."

"This time," Katie said. "But it was just lucky that Jake was around."

Sadie couldn't argue with that. It had been lucky, especially with as hard as Jake had been working—maybe more so on staying away from Katie than tending the cattle in the farthest pastures. "It was lucky," she agreed.

That was good. Maybe the fortunes of this family were finally about to change. They'd had enough tragedy to last several lifetimes. They were due some happiness.

So were Katie and her son.

"I don't trust luck," Katie said. "And I don't trust my son on the ranch. There are too many things that can hurt him here."

"Are you worried about Caleb getting hurt?"

Sadie asked. "Or are you worried about your-self?"

Katie's face flushed a deep red. "My first concern is for my son."

"Of course," Sadie agreed. She knew Katie was a good mother. She'd always known the young woman would be—from how fiercely she'd loved Jake. She'd been willing to make every sacrifice for him. But Jake had loved her back too fiercely to let her make any. "But you're also worried about yourself."

"I can't lose Caleb," she said. "I wouldn't survive if something happened to him too."

As she thought of losing her own sons, and then later her husband, an unbearable heaviness settled on Sadie's heart, and she closed her eyes as pain washed over her. It was so intense that she had to stop walking for a moment, that she had to catch her breath to ease that ache in her chest.

"Sadie?" Katie asked, concern in the young woman's voice. "Are you all right?"

"You'd be surprised how much a person can survive," Sadie murmured. She had survived, but that might have only been because she'd had no other choice, because people had needed her. Like people always needed Jake, never more so than now.

But he needed Katie. He just hadn't realized it yet. Or, remembering what Sadie had seen and overheard, maybe he had.

"I'm not as strong as you are," Katie said as tears welled in her eyes.

"Oh, you're stronger than you think," Sadie assured her. "Much stronger…"

But Katie shook her head. "I can't. I can't stay here. And it's not just because I'm worried about Caleb."

Was she going to admit it? That she was worried about herself, that she was worried she was falling for Jake all over again?

"I'm losing clients," Katie said.

Sadie furrowed her brow, confused for a moment. "Clients?"

"Mr. Herrema is furious that I'm staying out here," Katie said. "That was my meeting in town. He doesn't want to work with me anymore."

Sadie shrugged again. "So? He can't be paying you much. He can barely pay the lease on his building." She knew because she'd inherited that building and several other ones in town when her father had passed away twenty years ago.

Ben handled those for her, just as he handled other things in town. Maybe she'd put too much on his plate; maybe that was why he hadn't been out to the ranch much.

"I can't afford to lose any more clients, or I won't be able to pay my lease," Katie said.

"I'll cover the lease payments for you," Sadie offered. She didn't want the woman to lose her business; she just wanted her to see that she belonged here at the ranch. "Or you can let the building go and work with all your clients from here."

"But I can't," Katie persisted. "And I don't want to. I want to go back to town. You need to find someone else to help with the ranch finances."

"You can't just up and leave," Sadie said. "I need some time to find someone else. And Caleb needs to finish out the school year with his teacher and Ian."

Katie fell silent, as if she was trying to come up with an argument and couldn't.

To bolster her case, Sadie added, "It's only a few more weeks." Three. Would that be long enough for Jake to win her back? Maybe. If he had a little help…

Sadie had already done what she could; she'd brought Katie and her son out here. She needed more help.

Katie drew in a breath herself, as if she was

bracing herself. Then she nodded. "Okay. I'll stay, but just until the school year is up."

Sadie nodded. "Good." It wasn't much time, but it would have to be enough—enough to make her want to remain at the ranch forever.

"And I hope you're right," Katie added. "I hope I am stronger than I think I am."

CHAPTER THIRTEEN

OVER THE PAST few weeks, Katie had noticed that Jake wasn't the only one who got up early. Melanie did too. They shared the bathroom between their two rooms—it had become a jill-and-jill bathroom after Melanie moved in. And every morning, Melanie had rushed into the bathroom and gotten sick.

In the beginning, Katie had respected Melanie's privacy too much to ask. But now she no longer had any doubt. The young woman was pregnant. Pregnant and alone despite that she'd claimed she was married.

Where was her husband?

Had he abandoned her?

Katie couldn't imagine having gone through her pregnancy alone. Like Melanie she'd often gotten sick too in that first trimester. And every morning Matt had treated her with a cold washcloth, a glass of fizzy water and a packet of saltines.

Katie had started bringing those same things

to Melanie. As she mopped away the sweat that now beaded on Melanie's brow, she assured the other woman, "You'll live through this." And she found herself repeating the words Sadie had told her just a couple of days ago. "You're stronger than you think you are."

"Are you sure?" Melanie asked, her voice raspy.

"Yes," Katie said. "I survived my pregnancy with Caleb, and I was just as sick as you are."

"But you weren't alone," Melanie said. When she'd thanked Katie the first time she'd helped her, Katie hadn't been able to take credit for Matt's thoughtfulness. She'd told her how wonderful her husband had been to her—even during those many years they'd just been friends.

"You aren't alone either," Katie said.

Tears pooled in Melanie's dark eyes. "But you're the only one who knows and you're not staying much longer."

A pang of guilt struck Katie's heart. "I can't."

"I know," Melanie said.

"And Miller's healing quickly. You won't need to stay much longer either."

Those tears spilled over and trailed down Melanie's cheeks. Katie suspected it wasn't just hormones that had caused them even before

Melanie murmured, "I don't have any place else to go."

"Yes, you do," Katie said. "You are always welcome with me." Which was another reason she needed to get a place for her and Caleb, because she doubted her mother and her headaches could handle a crying infant.

Melanie had to have at least six months before she would give birth. So Katie had time to find a place for all of them. Because Melanie wouldn't have much more time before she started showing, Katie suggested, "You should tell the others."

Melanie wasn't as outgoing as the rest of them. Either she was shy, or she had trouble trusting people. Maybe with good reason. Maybe she'd already trusted the wrong person.

Melanie sighed but nodded. "I know. I suspect Taye and Sadie have figured it out too."

Taye, despite her youth, was just as perceptive as Sadie was with all her years of experience.

"And that's probably not all they've figured out," Melanie continued, her raspy voice dipping into an even lower whisper. Maybe she hadn't wanted Katie to hear her.

"What else is there, Melanie?"

But the other woman just shook her head. Whatever it was, she wasn't ready to share.

Katie understood. There were things she couldn't share with anyone, like her guilt over Matt, over never loving him as much as he'd deserved, as much as he'd loved her.

Shaking her head must have increased Melanie's nausea because all the color drained from her already pale face. She pressed the wet cloth to her mouth, but she didn't have anything left to purge. So she sighed with uneasy relief. "I see why you only have one child..." Melanie murmured.

Tears sprang to Katie's eyes. "I wanted more," she admitted. "We'd been trying for a while. We were just about to start IVF treatment when someone ran a red light and struck Matt on his way home from work."

"Oh, Katie..." Melanie surged weakly to her feet and wrapped her arms around her. "I'm so sorry..."

"The other driver was a teenager. He'd been texting and didn't see the light change."

Thinking about it, about the senselessness of it, always brought forth a surge of anger. Anytime she passed a driver who was texting, she was tempted to perform a citizen's arrest herself. Or at least offer them a stern warning, to share with them how much their distract-edness could cost someone else. A life, a husband, a father...

A best friend.

So much could be gone in an instant.

"You're the strong one," Melanie told her.

She shook her head. "I'm not nearly strong enough." She hadn't been strong enough to put her past behind her, not even for Matt.

"Do you think that because you're still grieving?" Melanie asked. "You need to give yourself some time. He hasn't been gone that long. It's not like you'll never move on, like you'll never love again."

"I won't love again," she said with absolute certainty. She had already loved twice. She'd loved Jake—even though he hadn't returned her love. And she'd loved Matt—just never as much as he had deserved. Katie had barely survived losing them. She couldn't risk that kind of pain ever again.

"I WON'T LOVE AGAIN..."

Grandma had warned Jake years ago that eavesdroppers never heard anything good about themselves. He hadn't known what she'd meant then, because in the conversations he'd been overhearing nobody had ever really been talking about him specifically—just him and his brothers as a group. As his father's father-less sons, as the boys whose mother had abandoned them.

Katie and Melanie hadn't been talking about him specifically, either, but he was part of the group of men Katie would never love. Because she would never love again.

Grandma was right.

Not that Jake would ever admit it to her. Or that he would admit to eavesdropping outside their guests' bathroom door. That had been rude, but he'd been surprised to hear anyone else up at dawn when he awoke.

So he'd approached the door to listen and make sure it wasn't the little boys up to some mischief again. Instead it had been two women, one of them apparently violently ill. Except that she wasn't.

As she'd said, Grandma probably already knew, and it wasn't his business to share anyway. Just as Katie wasn't his business either.

Not anymore.

He turned away from the door and nearly stumbled over the sleepy little boy standing in the hallway behind him, rubbing his bleary eyes. Jake didn't want the women to catch him eavesdropping, so he swept Caleb up in his arms and carried him back down the hall and through the open door of his room. Unfortunately a little giggle of surprise slipped out of Caleb's lips. Jake tensed and, just inside Caleb's room, he listened for the sound of a door opening. But he didn't hear anything except Caleb's question.

"Is it time for my riding lesson?" he asked, his hopefulness waking him up a bit more.

"No, it's still bedtime for you, little man," Jake replied as he laid him on his rumpled bed.

"You're up," Caleb pointed out.

"Yes, I have to work," Jake said.

"When I grow up, I wanna be a cowboy just like you, Mr. Big Jake," Caleb said.

Instead of flattering him, the thought saddened Jake. He shook his head. "No, you don't want to be like me."

Caleb's head cocked to the side on his pillow and he asked, "Why not?"

A chuckle slipped out of Jake's lips now. The kid was so inquisitive and positive despite the tragedy he'd endured. Jake couldn't tell him all the reasons he shouldn't want to be like him—like that he didn't want to wind up alone. "Being a cowboy is hard work," he explained. "You have to go out no matter what the weather's like."

"There are no snow days like we get in school?" Caleb asked.

"Nope. And you're out in the snow, freezing so you can make sure the cattle don't freeze."

"But you get to ride horses all the time," the little boy pointed out with longing.

Canceling his riding lessons had been the ultimate punishment for his sneaking out of the classroom with Ian. Somehow it had also punished Jake. He'd missed seeing the little guy the last couple of afternoons. Usually the kids were in bed by the time he got into the house.

So instead of rushing out to the barn, like he needed to in order to take care of Midnight, he found himself lingering. "Some of the cowboys ride in pickup trucks now," Jake informed him.

Caleb snorted. "Then they're not real cowboys like you, Mr. Big Jake."

Jake chuckled again. "They are—because they're taking care of cows. Bringing the hay out to them, bringing out medicine, whatever else they need."

"I asked Ian once, in school, why cowboys are called cowboys. I asked if they ride cows, and everybody else laughed at me. But Ian didn't. He said that sometimes his uncle Dusty rides cows, but it's because you all take care of cows that you're called cowboys."

"That's true," Jake said. "That's how it started." He studied the little boy's face and the curious wrinkling of his brow, as if that memory had been painful for him.

Jake had always been big for his age, so nobody had laughed at him in school. Only his brothers had ever been brave enough to try picking on him, and that was just because they had run to Grandma for protection when he'd tried to reciprocate.

"Was it hard for you when you moved to Willow Creek?" Jake wondered. "Did the other kids pick on you?"

The little boy's bottom lip quivered, and he nodded. But then he said, "Ian never did, though. That's why we're best friends."

That must have been why Caleb was so patient with him and his memory lapses—because Ian had been patient with him while he was adjusting after moving from the big city to cattle country. And that after losing his father.

"That's good," Jake said. "It's good that you have Ian. And especially good that you're here for him now. I appreciate that you help him remember things."

Jake hadn't had to remind Ian for a while that his parents were gone gone. Not just on vacation.

And that had eased some of his burden. He was concerned, though, that Caleb might have been shouldering more of that—and his best friend's grief—than a little boy could carry. Especially when that little boy was already dealing with his own grief.

"Who's your best friend, Mr. Big Jake?" Caleb asked.

It had once been Caleb's mother—back in school. Even before Jake had fallen for Katie O'Brien, he had appreciated her wit and her warmth. But after he'd broken up with her...

"Dale," he said.

"Who's Dale?"

"My brother. Ian's dad."

"He's dead," Caleb said.

"Yes." And that loss lay heavy on Jake's heart and his shoulders. He'd lost so much when he'd lost his younger brother. He'd lost the person who'd loved the ranch as much as he and Grandma did. And he'd lost his very best friend. Dale had been that person to whom Jake could tell everything. The person who'd known him best.

"My best friend—before Ian—died too," Caleb shared.

Shocked at the amount this kid had suffered, Jake asked, "You had a friend die?"

Caleb nodded, and tears pooled in his blue eyes. "My daddy. He was my best friend."

Jake felt the kid's pain as if it was his own; his heart wrenched with it. He wrapped his arms around the little boy and held him close. And those pooled tears spilled over and dampened Jake's shirt. He didn't care about his shirt or that he had so much work waiting for him. He held Caleb until his body got limp and his breathing grew soft. Then he lowered the sleeping child back to the bed and tucked him under the covers.

When he stood up and turned toward the door, he gasped at the shock of finding someone standing there—watching him. He opened his mouth, but she held a finger to her lips, then she stepped back into the hall.

Jake followed her out and pulled the door mostly closed behind him. He didn't dare shut it tightly and risk waking up the little boy.

Although Jake wasn't sure he wanted to be alone with Katie…

That he should be alone with her.

She was so beautiful with her thick red hair mussed from her pillow and her makeup-free skin as silky as the robe she cinched tightly around her small waist. He wanted to lean toward her—wanted to kiss her again.

But he knew now that she didn't really want that from him or from any other man. Maybe most especially not from him...

She stood stiffly in the hallway, her body tense. What had she heard? Did she think he'd upset Caleb? Had he—with his questions?

"I'm sorry," he said.

"You're sorry?" she asked, and she cocked her head to the side in the same way her son had just moments ago. "About what?"

Apparently she hadn't realized he'd been eavesdropping outside the bathroom door. Or maybe she'd dismissed that since she'd probably been doing the same outside her son's bedroom door.

"I'm sorry if I was the one who upset him," he said.

"It wasn't you who took his father," she murmured.

No. That had been a texting teenage driver, but he wasn't supposed to know that. The thought of it—the senselessness of it—turned his stomach so he felt like Melanie must every morning.

"I didn't know he still cried about him," she said. "He hasn't in the longest time."

Jake released a shaky breath. "It's probably

being here—with the other boys going through their loss…"

"I was worried about that—that it would be too much for him," she admitted. "But he was determined to be here with his teacher and with Ian. Now I know why he was so determined. He never told me that he was getting picked on when we first moved here."

Was she mad that her son had shared things with him that he hadn't with her? Or was she just upset—as he'd been—that anyone had picked on the child?

"It's rougher being a kid than I remember," he admitted.

"Especially a kid who moved here from the city," she said. "I grew up here. I didn't think how different it would be for him. How hard it would be…" Her voice cracked with emotion. "Maybe I am a terrible mother just like you've thought."

"I never said that," he insisted. He'd never even thought it; it was clear how much she loved her little boy.

"You never expressed it in those words," she agreed. "But you questioned my decision to move him out here."

He'd done that more for his sake than theirs. He hadn't wanted her here, reminding him of everything he'd given up. "I had no right." And now he knew that he never would.

"No," she said. "You didn't. But that didn't mean you were wrong."

"I was," he conceded. "That little kid is super special. And that's because of you, because everything you've done has been for the best for him."

She shook her head. "He's so special because of his dad, who was his best friend and mine."

"Tell me about Matt," he said, suddenly wanting to know about the man who'd been so important to her and Caleb.

Tears filled her eyes. "He was so funny. So quick-witted but also very kind. He had unlimited patience. And he was smart. An engineer but he secretly wanted to be a comedian. We spent a lot of time at comedy clubs."

He had to clear his voice to ask, "Where else? Did you travel like you planned?"

She nodded, and her lips curved into a slight smile. "Matt was more fun and knowledgeable than any of our travel guides. He always found the best places to eat, the most fun activities to try…" Her voice cracked now, and the tears spilled out of her eyes to trail down her face.

"I'm sorry," Jake murmured. "I—I shouldn't have brought it up."

"It's okay," she said, and she swiped her hands across her face.

"I need to get out to the barn, take care of that bronco so nobody else gets hurt," he said, reminding himself why he couldn't stay with her. Jake wanted to reach out to her, wanted to hold her like he had her son. But he was hurting too.

She'd done all the things she'd wanted to— without him. She'd lived the life they'd planned with another man. Too many years had passed for them to ever find their way back to each other. She wasn't the sweet teenager who'd adored him anymore. And he was a man with too many responsibilities to take on any more.

So even though his arms ached to hold her, he couldn't. He couldn't offer her comfort over the loss of another man. And not just because of the ugly jealousy that suddenly churned in his stomach but because he had nothing to offer her, nothing left to give anyone.

CHAPTER FOURTEEN

JAKE HAD COMFORTED CALEB, had held him while he cried. But then he'd just left Katie standing alone in the hallway, staring after him as he'd walked away from her.

That was what he'd done a dozen years ago by that fountain, so she shouldn't have been surprised. But she was.

She'd once thought she knew Jake Haven so well. That had changed that day all those years ago. Since moving onto the ranch, she'd caught glimpses of the man she'd once thought he was while he was taking care of his nephews and Caleb.

He'd been so sweet with him that morning— just an hour or so ago. He'd been so sweet that Katie's heart had ached with longing for what had once been between them. For the sweetness he'd once shown her.

But he hadn't taken her into his arms like he had Caleb. He'd just walked away, leaving her feeling so cold and alone and hopeless.

Was she never to love again, just as she'd told Melanie? Even Matt, with his big, loving personality, hadn't been able to fully replace Jake in her heart, so no doubt nobody else ever would. She and Jake had had too many good memories for that one bad day at the fountain to destroy. There had been too many moments of sweetness, of affection and what had felt like genuine love to her. Even though he'd given her heart back to her, he had been the first man to claim it, and it had felt to Katie like he had always held a piece of it.

"You're not eating," Taye remarked with some concern as she pointed toward Katie's full plate of cooling eggs and bacon. "Do you want me to make you some pancakes instead?"

Katie shook her head. "No, thank you. I'm just not feeling very hungry this morning." Maybe because she knew not even Taye's delicious food could fill the hollowness inside her. Nothing could. Even Matt's love hadn't been able to completely fill it.

A twinge of guilt roiled her stomach even more than the emptiness. She picked up her plate and headed toward the sink, trying to avoid the eagle-eyed gaze of Sadie, who sat quietly at the head of the table, her rigid back toward the hearth. She was always quiet in the morning even though she'd probably been up for hours already. Her bedroom was on the main floor, though, so there was no way of knowing for certain how long she'd been up or what she was ever up to…

Katie was certain that the older woman had a plan in bringing all these women to live at the ranch. That she wanted to set up her grandsons with potential wives, so that they could add to her family in order to fill some of the void of Dale and Jenny's loss. Katie could have told her that nothing would ever fill that void completely, but Sadie Haven had to know that already. She'd lost her son and her husband long before Dale and Jenny had died.

"You sure I can't tempt your appetite with something?" the cook asked.

Katie shook her head. "I'm sorry, Taye. I'm just feeling a little off this morning."

"I'm sorry," Melanie murmured.

"Did you give her that stomach bug you have?" Emily asked with a shudder of revulsion.

Katie waited for Melanie to take advantage of the opening and tell the other women that what she had wasn't catching. Her mouth was partially opened, as if she intended to share her secret. But then she glanced around the table at the children present and shook her head.

Katie understood that Melanie wasn't ready yet. So Katie assured them, "No. I feel physically fine." She glanced over at Caleb, who was sandwiched between Ian and Miller on the bench on the other side of the long dining room table. He was subdued this morning, not his usual bubbly self who tried every morning to make Little Jake laugh.

As if the toddler realized he was being ignored for once, he blew bubbles and some pieces of dried cereal across the table. That made Caleb giggle, but that was even more subdued than usual.

Emily must have picked up on it, too, because she studied him with her brow furrowed. She clapped her hands together and announced, "Class starts in ten minutes, guys. Time to brush your teeth and meet me in the playroom."

The boys got up from table—even Little Jake. They deposited their cereal bowls in the sink before running up the back stairwell. Instead of clinging to Emily, like he usually did, Little Jake toddled up the steps after his older brothers and Caleb. It was probably Caleb's attention he was still trying to seek. Because he passed Miller without a glance as Miller struggled yet with his heavy cast and his crutches. He couldn't put weight on that leg yet. But Melanie worked with him all the time to strengthen it in other ways.

"So you're concerned about Caleb," Taye surmised. "What's going on?"

Katie sighed. "He's missing his dad especially hard today."

"I thought he'd be okay after crying it out on Jake this morning," Emily murmured.

Katie gasped. She'd thought she'd been the only one who'd overheard their exchange. Heat rushed up to her face over how she must have looked standing out in the hallway, like she was mooning over Jake Haven. She wasn't the teenage girl she'd once been; she was a professional now, a mother, a widow...

And maybe that was what humiliated her the most about mooning over Jake again, that she was betraying the man who'd deserved her total devotion.

"My bedroom is on the other side of Caleb's," the teacher reminded them.

So she hadn't seen Katie standing in the doorway, watching them—probably with the longing that had intensified her hollowness this morning. Jake had been especially kind to Caleb this morning. He'd taken the time to listen to her son, to comfort him until he'd fallen asleep. He worked so hard on the ranch, for his family, and to take care of all of the boys—even hers.

"I couldn't hear everything they were saying," Emily continued. "But there's no mistaking Jake's deep voice." She gave an exaggerated little shiver and wiggled her blond brows.

Was Emily attracted to Jake?

A pang of jealousy struck Katie like a hard slap. But she had no right to feel jealous of Jake—not anymore.

"But then of course it had to be Jake with Caleb, since he's the only one of his brothers who's actually stepped up to care for the boys. He's the only one who takes responsibility seriously." Now Emily's face flushed, and she glanced at Sadie and murmured, "No offense."

"I didn't take any offense," Sadie said with a chuckle and she glanced toward the doorway between the kitchen and the hall that led from the front door.

The mayor leaned against the arched doorway, a slight grin curving his lips. "I didn't take any offense either," Ben Haven said, but then he clutched a hand to his heart as if it had been wounded. "I'm used to beautiful women falling for my big brother instead of me, aren't I, Katie?"

Heat burned her face with her embarrassment. Now these women—who'd become her friends—would know how she'd once mooned after Jake too. Like Emily...

Maybe the teacher was starting to fall for Jake.

Not that it was any concern of Katie's. But even though she knew that, she couldn't stop her mind from going there—to Jake with someone else.

Would he marry?

Even though he'd once promised he would marry her, he hadn't. And in all the years since they'd broken up, he hadn't married anyone else.

She had to stop thinking about Jake. So she forced a laugh. "You can't have every woman's heart, Ben," she told him. "Every once in a while someone can resist your charms."

He chuckled.

And Emily snorted. "Yeah, every smart woman."

He pressed his hand to his heart again. "But I only want the smart ones."

Emily shook her head, but her face was still

flushed. "The smart ones go for men of substance, men like your brother."

Ben sighed.

Sadie stood. "You can't deny your brother's a good man," the proud grandmother said. "He's stepped up even when I told him he didn't need to. He made sacrifices. For family. For the ranch. He made sacrifices nobody should have had to make."

Sadie looked at Katie then, and Ben's gaze followed hers. And they nodded as if in silent agreement.

What sacrifices were they talking about? That he hadn't finished college? Or were they talking about her?

Had he not really wanted to break up with her?

The question burned on her lips, in her heart, but she couldn't utter it. She didn't want to know the answer. It was all too late now.

Ben closed the distance between him and his grandmother, then kissed her cheek. Despite her being at least eighty, there weren't many lines on her face. "I'm sorry I haven't been around that much lately. There was stuff in town…" His voice trailed off as if he'd heard the lameness of his own excuse.

Or he'd heard Emily's derisive sniff, dismissing his reason.

"But I'm here now," Ben continued, "and Baker pulled in behind me. He headed straight for the barn."

"He should have stopped in for breakfast first," Sadie said.

"We're not here to eat, Grandma," he told her. "We're here to help."

"Good," she told him, and she patted his cheek instead of kissing it. The pat was hard enough that he flinched a little. "It's about time."

"Just don't hold your breath waiting for Dusty to show up," Ben warned her. "Anybody who does that would be a fool."

A gasp slipped out of Melanie, whose face had gone as deathly pale as it did every morning. With a hand pressed over her mouth, she ran from the room.

"What's wrong with her?" Ben asked.

Emily glanced after her. "I thought it was a stomach bug." She turned toward Katie now and stared at her with narrowed eyes. "You know…"

Katie shook her head. It wasn't her secret to share.

But she doubted Melanie's secret was the

only one being kept at Ranch Haven. Sadie had her secrets—about her plans. But was she holding another secret—one about the past? One that had affected Katie?

"COME ON, MAMA," Jake murmured, trying to coax the cow out of the ravine into which she'd wandered with her calf. "If you come out, your baby will follow. You don't want it getting hurt down there..."

Jake had already had to deal with pain that morning. But he was glad he'd been there for Caleb, to comfort the little boy. He just wished he'd had the right to comfort the little boy's mother. To make her feel better, even though her grief made him so uncomfortable.

How could he be so jealous of a dead man that he felt physically sick?

His empty stomach churned with it, but he pushed down the nausea and his thoughts of Katie. He forced himself to focus on the job he had to do—just as he'd done a dozen years ago.

He pressed his knees against Buck's sides, urging the horse farther down the steep bank. As he did, he raised his rope. He'd probably have to lasso the mama in order to help her out of there. But before he could toss his rope, another one sailed past him and expertly circled the cow's thick neck.

She let out a pitiful protest, but a shout of triumph drowned it out. Jake glanced behind him where his brothers were carefully maneuvering their horses down the steep slope.

Ben held the rope. "Told you," he chided their youngest brother. "I still got it."

Baker smirked. "An enormous ego? Yeah, you still got that."

"Says the calendar boy," Ben shot back.

A grin tugged at Jake's lips. Their baby brother was never going to live down getting roped into posing for a firefighter calendar, the proceeds of which were donated to charity. According to the local press Jake had read, the donations this year had been their most to date.

Baker was too proud to let it show if their teasing affected him. He lifted his head and said, "And I'm still more humble than you are."

"Hey," Ben exclaimed. "I will have you know that my ego took quite the blow this morning when I walked into breakfast and heard all the women singing Big Jake's praises instead of mine."

Jake shrugged. "Yeah, right…" He knew for certain that one of those women would prob-

ably never say anything positive about him—
the only one he wanted to…

"No, seriously," Ben persisted. "They were
talking about how you're the only one of us
who's been there for the boys."

Jake narrowed his eyes and studied Ben's
face. For once he looked serious—and ashamed.
So did Baker, from what Jake could see of his
face with his hat hanging low over it. His mouth
was pulled down in a deep frown.

Jake couldn't accept any praise, though. "I've
really not spent that much time with them. Not
like I could if I had help with the ranch…" But
his help had been Dale, and Dale was gone.

"I thought Katie was helping you," Ben said.
"I thought that's why Grandma dragged her
out here."

"Kicking and screaming…" Jake murmured.

"What?" Baker asked with genuine concern.
"Grandma kidnapped her?"

"I wouldn't put it past her," Ben remarked.

Jake sighed. "Let's just say Katie is not here
because she wants to be. And she definitely
has no intention of staying. She's just here to
help with the books."

"So convince her to stay," Ben said, as if it
were that simple.

"I can't…" He knew that for certain. "She wants nothing to do with me."

"Because you broke her heart," Ben said. "She hasn't realized you did that for her, has she?"

"You did?" Baker asked. He'd been so young and so consumed with his grief over Grandpa Big Jake's death that he probably hadn't realized what else had happened in the family back then.

"Jake didn't want her to give up going to college to stay here with him—with us," Ben said.

Jake gasped in shock that his younger brother had figured it out. But he shouldn't have been surprised.

Most people thought Ben Haven's good looks and charm were why he was such a successful politician despite his relatively young age. Jake knew it was because the man was highly perceptive, so perceptive that he knew how to charm everybody. Although—if his ego had indeed taken a blow that morning— maybe his charm didn't work on everybody.

"Is that true?" Baker asked Jake. "Is that why you never married anyone else? Because you never got over her?"

He sighed. "That makes me sound pretty pathetic…" Kind of like the cow stuck in the bottom of the ravine, unwilling to leave her baby.

The ranch was Jake's baby. Probably the only one he would ever have, and truly it had been enough. He'd gotten a great deal of satisfaction out of it and his family, even though he'd thought often of Katie over the years.

The cow let out another pitiful cry that drew their attention back to her. Instead of tugging on the rope he'd lassoed her with, Ben dismounted from his horse and walked over to her. "Let's push her out of here," he suggested.

Despite living in the city now, the mayor still had a soft spot for animals. Jake grinned and slid off Buck's back.

Baker sighed but dismounted, as well. He tried hard to hide his soft spot for the animals, or maybe just for the ranch. "So are you going to stay pathetic?" his youngest brother razzed him.

Jake nudged the cow just a bit in Baker's direction, enough that the firefighter slipped and went down…into what the cow had left behind her.

Ben burst out laughing. "Wish I had my camera. Not sure what kind of calendar that picture would make it in, though."

Baker wiped a smear of manure from his

chin and glared at Jake. "You're not pathetic. You're mean."

Jake flinched. He had been—once—to Katie. And he suspected she would never forgive him for it. "I'm busy," he said. "I didn't have any time for hearts and flowers these past twelve years. I certainly don't now."

Ben flinched this time. "I'm sorry we haven't been around much. We'll help out more." He glanced at Baker, who glared at him now.

"I don't have cushy office hours like you, Mayor," the youngest said. "But I'll come around whenever I'm not on a shift."

"So we'll make sure you have time," Ben said, then urged, "Katie's single now, Jake. You've got a second chance. Take it."

Jake shook his head. "She's not single."

Ben sighed. "I can understand you not wanting to take on another kid with us basically having dumped the boys on you alone—"

"I don't mean that she's not single because of Caleb. It's because she's still wearing her husband's rings. She's still in love with him. She's not ready to move on—with me or anybody else."

"Shoot," Ben said. "I thought I might have finally had a chance with her."

Jealousy surging through him, Jake nudged the cow toward Ben.

The mayor slipped but held himself off the ground with his grasp on the rope around her neck. "Hey, I'm just kidding!" Ben said. "Just like I was when I used to tease you back in high school that I was going to go after her, and you used to threaten that you'd beat me up."

"I was just kidding back then too," Jake said. But he wasn't entirely certain.

Katie brought out a possessiveness in him that he'd only ever felt with her, not that he'd seriously dated anyone but her.

Yet when he'd seen her that night sitting with Matt Morris beside the fountain, laughing and smiling at him, his protectiveness had been stronger than his jealousy. He'd wanted to protect her from himself and from the life of hard work and sacrifice he'd been facing back then. He'd wanted her to be happy, and she had been—with Matt.

Jake could never make her that happy. He would only ever disappoint her, like he had all those years ago. He was too busy to live out the dreams they'd once shared.

With all of his duties, he would never have time to travel to all the places they'd wanted to see, and with having his nephews to raise now, he wasn't sure he would want to have more kids for that big family she'd always wanted.

He already had too much to deal with, so maybe it was a good thing that he knew he had no chance with Katie. But why he did feel so very disappointed?

CHAPTER FIFTEEN

AFTER TUCKING CALEB into bed, Katie had returned to the office. More because she'd needed to be alone than because she had work to finish. Caleb hadn't shared anything with her that he had with *Mr. Big Jake*.

She'd even prodded him with questions about what it had been like for him when they'd first moved to Willow Creek. But he'd insisted that it had all been good.

Her little boy had lied to her. He'd had no problem telling Jake the truth. No problem crying in his big, strong arms.

But for her, Caleb forced a smile and assured her, "I'm happy, Mommy."

Then he'd asked, "Are you happy?"

And she'd forced a smile for him and claimed, "Of course. How could I not be happy when I have the sweetest son in all the world?"

He'd snorted then, recognizing her prevarication just as she'd recognized his. But she'd been honest with him. He was the best.

"I'm not *sweet*," he'd told her, his nose wrinkled with disgust.

She'd pretended to nibble on his cheek—the one without the scrape healing on it—and proclaimed, "You're definitely sweet. Must be all those cookies you're eating."

He'd giggled and had seemed very happy. But after that morning she knew better.

She knew she and the little Haven boys weren't the only ones still grieving. She wasn't grieving just the loss of her husband but the loss of the relationship she'd had with her little boy when he used to share everything with her.

A shaky sigh slipped through her lips as the sting of tears burned the backs of her eyes. She closed them for a moment, and when she opened them—just seconds later—she found she wasn't alone.

"You're falling asleep at your desk," Jake said from where he stood in the doorway, staring at her. "Why are you up so late?"

She glanced at the corner of the computer monitor and gasped at the time displayed. More time had passed since she'd tucked Caleb in than she'd realized. So much time that Jake must have come in from the pastures and showered. Or maybe it was raining outside. He wasn't wearing his hat, and his black hair was damp. But he also smelled fresh; that could have been the rain, too, or whatever soap he used in the shower.

The thought of him in the shower got her pulse racing. She acted like he'd startled her instead, pressing a hand to her heart, much as Ben had that morning at breakfast.

He repeated, "Why are you up so late?"

She blinked. "I tucked Caleb into bed and then came out here to finish up some work."

That hadn't been all she'd done, though. She'd been checking through the replies to the job she'd posted for a ranch bookkeeper. She'd also been checking on houses for sale or lease in town.

"I didn't realize how much accounting the ranch required," he said.

"Ranch Haven isn't my only client," she said, then murmured, "Although it might be soon."

His brow furrowed beneath a lock of damp black hair. For just a moment he reminded her of Caleb. But that wasn't possible—with his blond hair and blue eyes, Caleb looked nothing like his new idol. He looked like his father— his former best friend.

Tears stung her eyes again, and she had to blink furiously to clear them away.

"What does that mean?" he asked. "Is Sadie trying to get you to work solely for the ranch?"

She shook her head but then she wondered… "I don't think she has anything to do with my clients dropping me."

"Who's dropped you?"

"Mr. Herrema—"

"From the printing shop?"

She nodded. "And Mrs. Campbell." That had just happened that morning. Or maybe it had been yesterday, but she'd read Robert's email about it this morning.

"She owns what—the local bakery?"

She nodded again. "The one where Taye used to work."

"Grandma might have something to do with that," he agreed. "But I think it's more likely it would be Mrs. Campbell retaliating against Sadie for stealing Taye away from the bakery. So I wouldn't take that one personally."

"I do, though," she said. "I can't afford to lose any more business." Not if she was going to qualify for a mortgage or a lease for a house for her and Caleb and maybe Melanie—if she truly had no place else to go.

What had happened to the young woman's husband? She didn't wear a ring, so maybe she'd only claimed to be married because she was embarrassed about her situation. Katie didn't know what to think, but she was worried about the shy physical therapist.

"What do you need?" he asked. "To spend more time in town?"

"I need to move back to town," she said. "I need to focus on all my clients—not just one."

He sucked in a breath. "I'm sorry."

"You're not the one who talked me into coming out here," she said.

"I'm sorry Sadie roped you into whatever scheme she's cooking up," he said.

"So you think she's up to something too?" she asked, surprised that they had come to the same conclusion. But then they had once thought alike—when they were teenagers. Or so she'd thought at the time.

"I guess I shouldn't have said she's cooked up something," he said. "For one, because she can't cook—not like Jenny did. That's why she claims she hired Taye Cooper and because the boys have always loved the cookies from the bakery."

"And Ian loves his teacher," she said, "just like Caleb does." She watched Jake's face then for any reaction to her mentioning the pretty, young teacher. Had he noticed her like she'd noticed him?

But his handsome face, with all those sharp lines and angles, revealed nothing. Instead he seemed focused only on his grandmother and her motives. "Maybe I'm being too suspicious of her, and she does just want to help them."

Katie suspected it wasn't just the little boys that Sadie wanted to help. She wanted to help her adult grandsons, as well. Bringing Katie and Caleb to the ranch had been a mistake if Sadie had been hoping that any feelings would rekindle between Katie and Jake.

"I wish Sadie would help me…" Katie mused.

"With saving your clients?" Jake asked.

She nodded. "I told her that I can't stay here beyond the end of the school year, or I'm not going to have a business to return to…"

"And?"

"She agreed to look at applications for replacements for me." Out of loyalty to Dale and Jenny, she couldn't leave the ranch in the lurch without someone to handle the day-to-day business operations.

"I take it that Grandma hasn't looked at any of the applications," he surmised.

"Oh, she's looked. She's just dismissed every applicant I showed her." Probably because they'd been men, but she wasn't going to mention that and stir up anything between Jake and his grandmother—not when he'd just put aside his suspicions of her motives. "We need to hire one of them soon in case they need to give two weeks' notice to a previous employer. It would also help if I had time to train them before Caleb and I leave."

"Well, despite what my grandmother thinks, she's not the one running this ranch anymore," he said. "Show me these applicants, and I'll talk to them."

She sucked in a breath. She should have been relieved that he was willing to help her, but she felt a flash of hurt that he wasn't trying to keep her here. Not that she could stay. As much loyalty as she felt to her friends, Dale and Jenny, she owed more to Matt—to his memory. It was good that she'd placed that ad, good that she had a list of candidates to show him, to prove to him that she hadn't come out to the ranch to chase after him like she'd done in high school and when she'd applied and gotten accepted to the same college he had.

She had lived so much of her life just to be close to Jake. Apparently it was what Mr. Herrema believed she was still doing. That was another reason she needed to get back to the city; she wanted to be respected as the professional she was, not dismissed as having never gotten over her teenage crush.

Jake moved away from the doorway then, but he didn't stop at the front of the desk. He came around to stand behind her chair, to lean over her and peer at the computer monitor. And she sucked in another breath, a breath that smelled of his fresh scent that was either rain or soap…and Jake.

And that hollow feeling in the pit of her stomach intensified so much that she ached. "What…what are you doing?" she asked.

"I assume they emailed you their résumés, right?" he asked. "Show me."

"Now?"

"Unless you're too tired and want to head into the house," he said. "But I'm going to be busy for the next few weeks. We'll be starting to wean the babies from their mothers—"

"That's terrible!" She shuddered at the thought of someone separating her from her child. Remembering how Caleb had confided in Jake and not her, she'd felt like he was doing that with her too.

"That's ranch life, Katie," he said with a short chuckle. "And it's busy. This might be the only chance I have for a while to look at these applicants."

"Is that why you came out here?" she asked.

Had he intended to ask her to find her replacement then? He knew she was going to return to town when the school year ended.

She couldn't see his face, with how he stood behind her, so she turned her head and her cheek brushed across his. He'd showered, but he hadn't shaved. There was stubble on his jaw, stubble that rubbed against her skin and made it tingle. That made her breath catch...

JAKE HELD HIS BREATH, held in the scent of Katie that he'd inhaled. The sweetness of that soft floral fragrance.

Honeysuckle.

It must be honeysuckle.

He didn't want to move, didn't want her to move.

He wanted to go on standing there with her cheek pressed against his. No. He wanted more than that; he wanted her to turn her head farther so that her lips brushed across his.

"Jake..." She murmured his name.

"Yes..." Yes, he wanted her to kiss him.

But that wasn't the question she'd asked. She repeated the one he'd ignored, the one he couldn't really answer. "Why did you come out here?"

Had he let Ben get to him with all his urging for Jake to go after his second chance with Katie? He knew better than to listen to Ben.

Jake didn't want to get his heart broken. Not again. So he released the breath he'd been holding. She shivered slightly, and she pulled away from him.

"I, uh, I saw the light on out here," he said. "I wanted to check the office."

"For intruders?" she asked.

For her...

He'd wanted to see her. Had needed to see her, to make sure she was okay after that morning. He'd wanted so badly to hold her, to comfort her, but he didn't think she'd wanted it from him anyway.

She didn't want him anymore. She wanted the man she'd loved, and Jake couldn't replace him. He didn't have the time to give her what Matt Morris had.

"I just wanted to make sure everything was all right," he replied.

She nodded.

"Are you?" he asked. "Are you all right, Katie?"

She shrugged, but she didn't turn toward him. "I told you I'm worried about losing my clients."

He doubted that was the only reason she wanted off the ranch, though. He was the other reason.

"I shouldn't have agreed to move here," she said. "But I felt so bad about Jenny and Dale's boys, and the books and…"

"None of that was your fault," he said. "Nobody expected you to uproot your life to move out here."

She shrugged. "Your grandmother did."

He sighed. She did, and maybe she'd enlisted Ben's help and that was why he'd spouted all that nonsense about sacrifices and second chances. "I'm sorry about her pressuring you," he said.

"I'm a big girl," she said. "I could have refused."

"Why didn't you?" he asked.

"Not because I was chasing you," she said, and she whirled back toward him, her eyes wide but her face red. "I'm not that teenage girl I once was, Jake."

"You don't look any older," he mused. Especially when she looked at him like that, all embarrassed and wide-eyed. When she looked like that, the years rolled away, and he found himself leaning toward her, brushing his lips across hers.

For a moment she was utterly still.

And he waited with anticipation. With hope...

Would she kiss him back?

She jerked away instead. "Jake! I told you last time was a mistake. I know what real love is now."

He flinched. "You're a young woman. You're never going to love anyone else?"

He knew that he was giving away that he'd been eavesdropping on her and Melanie that morning, but he didn't care. He just wanted to hear it again. No. He didn't want to—he *needed* to—so he wouldn't make a fool of himself going for that second chance.

She shook her head. "I can't..."

"He must have been quite a guy," he acknowledged. He'd obviously been an incredible father, the kind a little boy could call his best friend.

Her eyes watered with tears, but she blinked them back. "I told you about him this morning. Everything he did—he did for me and for Caleb."

"You took *all* those trips you wanted?" he asked, his heart aching with regret that he hadn't been the one to make her dreams come true.

She nodded. "Yes..."

He sighed. "I can't even remember what places we talked about..."

"Hawaii. London. Paris. Sydney," she said.

"You saw them all?" he asked, and he marveled at how hollow and empty he felt inside.

She nodded again and then asked him, "You didn't go anywhere?"

He shook his head. "No. I was too busy with the ranch." And he was even busier now that the ranch had expanded, and he didn't have Dale and Jenny to help him. And he had the boys to think about...

He couldn't think about himself, about the dreams he'd abandoned when he'd left Katie behind all those years ago. He had to stay focused on the present, and because of that, he had no future to offer her.

"So you can't say anything about me wanting to focus just on my business and my son now, since that's what you did when your grandfather died," she said. "You threw yourself into work. That's what everyone says. You quit college and buried yourself on the ranch along with the original Big Jake."

That wasn't all he'd done. He'd given her up. Them...

"I dated," he said, defending himself. Just as she clearly didn't want him thinking she was mooning over him, he didn't want her thinking that he'd pined for her all these years either.

Even though he might have...

When he'd allowed himself to think about her at all.

"You didn't get married," she said. "You didn't have that big family we talked about having."

He could have said that neither had she, but he knew why—because of his eavesdropping. "I have that big family—with my brothers. With my nephews. I don't have time for anyone or anything else."

"You're busy," she agreed. "I know you have a lot to do, so we should probably take a look at these applications now."

Jake nodded in agreement and understanding. Even if she had been willing to give love another chance, she probably knew he would just disappoint her again and now Caleb too. She turned back to her computer, tapped the keyboard and pulled up those applications to show him. She couldn't wait to get away from the ranch. No. She couldn't wait to get away from him.

So much for that second chance his brother

had urged him to take. Ben wasn't nearly as perceptive as Jake had once thought. And neither was he...

CHAPTER SIXTEEN

SADIE HAD NEVER considered that her plan might fail. But maybe grief had distracted her from thinking it through carefully enough, so that she would have been prepared for this.

Jake waved a sheaf of papers in front of her, prompting Feisty to jump up and down on her lap as she snapped at them. Sadie smiled as the dog's teeth snagged a couple of papers, tearing them apart.

Good dog...

Of course Feisty thought Jake was playing with her, but it was clear from the rigid set of his jaw that he wasn't playing.

"What are you doing?" Sadie asked him. She'd figured he would have been in bed hours ago with as early as he got up.

But he'd just stomped into her private suite moments ago, waving around those papers like they were on fire. He'd startled her and Feisty into waking up from where they must have dozed off sitting in front of the television. She usually watched the nightly news in the little room off her main floor bedroom, so that she didn't wake up the kids. Not that they probably would have been able to hear the set in the living room either.

"I'm showing you the applicants you refuse to look at for Katie," Jake said.

No wonder his jaw was so rigidly set. Katie must have told him how desperate she was to leave the ranch when the school year ended. He looked a little desperate himself. Desperate for her to leave? Or desperate for her to stay?

Sadie shrugged. "I already know nobody's going to be as perfect as she is. You must have concluded the same thing since you never proposed to anyone else."

He narrowed his eyes and glared at her. "I knew you were up to no good. You're matchmaking."

She blinked at him, trying to act all innocent. "Matchmaking who? None of you boys are around the place. It's just me and my girls."

The young women she'd hired had become her girls—the granddaughters she'd always wanted. She'd had one in Jenny. A sweet, smart, wonderful girl...

Tears filled her eyes, and she lowered her gaze to her lap, to the rings she wore. The ring she should have given to Jenny when she'd had the chance. All Dale had been able to afford when they'd married had been a simple gold band, like the one Sadie wore with the diamond her husband had given her for their fiftieth anniversary.

Jake waved the papers at her again. "Oh, no. Don't you get all watery-eyed with me. I know you're just manipulating me."

"I was thinking of Jenny," she answered honestly. "I miss her."

Jake released a ragged breath. "So do I. I miss them both. But Katie's not going to replace them. She has her own life. And the longer she stays out here, the more clients she's going to lose in town."

Sadie shrugged. "So what? We'll pay her more. She deserves it for all the work she's been doing. She'll be fine."

"It's not what she wants, Grandma," he said. And his voice got gruff when he added, "I'm not what she wants."

She blinked again and tried for the innocent act. "I don't know what you're talking about."

"Just in case you are matchmaking, it's not going to work," he warned her. "She's not interested."

"What about you?" Sadie asked. "Would you

be interested if she was?" She was pretty sure he was, or she wouldn't have moved Katie and Caleb onto the ranch. Like she'd said, Jake had never found anyone else he'd wanted to marry. He'd never found anyone he'd even looked at like he still looked at little Katie O'Brien.

On the other hand, he was glaring at Sadie. "How can you even ask me that? How can you think that I have any time for romance, for anything but the ranch and those poor orphaned boys?" His brow wrinkled. "How can you find time for anything else?"

She glared at him now. "What do you think I'm doing? I'm making sure those boys are taken care of." All her boys—even her big ones. Maybe especially her big ones...because they could only help the little ones heal once they'd healed themselves. And they'd been hurting long before they'd lost Dale and Jenny. They'd been wounded since their father's death and their mother's desertion, and they'd never allowed themselves to trust or love anyone completely. Except for Dale. He'd loved Jenny so much, just like she believed Jake loved Katie.

"Then leave the ranch to me," he said. "Let me handle that."

She nodded. "Sure, you handle the livestock,

the ranch hands, the grooms, the breeders, the buyers. You got all that on your plate, Jake. Let me handle the office work."

He shook his head. "Your solution to that was manipulating Katie into moving her and her son out here."

She nodded in wholehearted agreement. "Yes, it was. She knows the books already, and we can trust her."

His jaw tightened again.

"Whitford didn't retire because he wanted to," she reminded her grandson. He'd retired because Jenny and Dale had figured out he'd been skimming a bit off the books. No wonder he'd spent the last few years of his employ trying to sweet-talk Sadie into moving south with him; it was her money that would have financed the move. It had probably financed his move despite his efforts at making restitution.

The money he had sent as reimbursement for what he'd taken, she and Jake had put into a separate account for Dale and Jenny's boys. A lot of the ranch money went into that account, too, at Jake's insistence because of all the work Dale had done to help him expand the ranch. She gestured at the papers Jake had stopped waving, the ones that Feisty had rightfully torn.

"How do we know that one of them wouldn't do the same to us? They're all strangers. We knew Whitford. Do you want to let one of them in here to steal from the boys?"

He sighed. "You don't know that any of them would embezzle."

"Neither do you," she pointed out. "And how in the world would you and I have the time to figure out if they were? Katie has to stay on. That's the only solution."

He shook his head. "Not for her. She's not going to stay, Grandma. All you're doing is putting off the inevitable. She has to protect her business."

And her heart, Sadie suspected. Katie had trusted him with it once and he'd broken it. She wasn't going to easily trust him with it again.

"And we have to protect ours," she said. "At least have her show you what to look for in case someone tries stealing from us again. Have her show you a few things."

Like how to be happy again.

"Grandma, I don't have time."

That was the problem. Jake was too busy; he needed more help. He needed Katie; he was just much too proud to admit it.

Or maybe he was trying to save Katie, like he'd done all those years ago, from the burdens he carried. He needed to realize that that weight would be lighter if he had someone to help share the load.

And most of all…if he had love.

HER FACE HOT with embarrassment, Katie rushed down the back stairwell to the kitchen. She couldn't believe she'd overslept—right through her alarm. Or maybe she'd come back to the house so late—after her conversation with Jake—that she'd forgotten to set it. The minute she stepped onto the kitchen floor, all conversation around the long table ceased and everybody looked at her.

Her face heated up even more. "I'm sorry," she said. "I don't know how I overslept."

"Because you've been working so hard," Taye told her, and she handed her a plate of warm blueberry pancakes.

"And because I shut off your alarm," Melanie told her. "I knew you got in late last night from the office, and when you didn't get up when it started going off, I figured you needed the sleep."

"And Emily got the boys up and their teeth brushed as usual," Taye added.

Warmth flooded her heart with appreciation for these amazing women. An only child, Katie had grown up longing for sisters and brothers. When she'd been dating Jake and coming around the ranch, she'd felt like she'd had brothers. But she'd never felt like she had sisters until now. Matt had been an only child like she was. They hadn't wanted their son to grow up as lonely as they'd been.

Caleb, planted between Emily and Ian on the bench, wasn't lonely now. He smiled at her. "You must've been tired, Mommy."

She still was because even though she'd slept in, she hadn't slept well. She'd kept dreaming about Jake, about his cheek pressed against hers. About their kisses. And how she'd longed for more.

"You're flushed," Melanie said. "Are you feeling okay?"

"She must have gotten that bug of yours," Emily said. "You look better now, though."

Melanie looked much better, so some of Katie's guilt over not helping her that morning eased. In fact the brunette was positively glowing. She could have taken the opportunity to share her news with everyone, and maybe she would have but Sadie slapped down some torn and crumpled papers next to Katie's plate.

"When everyone else heads upstairs, you

and I need to discuss these," the older woman remarked.

The applications. From her tone, Sadie wasn't too pleased that Jake had brought them to her. And from the condition of them, she hadn't been impressed with any of them.

"Did Feisty eat your homework, Miss Sadie?" Caleb asked.

Katie chuckled despite herself. Her son was so much like his father, so bright and witty. "I have a feeling that Miss Sadie fed these papers to her," she said.

Sadie chuckled too. "I've seen you try to do the same," she teased the little boy.

His face flushed now, and he glanced guiltily at Emily. "I... I..."

"Didn't fool me," the teacher assured the little boy. "And doesn't get you out of the assignment either. We have a lot of things to learn today, so let's get going." In her Mary Poppins way Emily got the boys to quickly clean up the kitchen and head for the stairs.

Melanie helped Miller hobble up behind them with his cast. Poor kid—everything still took him so much effort. It was going to be a long time before he no longer needed his physical therapist. Melanie was going to have to share her news soon.

Taye cast Katie an apologetic look. "I need to pick up some supplies from town."

And suddenly Katie was alone with Sadie Haven and those torn and crumpled papers. Well, she was alone but for the traitorous ball of fluff that sat on Sadie's lap, her dark eyes half-closed as she dozed.

Katie braced herself for a rebuke over sharing those applications with Jake. She'd felt guilty about doing that, knowing that he already had so much to handle with the ranch and the boys. But she'd felt as if she'd had no choice, as if Sadie was deliberately trying to keep her here longer than they'd agreed. And she had to leave before she did something stupid, like fall for Jake all over again.

That couldn't happen; she couldn't betray Matt any more than she already had. He'd hated how much Jake had hurt her all those years ago. He wouldn't have wanted her to risk getting hurt all over again.

"I looked over these," Sadie said with a sigh. "But I didn't recognize any of the names. Do you know any of them? Would you personally recommend them?"

Katie shook her head. "I don't know them, but I've been gone a long time."

"But Dale and Jenny must have told you about Whitfield," Sadie prodded.

Katie nodded now. "He was padding his paycheck." Reimbursing himself for things for which he hadn't paid, using the ranch credit card for personal items.

It hadn't been a lot, but in the days when they'd been struggling, it had been too much. The ranch wasn't struggling any longer, but that only made its cash accounts more tempting. "We could run extensive background checks," Katie suggested.

"We would," Sadie agreed. "But that might just mean they didn't get caught or maybe they haven't committed a crime yet. Not that they're not capable."

"Why do you trust me?" Katie wondered aloud.

Sadie smiled, and it warmed her dark eyes. This was the way she smiled at the boys—with warmth and affection. "Because you're family, Katie," she replied as if it was obvious.

It wasn't obvious to Katie. She furrowed her brow and said, "But I'm not…"

Because Jake had broken his promise and her heart. He'd made a promise with that little opal ring; the one she'd returned to him when he'd returned her heart to her. She'd waited a few weeks for him to come back to her, to tell her that he'd been lying when he'd said he didn't love her. But he hadn't come back, and so she'd mailed his ring to the ranch.

"You nearly were," Sadie said. "You should have been, would've been if my grandson wasn't so darn stubborn."

A dull ache started behind Katie's furrowed brow. "I don't understand…" What had Jake been stubborn about…? "But it doesn't matter," she told herself as much as she was telling Sadie. "I still can't stay here. I have a business to run, and that business is in town."

"You could spend more time in town," Sadie suggested.

She shook her head. "That's a long drive." And she was reluctant to leave Caleb out here without her. He was too inquisitive about the ranch and the animals, and she didn't want to put the responsibility of watching him onto someone else's shoulders. Everybody else was already doing more than their share. She didn't want them doing hers, as well.

Raising her son was her responsibility, and hers alone now that Matt was gone. She needed her business and her income to provide for them both.

"I don't want to be away from my son that

much," she said. "I can take care of the quarterly taxes and the things that I did for Dale and Jenny, and you can hire someone just for payroll and purchasing and accounts receivable." That was a full-time job on its own. Maybe two full-time positions that Jenny and Dale had managed to take care of part-time. They'd been an amazing, hardworking people. "And when I do that, I can audit the accounts—make sure whoever replaces me isn't embezzling."

"Teach Jake," Sadie said.

"What?" she asked. "He already has too much to do."

"Not to do the bookkeeping, but how to monitor the bookkeeper so that nobody steals from us again."

Katie flashed back to last night, to Jake's cheek pressed against hers as he'd leaned over her chair, over her, and she nearly choked on the sudden dryness of her throat. She reached for the coffee that had cooled sitting next to her plate of now-cold pancakes. She took a quick sip and shook her head. "I doubt he has time for that."

And she wasn't sure she had the willpower. It wasn't fair. Not to her. But most especially not to Matt. He'd spent so much time in the friend zone because she hadn't been willing to trust anyone with her heart after Jake had broken it. But he'd been patient and won her over with his unwavering friendship.

She drew in a deep, unsteady breath—filling her lungs and her heart with resolve. She would not—*could not*—do anything to dishonor her husband's memory. She couldn't go back to the man who'd made it so difficult for her to love him.

"Jake will make time, just like he does for Caleb's riding lessons," Sadie said. "He wouldn't miss those. He wouldn't do anything to disappoint your son."

But she would?

Maybe Sadie hadn't implied it, but that was how Katie felt. Guilty over how devastated Caleb would be when they had to leave the ranch. But they had to leave.

For both their sakes.

Caleb could not get any more attached to Mr. Big Jake than he already was.

"You find a candidate that you know and trust," Sadie said. "And I will hire them to replace you…if you really want to leave…"

"Of course I want to!" Katie said. "This was never supposed to be permanent." She'd only wanted to help out because she'd known, personally, how hard it was to suddenly lose someone.

Sadie reached out then and covered Katie's small hand with her big, callused one. Veins crisscrossed the back of it, and the fingers were crooked with swollen joints. It was a hardworking hand. "I just want you to think about what *you* want, Katie," she said. "What you *really* want."

Then she scooped up her little dog and walked out of the kitchen, leaving Katie alone with her cold breakfast and her guilt. She knew what she really wanted, but it didn't matter.

She couldn't have it.

Even if Jake was willing to really give his love to her this time, she couldn't accept it. She couldn't betray Matt any more than she felt like she already had. This past year she should have just been missing him, mourning him, but guilt had been mixed in with all her other emotions—guilt that she hadn't loved him as much as he'd deserved. She couldn't fall for Jake without feeling even guiltier than she already did.

JAKE STOOD AT the bronco's stall, staring over the door at him. The horse stared back at him, his big eyes watchful, but he didn't paw the ground like he did for everybody else. He didn't rear up or whinny. He just stared back. Calmly.

It was strange how the horse was getting less restless but Jake was getting more. He felt trapped, smothered almost under the weight of all his responsibilities.

Was this feeling why his mother had taken off all those years ago? She'd returned to the rodeo circuit for a while. She'd sent them letters from each stop on the tours. Jake had never opened his.

As far as he knew, only Dusty had.

His brother was the one who'd told him when she'd retired and settled down with another rider, on a ranch they'd started together. Jake might even have more siblings for all he knew, but he didn't care. He already had more than he could handle right now.

Midnight shifted his hooves against the ground, drawing Jake's attention to him. He'd been so deep in his thoughts that he hadn't noticed he was no longer alone. A little hand slipped into his, and Caleb tugged at his arm. "When can I ride Midnight?"

Jake snorted, a sound the horse echoed. "Never. Midnight was trained to make sure that nobody can ride him. That's his job with the rodeo. So he isn't safe for anyone to ride."

"But he's so pretty…" Caleb murmured.

"That doesn't make him safe," Jake said, and he thought about Caleb's mother and how pretty she was. But falling for Katie wasn't safe. She was still in love with her husband, and even though he was dead, Jake couldn't compete with him. He could never offer her what Matt Morris had. The travel, the time, the attention…and disappointing her would hurt Jake more than letting her go again.

"But Midnight and me are going to be friends, and he'll let me ride him then," Caleb said, and he reached into his pocket and pulled out some crushed cookies. "I'm going to give him these."

Jake shook his head again. "No. You're not going to win him over with cookies."

"But everybody loves cookies," Caleb insisted.

"Not horses," Jake said. He reached into his own pocket and pulled out a carrot. "Horses like carrots."

"Who'd want carrots?" Caleb asked, his little face all screwed up with disgust. "Instead of cookies?"

Jake chuckled, and a laugh echoed his, a

soft, musical laugh. He wasn't surprised Katie was with her son. He knew she wouldn't let Caleb come out to the barn alone. Ever since he'd been hurt, she'd been extra vigilant, like she didn't trust him out of her sight, like she couldn't risk losing her son like she'd lost her husband.

She wasn't going to be happy about Jake's plan for today's lesson then. But Caleb had been complaining over only being able to ride inside the corral. And Jake couldn't blame him for getting bored with the same scenery, especially when there was so much of the ranch he hadn't seen yet.

"Forget about Midnight," Jake urged the little boy. Caleb's preoccupation with the horse unsettled him. "I have our horses all saddled up for a ride around the ranch today."

Caleb's eyes widened, but the gasp Jake heard wasn't his. He glanced over at Katie, whose lips had parted with that gasp. She shook her head.

"Can we, Mr. Big Jake? Can we ride around the *whole* ranch?" Caleb asked eagerly.

Jake chuckled. "That would take more than an hour," he said, and unfortunately that was all the time he'd managed to cut out of his busy schedule for these lessons. How was he going to be able to find time for lessons from Katie, so that he could catch any embezzling from her replacement? "It would take days to ride around the *whole* ranch."

"Can we? Can we?"

"You have school," Katie reminded her son.

"Only for a couple more weeks," Caleb said. "I'll have a lot of time on summer break. I can ride around the whole ranch *then*."

A twinge of pain struck Jake's heart. They wouldn't be here in the summer. Katie had already made that clear. They would probably be leaving even sooner—if she had her way. Apparently she hadn't told her son that yet, though.

It was going to break his heart to leave here.

And that wasn't the only heart that was probably going to break…

CHAPTER SEVENTEEN

OH, NO...

Tears stung Katie's eyes as she realized how attached Caleb already was to the ranch and to Jake. Leaving here was going to devastate him. But she had to. She couldn't stay.

She wasn't going to explain all that to him now, not when he was so excited.

"Let's not waste any of your riding time making future plans," she suggested. Especially plans that weren't going to work out—because of her plans. "You need to get going."

"What about you?" Jake asked, his voice a deep rumble.

"What about me?" she asked.

"I assumed you were going to go with us," he said.

Her pulse quickened, but it had to be at the thought of getting on a horse again. Not at the thought of spending more time with Jake.

"I..." She had no reply. Usually she watched their lessons, but that was from the safety of the other side of the fence from the horses and from Jake.

"Please, Mommy!" Caleb implored her. "Come with us! Ride with us!"

Her stomach plummeted. But since she was going to disappoint her son soon, maybe she could give him this. It wasn't as if she'd never ridden before; she just hadn't in a long time. That might have had more to do with the memories—of Jake—than her fear of large animals, though. And maybe she'd just built up that fear in her mind as a way of reinforcing how unsuited she and Jake had been, as a way of trying to assure herself that Matt had been the better match for her. But now she saw that Jake was still the man she'd fallen for—with how much he loved his family and the ranch and with how sweet he was with her son.

"I saddled Matilda for you," Jake said. "She's extremely gentle and not very big. You'll be comfortable."

Katie wasn't, though. Not when he led the horse out of a stall and toward her. As small as the brown mare was, Katie doubted she would be able to climb into the saddle on her own. And sure enough, as she tried to lift her foot into the stirrup, she was just a little bit short.

Jake chuckled, like he had at her son when

Caleb had tried to feed the bronco cookies. She was glad that he'd stopped the little boy— who already knew he was supposed to stay away from that horse. She'd made that clear to him. She wasn't glad that Jake had to help her now. His big hands circled her waist and he lifted her as easily as he lifted Caleb. Even after she was settled into the saddle, grasping at the horn of it, around which he'd wrapped the reins, his hands lingered. "Are you okay?" he asked.

"No." But it wasn't because of the horse. It was because of him—because his touch brought so many memories to mind and so much longing...

"You don't have to go with us," Jake said, his voice pitched low so Caleb wouldn't hear. "I'll make sure nothing happens to him."

That wasn't a promise he would be able to keep—because of her. Because she was going to hurt her son when they left the ranch.

She forced a smile. "I'll be fine."

"Do you remember what Mr. Big Jake taught you?" Caleb asked. "If you don't, I can remind you—like I remind Ian of stuff."

A smile twitched at her lips. "You do a very good job of reminding Ian."

Unfortunately the little boy still struggled—

so much that Emily was giving him extra lessons. That was why he hadn't tagged along, like he often did, on this lesson. She wished he was here, though. That anyone else was here... to help distract her from the feelings rushing through her.

Finally Jake moved his hands from her, and he led the other horses out of their stalls. He barely had to help Caleb into the saddle. The little boy was so eager to go that he just about vaulted onto the horse like a rodeo rider.

Her heart stopped for a moment as she considered that he might want to be one when he grew up. Or a rancher...

That he might choose a hard or dangerous career for himself. Would he have if they'd stayed in Chicago?

But then Matt's career as an engineer hadn't been dangerous at all, and he'd still died much too young. There were no guarantees in life. No promises that could be kept.

She'd learned that even before Matt had died. She'd learned that from Jake, just like she'd learned to ride. The lessons did come back to her, and she found herself relaxing on the gentle horse.

Jake swung into his own saddle, on his much bigger horse. And her heart started pounding fast again. He looked so big. So strong and so very handsome.

She forced herself to look away from him, to focus instead on her son. Caleb rode close to her, sharing all his recent lessons with her like he'd been the teacher rather than the student.

He was so smart, like his father had been, and a good student in all subjects. But he had taken to riding like a natural. His body moved with the horse, like Jake's. Unlike herself, who bucked up and down in the saddle when the mare tried to keep up with the other horses.

Katie was going to be sore later. She remembered that almost as vividly from her old riding lessons as she remembered Jake's kisses, his touch…

Warmth suffused her body, and it had nothing to do with the afternoon sun shining down on them. They rode their horses down a gravel drive that didn't lead them toward town but deeper into the ranch.

"Mommy, you gotta go faster," Caleb chided her. "Or you're going to fall behind."

She felt like she'd fallen back twelve years into the past. She felt like that teenage girl who was riding for the first time, seeing the ranch for the first time.

She'd been so overwhelmed back then at the

size of the animals and the place and how different it was from the life she'd known in the city. She was still overwhelmed.

But now she could also appreciate the beauty of the land. Spring had been late coming this year, but it had arrived fully now, painting the landscape with vivid colors of greens and golds, with bright pops of purples and yellows and blues in the wildflowers.

Jake used to bring her bouquets of those wildflowers, and she'd treasured them more than her mother's elaborate flower gardens. They'd been wild and unique, like she'd always thought he was.

He was such a part of this land. Of the ranch...

No wonder he'd never wanted to leave it—despite those plans they'd made to travel, to live in a city. She wondered now why he had even agreed to such things when it was clear that this was where he belonged. Had he just been humoring her then because she'd been so besotted with him? But then he had always intended to return and settle down on the ranch. He'd just had to do that sooner because of his grandfather's death.

A sigh slipped past her lips.

"You're bored because you're going too

slow," Caleb said. "Go faster! Like me!" He urged his horse into a gallop.

She nudged her knees gently into the mare's sides, and instead of feeling nervous when the horse sped up, excitement coursed through Katie just as the wind coursed through her hair, whipping it around her shoulders. A laugh escaped her.

Caleb's laugh echoed hers. "See, Mommy, it's fun!"

It was, just as it had been in the past. She'd just been forcing herself to deny that she'd ever had the fun with Jake that she'd had with Matt.

The ride was exhilarating, maybe more so because of how close Jake kept to them. He might have just been being careful, so they wouldn't get hurt.

But there was something so intense about how he watched them…

Not that she could see much of his face beneath the brim of his hat. And it seemed like he might have pulled it lower, as if he was trying to hide some of his feelings from them. Maybe he was impatient.

She knew he didn't have much free time, and they'd taken more than the hour that he usually allotted for his lessons with Caleb. "We can turn back," she offered.

"I wanna see the cows, Mommy!" Caleb insisted.

Jake pointed toward the pasture they approached. "Here are the calves," he said.

"Those are baby cows?" Caleb asked, his little brow furrowing beneath that fall of blond bangs.

"They've gotten bigger now than when they were born a couple months ago," he said. "That's why we separated them from their mothers."

"They must grow up superfast," Caleb said. "I wish I could grow up that fast!"

Pain squeezed Katie's heart. "You're already growing up too fast," she said.

He shook his head. "I'm still too little. I wanna be big like Mr. Big Jake."

With as short as she was and how short Matt had been, she doubted Caleb would ever grow tall. But she wasn't about to share that with him any more than she was ready to share that they had to leave the ranch soon.

Jake, already at the fence, swung easily out of the saddle of his horse. He did it with such grace, so effortlessly, as he always seemed to do everything.

Caleb tugged back on the reins and stopped his horse at the fence. Then he wriggled down from the saddle. Holding the reins in one hand, he headed toward Jake. Actually he headed toward the calves that must have recognized either Jake or his horse because they approached the fence.

Katie pulled on her reins, and the mare dutifully stopped for her. But she hesitated for a moment, uncertain how to dismount.

"Need a hand?" Jake offered. And he reached for her waist again.

She didn't want him to touch her again. Didn't want to want him...

So she swung her leg over the saddle on the other side of her horse and slid down the animal. The mare was small but sturdy enough that she barely moved. Maybe horseback riding wasn't as difficult as Katie had persisted in thinking it was.

"Come see the baby cows!" Caleb urged her.

There were so many of them. Some brown. Some black and white. Some brown and white. All different sizes and builds, as well. "Wow," she murmured. "They all look so different from each other. I don't remember you having so many of them before."

"The ranch operations have expanded a lot in the last twelve years," Jake said with pride. "I owe that to Dale."

So his pride was in his brother, not himself. She could hear the gruffness in his voice, hear how much he missed his brother—the one he'd told Caleb had been his best friend. Who did he have now? He seemed to be shouldering all the responsibility alone.

He continued talking about his brother with that pride. "Dale was a great ranch foreman. He was the one who started our horse-breeding division. As well as breeding horses, we breed a bigger variety of cattle. We breed some for beef and some for dairy and—"

"What about to ride?" Caleb asked, turning away from the fence to look at Jake. "Do you have any rodeo bulls?"

Jake shook his head. "No way. It's bad enough that Dusty sent that bronco here. I don't want any other dangerous animals around. Most of the breeding is done with artificial insemination, so that we don't have to keep the bulls."

"Artificial what?" Caleb asked.

Heat rushed to Katie's face. "That's a conversation we don't need to have yet," she said. Hopefully not for a long time.

"Why don't you grab some grass for the cows?" she suggested.

Caleb, as if reluctant to leave his cute new

friends, reached around the fence, grabbing at the weeds and wildflowers. He held them out, luring the animals even closer.

There really were so many different kinds. But the one thing they had in common was that they all cried out pitifully for their mommas. "They seem so upset," she murmured, and she shot Jake a glance. "I can't believe you have to separate them this soon." It seemed heartless to her.

He held up his hands. "I'm sorry. But again, that's ranch life." A life he seemed to love as his dark eyes warmed with appreciation as he stared out at the pasture crowded with calves. "It was time for them to be weaned."

She found herself reaching out for her son, circling her arm around his shoulders as he shoved grass through the fence for the bawling calves. He giggled when they licked his fingers with their rough tongues.

"Nobody's taking him away from you," Jake assured her.

But she wasn't so sure about that.

Caleb stared up at the cowboy with such adulation. She had no doubt that Caleb would be as upset at being separated from Jake and the ranch as these babies were over being separated from their mothers.

She'd warned Caleb before they'd moved to the ranch that this wasn't going to be permanent. That they weren't going to stay indefinitely. But she doubted he would remember that like he remembered his riding lessons.

He was going to be upset no matter when they left. How was she going to remind him that they were leaving when school was done?

JAKE HAD SPENT longer on Caleb's lesson earlier that day than he'd intended. But the boy had been so excited. He hadn't been the only one.

Even Katie had seemed to enjoy herself.

Jake had enjoyed himself too much, had enjoyed sharing the ranch with the boy and his mother. Mostly he'd enjoyed the sight of Katie in the saddle, her face aglow with the sun, her red hair flowing around her shoulders. She was so beautiful that she had taken his breath away.

He was lucky that Buck was such a good horse, or Jake might have toppled out of his saddle. Caleb wouldn't have been so impressed with him then. The little boy probably wouldn't be impressed with him at all if he knew how hard Jake had once made his mother cry. His heart was heavy yet with guilt over how he'd treated her that day. It didn't matter that he'd thought it was for the best—for her.

It had never been for the best for him.

But that was the past. And Jake couldn't undo it. He couldn't go back and make that day never happen. He could only wonder how different things might have been...

Today he'd seen a glimpse of how it might have been with Katie and Caleb riding out to the pasture with him. With her smiling and laughing...

That was why he hadn't wanted the ride to end. But it had. And he'd had to go back to work afterward. Katie must have, as well. He'd just finished up with Midnight, but apparently she was still working because when he stepped out of the barn he noticed light spilling out of the windows of the old schoolhouse. Had she gone back to work after dinner? Or had she been in the office the entire time?

Was she working hard on the books? Or was she working harder to find her replacement at the ranch?

He had to know, so instead of heading straight to the main house, he stopped at the office, pushing open one of the double doors to step inside the building. She must have heard his boots on the porch because he didn't startle her this time. She obviously hadn't dozed off at her desk. It was almost as if she'd been watching the door for him.

"You're really here for the lessons?" she asked, her tone incredulous.

He pushed his hat up a bit on his forehead to focus on her. "The lessons…" He'd thought of them earlier today, but then after their ride, he'd forgotten all about them.

"Accounting lessons," she said. "Your grandmother mentioned them this morning, but I didn't think you'd have time, especially after Caleb's ride went so long."

He uttered a weary sigh. "I really don't have time."

"How do you do it all?" she asked incredulously. "Without Dale, without Jenny, how are you managing everything on your own?"

He shrugged. "Not very well…" He felt stretched too thin, unable to make the boys as happy as they deserved to be. But at least Grandma had hired the teacher and the cook and the therapist. And Katie…

"You need to hire more than a replacement for me," she said. "You need to hire somebody to help you more with the cattle and the horses."

His shoulders sagged with the burdens he

carried. "There's no replacing Dale," he said, his heart aching over the loss of his brother.

"Jake…" Her green eyes glistened with tears of sympathy—for him. "You look exhausted. Go get some sleep."

His heart clenched over her show of concern for him. She'd always been so kind, but he didn't deserve her caring anymore. He shook his head. "I have to do this for the boys," he said. "So the new accountant doesn't steal money that will be theirs one day."

"You really want me to give you lessons?"

It had been a long day. The last thing he wanted was to sit in front of a computer. But he remembered the last time he'd been near it— near her—so close that her cheek had pressed against his.

His breath caught somewhere in his throat, nearly choking him. He swallowed hard and walked across the floor, closing the distance between them. But when he started to move behind her chair, she shoved it back—her body tense—so he couldn't get behind her. And he noticed that she was sitting higher in the chair, on a pillow. He chuckled. "A little sore?"

Her face flushed a deep red, clashing with her auburn hair. "I haven't been on a horse for a long time," she said.

"Caleb said you don't even ride them on the carousel," he said.

"My son shares a lot with you…" she murmured with a little catch in her voice.

"Is that a problem?" he asked.

"Is it?" she asked. "You already have so much going on with your nephews and the ranch and…"

Fighting his feelings for her. But she didn't know that, didn't know that he was falling for her all over again. Or maybe he'd never picked himself back up from that first fall all those years ago.

"I enjoy Caleb," he admitted. "He's a neat kid."

"He idolizes you," she said.

He grinned. "That's not a problem for me."

"Your nephews do too," she said.

That obviously didn't bother her, though. "Is it a problem for you—that Caleb and I are getting close?" he asked.

"I don't want him getting hurt," she said.

Then don't leave…

The words caught in the back of his throat. He couldn't utter them. For one, he knew she no longer had an interest in a life with him. And even if she did, he would be asking her to make as many—if not more—sacrifices than she would've had to make twelve years ago. He had more responsibilities now. His nephews…

And the ranch was even bigger than it had been back then. It took even more of his time, especially now that he didn't have Dale to help him.

It wouldn't be fair to her. Or to Caleb…

She had her business to worry about and her son. He wouldn't be able to give either of them enough time or support. And that wasn't fair…for any of them.

He glanced then at her computer monitor, and that glance answered the question he'd had earlier. She wasn't looking at ledgers but at résumés for her job.

The name on the application on the screen immediately struck a chord in his memory. This was someone from town, someone his grandmother would know and probably wouldn't be able to veto.

Katie would be able to leave. Soon.

"I don't want Caleb getting hurt either," he said.

She followed his gaze to the computer. "I can't stay here, Jake."

"I know." The longer she stayed, the more clients she would lose. And the more of his heart he would lose.

"I'm sorry…" she murmured.

Did she know how he felt? That he was already falling for her and for her son?

"I know you already have so much to deal with," she continued. "And now your grandmother is making you take these lessons from me."

A grin twitched at his lips. "Sadie's not making me do anything. She's not the boss of me like she thinks she is of everyone else."

Katie smiled then. "You sound like one of the boys now," she teased.

That smile of hers had his heart clenching in his chest, had his stare slipping to her lips. He wanted—no, he needed—to kiss her. He was moving toward her when a door creaked open behind them.

He jerked upright and stumbled back, away from her. His grandmother stood in the doorway.

And Jake realized she wasn't alone. A little boy held her hand.

"Caleb," Katie said, and she rushed around Jake toward her son. "Why are you up? What's wrong?"

"I think Little Jake woke him up," Sadie replied.

"Oh…" Katie murmured sympathetically. "I thought he was getting over those nightmares."

Jake wondered if he ever would—if anyone could ever get over losing someone they loved.

"Emily's calming him down now and dealing with the other boys, so I offered to walk Caleb out here since he couldn't get back to sleep without being tucked in."

Caleb released Sadie's big hand and held out his own as he walked farther into the room.

"I'm sorry I wasn't in my room, honey," Katie said. "Of course I'll tuck you back in." She reached for his hand, but he stepped around her.

And reached for Jake. "Will you tuck me back in?" he asked.

Jake felt that painful clench in his chest again, like someone was literally squeezing his heart. Or at least wrapping himself completely around it. Instead of his hand, Caleb held up both arms like Little Jake did when he wanted to be carried.

And Jake remembered that Caleb was only a few years older than the toddler. He was still just a little boy—a very little and lightweight boy. Jake lifted him easily into his arms.

And the sleepy kid wrapped his arms around Jake's neck and snuggled against his shoulder.

Jake had no doubt now that the little boy was already wrapped around his heart…just as the boy's mother was.

Had always been…

If he was a more selfish man, he would have figured out a way to keep them. But it wouldn't have been fair to them—when he had so little to offer them.

No. It was better that it wasn't fair to *him* than to either of the people he'd come to love so much.

CHAPTER EIGHTEEN

IT WAS A PROBLEM. A big problem for Katie when her little boy walked right past her, seeking comfort from the man Matt had resented for making her so sad. How would he feel about their son idolizing this man? Not happy…

And all he'd ever wanted for her, for Caleb, was their happiness. She wanted the same for Matt even though he was gone. She didn't want to do anything that would have made him unhappy had he still been here.

But Jake held her son so carefully now, so affectionately, that she couldn't protest. She could only watch as Jake carried her son away from her.

And she felt like those mother cows must have when they had been separated from their babies. Her baby wasn't crying like those calves had today. He was nearly asleep, his blond head resting on Jake's broad shoulder—his bright blue eyes closed.

Sadie opened the door for them, but before

Katie could follow them out, she closed it behind them. And Katie felt even more like those mama cows.

"I need to go to my son," she said.

"Jake's got him," Sadie assured her. "That's who he was asking for when he came downstairs."

Katie sucked in a breath.

"I didn't say that to hurt you," Sadie said, and there was sympathy in her dark eyes. "I say that to make you feel better, that they're bonding."

Katie shook her head. "I don't want that." It was only going to make it harder for her to leave. But that was exactly what Sadie wanted. To keep them here.

"He'll always remember who his daddy is," Sadie said.

Katie had to make certain that he never forgot Matt. She had to make certain that she never forgot him either. Guilt pressed so heavily on her chest that she struggled to draw a breath now.

"It's clear he had a close relationship with his father, or he wouldn't be so drawn to Jake," Sadie said.

Katie shook her head again. "No. You're wrong."

Sadie arched a brow that was still dark, unlike her white hair. "They weren't close?"

"No. They were very close." His best friend. That was what Caleb had called Matt. "But that's not why he's drawn to Jake. Jake and Matt are nothing alike. Absolutely nothing."

"Matt wasn't a good man?" Sadie asked.

Katie gasped, shocked that the older woman could even imply such a thing. "He was the best. He would have never hurt me. Not like Jake did."

Sadie sucked in a breath now. "I'm sorry."

Katie blinked against the sudden sting of tears. "That wasn't your fault."

Sadie released a heavy sigh then. "I think it was. When his grandfather died, it hit me hard. I tried to hide it, but Jake could always see right through me. Even when he was a kid." Her lips curved into a slight smile as if she was remembering him then. "Just like his grandfather. The first time I met the original Big Jake Haven, he looked at me, and I think he was the first man who really saw *me*."

Katie remembered the first time she'd seen Jake—really seen him. Her first day of high school. He'd been a couple of grades ahead of her. The oldest of the Haven boys. But even then, at sixteen, he'd looked like a man. And when he noticed her, she had felt like a woman for the first time in her life.

"After my husband died," Sadie continued, "Jake was the only one of my grandsons who saw how much I was hurting, how much I was falling apart."

The warmth of sympathy filled Katie's heart. Sadie Haven was legendary for her strength, but that didn't mean she couldn't be hurt. That she couldn't feel pain and loss. She'd had so much of it in her life. "I'm sorry…"

Sadie blinked as if fighting back her own tears. Then she focused on Katie with dry eyes. "No. I'm sorry because I couldn't convince him to stay in college. I couldn't convince him to stay with you."

Heat burned Katie's face. "If he'd loved me, you wouldn't have had to convince him."

"That's why I had to try so hard," Sadie said. "And why I ultimately failed to convince him, because he loved you so much…" Her voice cracked now.

And Katie's heart cracked. She shook her head, unwilling to believe it. "No…" All those things he'd said to her, those horrible things about her chasing him, suffocating him. But that had been one day; he'd never talked to her with anything but love and affection every day other than that one. Yet that day he had hurt her so badly. "No, he didn't love me. Not like Matt did."

If only she could have loved Matt as completely as she'd loved Jake, but her heart had never fully belonged to her husband because Jake had always held a piece of it.

"Your husband is gone," Sadie said. "I'm sorry about that. He sounds like a good man, a good father, a good husband..."

Tears flooded Katie's eyes now and trailed down her cheeks.

"He would want the best for you, Katie," Sadie said. "He would want you to open your heart to love again."

Katie wiped away her tears with shaking hands. She and Matt had never had that conversation—had never talked about what one would do if the other was gone. They hadn't expected to lose each other so soon.

Or maybe Matt had always known he didn't completely have her anyway. He, better than anyone, had known how much she'd loved Jake.

Defensive, Katie turned on the older woman. "What about you?" she asked.

Sadie's eyes widened. "What about me?"

"Your husband has been gone for twelve

years," Katie said. "You haven't opened your heart to anyone else."

Sadie chuckled. "I'm eighty years old. Too old for romance."

"You weren't eighty when he passed away," Katie pointed out. "You were still in your sixties."

Sadie snorted. "Barely. And I had boys to raise, a ranch to manage. I was too busy to look for love again."

"So am I," Katie said. "I have a business to run. A boy to raise."

"A boy who needs a father," Sadie said. "A boy who's already fallen for Jake."

"Those boys you had to raise needed a father, too, and a grandfather." Katie tossed her words back at her. "But you never got over your husband."

Sadie uttered a very heavy sounding sigh. "You're right. I didn't. I guess I'm a lot like Jake that way."

"He never got over losing his grandfather," Katie agreed. To the point that he'd tried to replace him—as the head of the family and the ranch.

"I wasn't talking about his grandfather," Sadie corrected her. "Jake never got over the loss of you."

"He didn't lose me," Katie reminded them both. "He shoved me away."

"For your sake," Sadie insisted. "He didn't want you making sacrifices for him. Giving up your education. Your dreams."

Katie's heart was beating fast as she wondered. Could it be true? "Did he tell you this?" she asked.

Sadie's mouth opened, but no words came out. She obviously couldn't lie.

"He didn't," Katie said.

"It was obvious," Sadie insisted. "He wouldn't talk about it. Wouldn't talk about you. But it was obvious why he broke up with you."

"It was to me too," Katie said. When he'd said all those things to her...

"He did it for you," Sadie stubbornly insisted. "For your happiness."

Katie had been happy with Matt. With the traveling they'd done. First as friends, then as newlyweds. She'd been happy with their son and with the life she and Matt had built together in Chicago.

But what if Sadie was telling the truth? What if Jake had sacrificed his happiness for hers?

What had he been left with?

He hadn't married. He hadn't had children

of his own. All he had was responsibility. For the ranch. For his family...

What about happiness?

CALEB HAD BARELY lifted his head from Jake's shoulder since climbing into his arms. Only when Jake stepped inside the house and Feisty went into their usual routine of tugging on his jeans and yapping and growling did Caleb rouse...just enough to giggle. Jake reached down and plucked the dog off the floor, letting it snuggle against him and the little boy.

The little dog closed her eyes too. Like Caleb, Feisty was up past her usual bedtime. Because of the nightmares...

Would they ever go away? Would Little Jake return to the happy, babbling toddler he'd once been?

Life would never return to normal; Jake knew that, knew they were all going to have to come up with some new normal for them. Just as they had in the past...

Just as they'd dealt with all their losses, as stoically as Havens had always dealt with them. Or they ran from them...like Jake's mother and Dusty.

Caleb and Katie weren't Havens but they'd suffered, as well. Jake's heart ached for the little boy's loss, just as it ached for his nephews' losses. They were just kids. It wasn't fair.

He blinked against the tears stinging his eyes and focused on the stairs, wearily climbing them with his armload of little boy and little dog. When he stepped through Caleb's open door and laid him on his bed, the dog jumped down onto the mattress too. She curled up next to the sleeping child, as if she'd somehow sensed he needed comfort tonight.

What had brought him out to the office with Sadie? Why hadn't he been able to get back to sleep?

Jake was tempted to wake him to ask those questions. But Caleb slept so peacefully now that Jake could only pull the blankets over him and quietly walk backward out of the room. He left the door open enough for Feisty to fit through should she wake up and want out. Then Jake stood in the hall and listened. He heard no cries from Little Jake, no murmur of voices from Ian or Miller.

Emily must have gotten whoever had woken up back to sleep. Taye called her the kid whisperer, and it was no exaggeration. Grandma had done really well with hiring those women. The teacher and the cook and, despite Miller's frustration with his slow progress, the physical therapist.

But Katie…

Katie was going to hurt more than she was going to help. Because when she left, she was going to hurt her son. And she was going to hurt Jake.

Remembering the name he'd seen on the application, he suspected that would happen soon. The sound of a door opening and closing drew him toward the stairs, because the sound must have been the front door.

He was surprised that Katie hadn't been right with him when he'd carried Caleb from the office to the house. But she must have stayed behind to talk to Sadie. She was in a hurry now, as she trotted quietly but quickly up the steps. She passed him without a glance, her head down, as if she couldn't look at him. What had happened?

What had his grandmother done? Because he had no doubt that she'd done something to upset Katie. Or had he?

Did she have a problem with her son getting close to him? Was she worried that he'd get too attached when she was determined to leave?

He watched as she hurried to her son's room and stepped inside to check on him. A twinge of pain struck his heart. He didn't want the boy getting hurt, but he had no doubt that Caleb would be hurt. Soon.

Instead of heading toward his room, Jake descended the stairs to the main floor to find his grandmother. She was moving slowly, so slowly that he caught her before she reached her suite at the back of the house. Was she finally starting to feel her age?

Or was it the grief that was hitting her just as it had seemed to hit the boys tonight, making Little Jake awaken in a nightmare and Caleb unable to get back to sleep? It seemed to come in waves. For a while the surface was calm, everything seemed to settle, and then another wave rose and swept over her...

How many more waves of grief could Sadie withstand?

"Are you okay?" Jake asked her, his heart filling with concern and love for her.

She tensed and stopped walking. Paper crinkled as she clutched something in her hand.

The résumé...

Katie must have printed it for her. Or maybe that was her resignation that Sadie crumpled up in her hand.

Keeping her back toward him, Sadie murmured, "I'm just tired..."

He probably should have let her go to bed. He probably should have gone to bed himself; it was late for him too and the morning was going to come much too soon. But he couldn't leave it.

Couldn't let her leave without knowing.

"Did something happen between you and Katie?" he asked. "Is she okay?"

Sadie sighed and she turned toward him. "This is what I'm tired of, Jake. I'm tired of you making all these sacrifices nobody's asked you to make. I'm tired of you giving up what you want."

She knew then. Knew that Katie had probably found a suitable replacement. That she was leaving.

"You must be tired," Jake said. "You're not making any sense."

She drew in a sharp breath. "You're the one not making sense. Or maybe it's that you have no sense, Jake Haven."

He tensed now, offended. "What are you talking about?"

"If you let that woman go again, you're going to be making the second-biggest mistake of your life," she warned him. "The first was when you let her go twelve years ago."

"I did the right thing," he insisted. "She fell

in love. She got married." She'd realized all those dreams she'd had. "She had a son. A life…"

"All the things you gave up," Grandma said.

"I didn't give them up," he assured her—though it was a lie. He'd never admitted to anyone what he'd done—not even Dale. But he suspected Dale and his grandmother—and apparently Ben—had guessed. "I didn't have time for them."

"You could have made time," she said.

He grimaced. "When? There is no time."

"You're making time for those riding lessons with her son. For a ride today with Katie and Caleb."

"They deserve more than an hour here or there," he said.

"Then hire more help," she said.

"Like you did?" he asked.

She nodded. "You think I could handle these boys on my own? Without these women? I'm too old to raise any more kids, Jake."

He knew that. He'd known it twelve years ago when Grandpa Jake died. "You've done the right thing," he told her. "With Emily and Taye and Melanie, they're all exactly what the boys need."

"Just like Katie is what you need," she insisted.

"But I'm not right for her," he said. "She deserves better." From the sound of it, from all the praises she'd sung about Matt Morris, she'd had better.

"She deserves you," Sadie insisted. "And so does her son."

He shook his head, shook the temptation out of it. "It wouldn't be fair. Not with how busy I am."

"Hire a good foreman for the ranch," she told him.

He'd intended to hire some more help but not a foreman. "I had a good foreman." Dale. "He's gone now, and there's no replacing him." Just as he suspected there was no replacing Matt in Katie's heart.

She was still in love with her husband.

Just as it had been twelve years ago, now was not the time for them either.

"Jake…" his grandmother murmured, her voice gruff with grief and frustration.

He closed the distance between them and kissed her cheek. It was only slightly wrinkled, only slightly leathery from age and all the time she'd spent in the sun over her eighty years. But he had to remind himself that she wouldn't be around forever.

No. He didn't have to remember that—he knew that nobody was ever around forever.

At least not in his life. Maybe that was another reason he'd been reluctant to risk a relationship. He'd known it wouldn't last, just as Katie's time here at the ranch wouldn't last. He could have asked Sadie then about the paper she held yet, crumpled into a ball in her hand. But he already knew what it was: the end of Katie and her son's stay at the ranch.

They would be gone soon. And they would take with them a big chunk of Jake's heart when they left.

CHAPTER NINETEEN

KATIE HADN'T SLEPT well the night before—
maybe because she'd slept in Caleb's small
bed, sharing it with him and that little dog.
Feisty had insisted on sleeping between them,
as if she was protecting the child from her.

From his mother…

Maybe somehow the pooch had figured out
that Katie was going to take him away. Sooner
rather than later.

Katie wasn't the only sleep-deprived one
gathered around the long table over breakfast
that morning. Sadie hadn't even shown up yet,
but she'd been awake later than usual dealing
with Caleb and her grandson. Jake, as usual,
was already gone; he had to be more sleep-
deprived than she was. He'd gone downstairs
instead of to his room after he'd tucked Caleb
back into bed.

She hadn't thanked him for that, for carrying the little boy back to his room. She hadn't

even been able to bring herself to look at Jake when she'd passed him at the top of the stairs.

Sadie had told her too many things, made her wonder about too much…about Jake. About the sacrifices he might have made.

Sacrifices for his family. For the ranch…

And for her?

Was it possible?

Even if it was, it shouldn't matter to her. The past was the past. They couldn't go back—they couldn't undo what had been done.

And she wouldn't want to. She'd had a good life with Matt; he'd made everything fun and happy. It wasn't fair that he was gone, and it wasn't fair that she could fall for anyone else. Ever…

"More coffee?" Taye asked.

"Yes, please," she replied with such urgency that the cook laughed as she filled her cup from the pot she held.

Emily pushed her cup across the table. "More…" she moaned as she laid her blond head next to her untouched plate on the table.

"Are you okay, Miss Trent?" Caleb asked with alarm from his usual seat on the bench next to his favorite teacher.

But Emily wasn't his favorite person.

Katie suspected his mother wasn't anymore either. Jake was. And when Katie took her son away from him, away from the ranch, she would probably never regain her title of favorite person. She would probably become her son's least favorite person.

"I'm fine," Emily assured her concerned student. "Just tired…" She punctuated the statement with a yawn.

"You should have let me take over with Little Jake," Melanie said.

Emily moved her head against the table where it lay, as if she was shaking it like she shook the table a bit. "You need your sleep more than I do."

Melanie glanced quickly at Katie, as if wondering if she'd shared her secret with the teacher. Katie shook her head in reply to the silent question.

"Physical therapy isn't easy work," Emily said, and she lifted her head and then the full mug of coffee to her lips.

Physical therapy probably wasn't easy work for a pregnant woman, struggling to handle a seven-year-old boy in a heavy cast. Miller had gotten over his initial shyness with his therapist and let her help him more. He also helped himself more now, though.

At least that was one responsibility Jake hadn't had to shoulder alone.

"We're making progress," Melanie said with a smile at Miller, who sat sideways on the bench, the cast propped up on it straight in front of him. "We'll make more when the cast comes off in a couple of weeks."

A couple of weeks. After school was done, after Katie intended to be gone. She needed to go to town, to start looking for houses. In the meantime she would have to move back in with her parents.

Her mother might have been nervous with a rambunctious little boy in the house, but she would never refuse to let them stay. And her father would warmly welcome them, as he had when they'd moved back from Chicago. Maybe he'd been happy to not be the only one messing up the house for once.

"I want this cast off now," Miller muttered, his cute little face contorted with a scowl. "And I want Little Jake to stop screaming at night. Why can he talk then, but never during the day?"

"To be fair, he's not talking then," Emily said with a heavy sigh. "He's crying."

"Who's crying?" Ian asked.

Miller groaned in frustration. "And why

can't you remember anything for more than two seconds? When's your head going to get unbroken?"

"My head's not broken!" Ian yelled in protest, but he raised his hands to it, as if checking to be certain.

Emily must have been tired because she froze, not jumping in as she usually did to stop the arguments between the brothers.

"Come on, guys," Melanie murmured. "Let's not fight."

A piece of hard cereal flew across the table and struck Miller in the nose. Then another one bounced off Melanie's cheek.

And Caleb started laughing. She glanced at him, but he raised his empty hands. "It wasn't me. It was Little Jake."

The toddler, fists full of cereal, hurled some more pieces, but these fell on Caleb's and Ian's heads and plates and splashed into Emily's coffee cup. Then a piece struck Katie on the chin and bounced onto her plate, as well.

"Hey!" Taye yelled as one was hurled toward her.

"What's going on?" a deep voice asked—a deep female voice.

And Little Jake, with a giggle, hurled a piece

of hard cereal at his great-grandmother, who'd just walked into the kitchen.

It struck her right in the middle of her high forehead and stuck there on her brow, which she had furrowed in confusion. Everybody froze, as did she…until she started laughing full belly laughs. The little boys immediately erupted with laughter. A laugh tickled Katie's throat and bubbled out of her mouth. Emily started laughing, then Melanie. And Taye laughed until she snorted.

Warmth flooded Katie's heart with appreciation and affection for them all. Even Sadie…

Maybe most of all Sadie, because she doubted anyone loved as fiercely as Sadie Haven loved. She would obviously do anything for her family.

How hard would Katie have to fight her to leave the ranch? How hard did she want to fight her?

Katie had printed off and given her that résumé last night. The name had been familiar to her, and it would be as familiar to Sadie. The certified public accountant was a Lemmon, widowed son of the current deputy mayor, once former mayor. Like Katie, Bob Lemmon had returned to Willow Creek after losing his spouse. He was older than Katie, his children already grown. And he wanted to come home to be closer to his father, but as he'd said in his cover letter, not too close.

He was trustworthy and experienced and perfect for the position. Even Sadie had to see that.

Yet she'd barely glanced at the résumé, saying she needed her glasses and was too tired to try to read the small print without them. Then she'd headed out the door of the office and back to the main house, crumpling the paper in her hand as she'd walked.

Katie would just print off another when she got into the office today. And if Sadie refused to hire him, she would ask Jake to do it. If she trusted herself to be alone with him…

Every time they'd been together without a pint-sized chaperone, they'd kissed. Her pulse quickened at just the thought of it, of his lips brushing across hers. She sucked in a breath—and then a piece of cereal as one struck her right in the mouth. She choked and sputtered.

Emily clapped her hands together and resumed teacher-mode. "Okay, guys, let's clean up our plates. And you, little man, need to clean up all the cereal, and then we get to our lessons." All the laughter must have roused her from her sleepiness because her blue eyes were bright now despite the dark circles beneath them. "Summer break will be here before we know it!"

Yes, it would. The time had already passed so quickly. Katie's entire day passed that way, so quickly that she even missed Caleb's riding lesson. He wasn't alone, though; the other boys and Melanie and Emily had gone out to the barn with him. Longing pulled at her as she watched them ride past the office. Jake had somehow even gotten Miller, with his heavy cast, up on a horse.

He must have gone back to work after the lesson, though, because as usual he wasn't at dinner that evening. They avoided any more food fights and got everyone asleep early enough that Taye and Melanie insisted Emily take the night off. She'd refused to leave the ranch, though, and wanted only a long bath and some quiet time.

Katie had returned to the office, and it felt entirely too quiet for her in the empty old schoolhouse. During the day with the sun pouring in, with clients and with Robert either on the phone or email, she didn't feel so lonely.

But at night…

At night whether in the office or in her empty bed, she felt the most alone. Did she really want to spend the rest of her life like this? So solitary?

Was Sadie right? Would Matt have wanted more for her?

He would have. He'd loved her that much, but he wouldn't have wanted Jake for her. He knew how badly Jake had hurt her; he'd been the one who'd picked up the pieces of the heart Jake had broken so badly.

No. It was better for Katie to spend the rest of her life alone than to spend it with Jake. Not that he really had any room in his life for anyone or anything—not even sleep.

Katie's skin suddenly tingled, and she realized she wasn't alone in the office any longer. She glanced at the doorway to find Jake there, leaning wearily against it. It looked like it might have been all that was holding him up.

"What are you doing here?" she asked.

"We were interrupted last night," he reminded her.

Her pulse quickened. They'd been interrupted just as he'd seemed about to kiss her. Was that what he'd come here to finish? And why was she so hopeful that it was?

"But you look exhausted," she said.

"I am," he admitted with a heavy sigh.

"Then what are you doing here?" she asked. "You should be in the house sleeping."

He nodded in agreement but instead of turning and heading out the door, he crossed the room to her. "Last night you were going to show me how to spot embezzling. I'm here for that lesson."

She felt a small jab of disappointment. "Did your grandmother tell you about the résumé I gave her?"

"Mayor Lemmon's son?"

She nodded. "She told you?"

He sighed again, even more wearily. "No, but I saw his résumé on your computer last night. I recognized his name."

"He's the perfect candidate for the job," Katie insisted. "Will she give him a chance?"

"She'll have to," he insisted. "If you really want to leave."

She thought of that morning—of all the laughter around the long breakfast table, of how happy Caleb was here with everyone else. It was going to be so hard on him to leave. And it was going to be harder for her than she realized. But then she reminded Jake and herself, "I can't stay."

"Because of your business?" he asked.

She nodded. But that wasn't the only reason and she suspected he knew that, knew that she didn't want to stay here with him. It would only make her long for him more, and that wasn't fair to anyone, especially not Matt.

"Maybe you should hire Lemmon to help you with your business, and you and Caleb can stay here," he suggested, and there was such hopefulness in his deep voice.

Did he want them to stay? Didn't he already have more to deal with than one man could handle?

"That's not a good idea for any of us," she said.

"Are you sure about that?" Jake asked, and he moved a little closer, so that his long shadow fell across the desk. The brim of his hat shadowed his face, so Katie couldn't see his eyes, couldn't see his expression.

Was he serious? Did he want them to stay?

It didn't matter. It didn't matter what he wanted now. She couldn't.

"I'm very sure," she insisted. "And I doubt Mr. Lemmon would be interested in this job if it wasn't at the ranch. I don't think he wants to be in town, in such close proximity to his father."

Jake chuckled. "Yeah, Old Man Lemmon is a lot like Grandma. Overbearing and stubborn."

"She loves you," Katie said. "She loves all of you so much." So fiercely...

But after losing some of her loved ones, Sadie no doubt thought that she had to fiercely love the ones she had left, in case she lost them too.

Katie understood that; she loved Caleb fiercely. Would he understand that? Would he accept that leaving the ranch was best for them? That they needed to build a life for themselves in Willow Creek?

"The problem with Sadie isn't her loving us," Jake said. "It's with her trying to control us."

"She doesn't seem to have been very successful with you," Katie pointed out.

If Sadie had been telling the truth, if she'd urged her grandson not to break up with Katie all those years ago...

Could that have been true?

Could Jake have thought he was doing what was best for Katie back then? But how could breaking her heart so cruelly have ever been for the best?

She was tempted to ask him, but then he might think that it mattered to her. That he still mattered to her...

And she'd already made enough of a fool of

herself over Jake when they were teenagers. She'd loved him so much then. And because she'd once loved him so much, she still cared about him. "You're wearing yourself out, Jake, trying to take care of everything on your own."

"You sound like Grandma now," he said, his lips curving into a slight grin.

She ignored his teasing and lifted her chin with pride in the comparison. She wished she was half as strong and confident as his grandmother. "Sadie Haven is a wise woman." If sometimes misguided, at least with her matchmaking efforts.

"Then you're not still upset that she manipulated you into moving onto the ranch?" he asked with a slightly mocking smile.

"I won't be here much longer," she reminded him. "School will be over soon. Caleb and I will be able to move back to town."

He sighed again, a ragged-sounding sigh as if he was resigned.

"Then you'd better show me how to spot embezzling," he said, and he gestured to the computer.

"I don't think you'll need to worry about that with Mayor Lemmon's son."

Jake shrugged. "I didn't think we'd have to worry about it with Whitford either. And

Lemmon's been gone a long time from Willow Creek. He might have changed."

"I was gone a long time too," she said.

"You've changed," he said.

"Not into an embezzler."

He chuckled. "I don't know if that's true," he said. "You seem reluctant to show me how to check for embezzling. Maybe you've been ripping off the ranch."

She chuckled. "Yeah, right. I'm too smart to try to swindle Sadie Haven." She turned her attention from him to the keyboard and pulled up the ranch records. She spent the next hour showing him how to check for cash reimbursements and how to verify accounts payable recipients.

He'd pulled up a chair next to hers, too close, and he seemed to be paying attention. But his head began to nod toward his chest, as if he was struggling to stay awake.

"I think that's a long enough lesson for today," she told him. "You need your sleep. And you really need some help around here."

He turned away from the computer monitor and stared at her now, his dark eyes warm with gratitude and maybe something else. "You've been a lot of help. Thank you."

His sincerity touched her. "You're welcome. But it's not enough, Jake, to have someone in the office. You need someone to help you on the ranch."

"That's what my grandmother says…" he murmured with a sigh. "She wants to me to replace Dale. She doesn't understand that that's not possible…" His voice cracked with grief, grief he'd probably buried so that he could deal with his nephews' grief instead.

And Caleb's…

Caleb had grieved with Jake about his father more than he'd grieved with her.

"I understand," Katie said. All too well.

"I'm sorry," Jake said. "I don't know if I ever expressed my sympathy over your husband dying."

"You didn't send a card or a note…" Heat rushed to her face that she'd admitted to having noticed his slight.

"I didn't know if you'd want to hear from me," he said. "After that day…"

The day he'd broken her heart. Had he done it out of malice like she'd thought, or maybe even out of his own grief over losing his grandfather? Or had he done it to stop her from making the sacrifices he had?

Instead of asking those questions, though, she asked the other one that had been niggling in her mind for the past hour. "You said earlier that I've changed. How have I?"

"You're not *my* Katie anymore."

Her heart thudded hard in her chest, but she summoned her pride again and said, "No. I'm not going to fawn all over you like I used to."

"I know you got over me a long time ago," he said.

She wished she really had—for Matt's sake as much as her own. He'd deserved better.

Now she realized that Jake had too. He looked so defeated, his broad shoulders and his head bowed with exhaustion, that her heart went out to him. And then so did her hands as she reached out and touched the slouched shoulder closest to her. "I still care about you," she admitted. "I hate to see you wearing yourself out like this. I wish…"

She didn't even know what she wished for anymore. She couldn't stay here. And while she cared about Jake, she couldn't love him—not without betraying Matt.

JAKE HAD BEEN so exhausted earlier that it had taken all his effort to stand in the doorway and then to focus on her accounting lessons.

Now.

With her admission, hope coursed through

Jake, energizing him. He wanted to reach for her, wanted to take her into his arms and apologize for how he'd treated her all those years ago.

And explain…

And beg her forgiveness…

But it wasn't just her forgiveness Jake wanted. He wanted her love.

He didn't deserve it, though.

Not after how he'd treated her. And even if he could earn her forgiveness and her trust, he would never have her love. That belonged to another man—a man she'd just confirmed could never be replaced.

Just as Jake couldn't replace Dale.

"I'm sorry," he said again, as he had just moments earlier.

"For what?" she asked, her head cocked to the side so that her long red hair fell across one shoulder.

She was so beautiful, her green eyes so bright as she stared at him. Waiting…

For his confession? What had Sadie told her?

Not that Sadie knew anything. Not that anyone knew anything for sure. Not even Dale. And Dale had been the only one in whom Jake had ever been able to confide. To trust…

He sighed. "I'm sorry you lost your husband so young. That Caleb lost his father."

"It wasn't fair," she said, and her lashes fluttered as she blinked away tears glistening in her eyes. "Just as it wasn't fair that Dale and Jenny are gone so soon."

He nodded in wholehearted agreement. "No. Those poor kids…" He reached out and touched her cheek. Her skin was so silky, so smooth. "And poor you," he said. "Matt sounds like he was a good man."

"The best," she said, and she lost her fight against the tears. One spilled over and trailed down her face.

Jake stopped it with his thumb, and his heart ached with her pain. With his…

He'd lost so much when he'd given her up. He'd lost the chance of ever being the best man she'd known, the best man she'd loved. She'd loved a better man.

And it sounded as though she would never stop loving him even though he was gone. "Despite dying so young, Matt was a lucky man during the time he had on earth," he assured her. "He had you. He had Caleb."

He forced himself to pull his hand from her face then, because if he kept holding it, he was going to lean forward. He was going to kiss her. And while she'd admitted to caring about him, she certainly didn't love him.

She would never be *his* Katie again.

He'd decided long ago that there was no point in apologizing to her—not when everything had worked out for the best. For her. But still, he felt compelled to say it now. "And I'm sorry for how I broke up with you," he admitted. "I was so harsh, and that wasn't necessary..."

"No, it wasn't," she agreed. "Unless you were worried about me following you back to Willow Creek..."

She paused, waiting for him to continue then. As if she already knew.

He couldn't bring himself to admit it now, not when they'd just discussed how great a man Matt was. "But you had Matt...and Caleb..."

"And what did you have?" she asked him.

He shook his head. "I can't talk about this now. I need to go to bed..." Before he did something stupid, before he begged her not to leave the ranch. Not to leave him...

But before he could rise from the chair next to hers, she reached for him. Her mouth touched his, her lips moving softly across his lips.

His breath backed up, choking him along with the emotion rushing over him. The pleasure.

The love.

He'd never stopped loving Katie. He didn't want the kiss to stop either, but Katie jerked back. Her face was red with embarrassment.

"I... I don't know why I did that," she murmured, and she flattened her hand across her mouth, as if she wanted to wipe away his kiss. She'd admitted to caring about him.

Maybe he needed to ask her for that second chance he so very badly wanted. But how could he ask when he couldn't give her and Caleb the time and attention they deserved? While he needed her—them—they needed someone else. They needed Matt Morris or a man like him, one who could devote himself solely to them.

CHAPTER TWENTY

WHAT HAD KATIE been thinking to kiss Jake? She hadn't been thinking; that was the problem. She'd been reacting to Jake's apology. But he hadn't finished it. He hadn't explained himself. And she wasn't sure that she wanted him to, that she wanted to completely forgive him, because then she would have no reason to not fall for him all over again. Except Matt…

Since that kiss the other night, she'd intended to avoid Jake. But that wasn't possible—not unless she was comfortable with Caleb attending every riding lesson without her.

Not that Caleb really needed riding lessons anymore. He was riding well. And thanks to her accompanying them on their jaunts around the ranch, she was riding better herself. Though she still got a little sore from the saddle.

How did Jake spend so much time in it? So much time with the livestock and his ranch hands? And yet, he still carved out some time for his nephews and for her son.

And her.

He'd been taking lessons from her at night—after the kids were in bed—when he should have been sleeping. He was every bit as smart as she remembered from when they were teenagers. The accounting principles that she'd struggled to learn came easily to him. So easily that he probably hadn't needed more than that first lesson. But he'd returned the next couple of nights after that one to learn more.

Or was he waiting for her to kiss him again?

She wanted to—so badly. So badly that she wouldn't resist if he'd kissed her. But he hadn't. He wasn't the only one not doing what Katie wanted.

Sadie wasn't either. She refused to hire Bob Lemmon, so Katie had. Actually she'd proposed a partnership with him, and he'd already started working with Robert in town, handling her clients who wanted to come into the office.

It wouldn't be long now before she could move back to town. School was nearly done. And then Bob could switch places with her—in work location and living location. He had a house in town, one that was bigger than he needed, he'd told her during their online interview.

On the computer in the office, she studied the photos he'd sent her. With four big bedrooms and two full baths and a big backyard close to the elementary school, it couldn't have been more perfect.

Even though they'd moved away ten years ago, Bob and his late wife had kept the house because they'd returned often to see Bob's dad and his mother. But now his mother and his wife were gone, and his kids rarely visited Willow Creek, so the house was too much for him.

It was perfect for Katie. He'd even offered to sell it to her. She should have been excited. Why wasn't she excited?

Why, instead of excitement, did she have this hard knot of dread twisting her stomach in knots?

Because of Caleb.

Because he was so happy here.

And she had to admit he wasn't the only one. She enjoyed riding around the ranch now. She enjoyed the women Sadie had hired, the women who had become Katie's friends. She loved the little boys.

And Jake...

No. She couldn't love Jake again. Still...

She waited here, in the office for him, so they could spend that time alone going over lessons he really didn't need. But yet…

Those lessons, seeing him, sitting so close to him…had become her favorite part of the day. Her skin tingled and her pulse quickened at the thought of his closeness, and because the door creaked open, she knew he was close.

She had to leave. Soon…because she was already falling for Jake all over again.

JAKE WAS EXHAUSTED. So exhausted that he should have gone straight to bed. Not just tonight but the last few nights. But he couldn't sleep until he had this time with Katie, this time that was just the two of them. As wonderful as it was to sit close to her, to smell that sweet floral scent of hers, it was also torture. Because he knew she was leaving.

As he pulled up a chair and dropped into it beside her, he noticed the pictures on the computer monitor. It wasn't a résumé this time but a house. Katie was moving on—moving away from Ranch Haven.

Away from Jake.

"Nice place," he murmured.

She tapped the keyboard so that the pictures disappeared—replaced with ledgers. The figures blurred before his eyes, and his head pounded. He had to lower his lids for a moment, had to draw in a deep breath.

A small hand gripped his forearm. "Jake? Are you okay?" Katie asked with concern. Her hand touched his face now. "Jake? What's going on? You don't look well."

He wasn't well. Seeing that house, knowing she was making her plans to leave…

And that it would be soon.

He felt sick. He wanted to tell her about the past and explain his reason for breaking his promises. But it wasn't fair now. He couldn't undo what he'd done. He couldn't make up to her the pain he'd caused, the pain she suffered now over losing her husband. And he certainly couldn't replace her husband.

"I'm just tired," he murmured.

"Then go in the house," she urged him. "Go to bed."

He wanted to but not alone. He wanted her with him, just lying in his arms, close to his heart. He wanted that so badly his body ached. A soft groan slipped through his lips.

"Jake, you need to take care of yourself instead of just everyone else," she said, her voice barely louder than a whisper. "You're so sweet and patient with Caleb and your nephews. And you're taking these accounting lessons your grandmother wants you to take, but it's too much. You need your rest."

That wasn't all he needed. He needed her. But she'd made her plans. So he wasn't going to beg.

Instead he forced himself to draw in a deep breath and shove himself up from the chair. "You're right. I need to go to sleep…" But he stopped himself from heading to the door. "Has Sadie hired Bob Lemmon yet?"

Her pretty mouth pulled down in a frown and she shook her head.

"I'll talk to her."

She stood up then and reached for his face again, sliding her fingertips along his jaw. "Go to sleep," she told him. "I'll deal with Sadie myself. I've worked out my own solution."

"She's not your problem," he said. And he uttered a ragged sigh. "She's mine…" Like Katie had once been, like he wished she could be again.

She rose up on tiptoe then and kissed him, just his cheek. Her lips brushed softly across his skin. He wanted to turn his head, wanted to properly kiss her. But he didn't want to push his luck.

Just because she was concerned about him

didn't mean that she could ever love him. And even if she could, she'd just pointed out to him how thinly he'd spread himself. What did he have left to offer her?

A WEEK HAD passed since Katie had first handed Sadie that résumé. And for a couple days after that, she'd printed out a new copy of it and brought it to her. There were a few of them now on the small desk in the corner of Sadie's master suite.

She'd barely glanced at the résumé. She didn't need to—she knew Lemmon's kid was a good egg. He wouldn't steal from them like Whitford had. She could trust him, and she should have already hired him. But maybe if Sadie took her time, the guy would find some other job.

And Katie would realize she was where she belonged—on Ranch Haven—with Jake. Her boy certainly belonged here. Sadie's heart ached at the thought of little Caleb leaving. He was one of Sadie's own now, just like Katie had always been since the shy little girl had first shown up at the ranch more than a dozen years ago.

She'd been so bright and happy then— so completely in love with Jake. She would have done anything for him. That had to be why Jake had given her up, because he hadn't wanted her to give up anything.

But him…

Was it too late for them now? Too late for him to take it back—for Katie to take him back?

Ever since that night Katie had handed her the first résumé, Sadie had been thinking about their conversation—about Katie's accusation that Sadie hadn't moved on from her loss either. That conversation had weighed as heavy on Sadie's mind as Big Jake's loss weighed yet on her heart.

Sitting in her favorite easy chair, with Feisty curled up on her lap, Sadie looked down at her hands. With all the veins and spots on them, they showed her age more than her face did. They also showed her hard work with the calluses and the swollen knuckles and crooked fingers. The only thing that still made them beautiful was the ring on her left hand. Big Jake had given her the diamond on their fiftieth anniversary to go with the simple gold band she'd worn since their wedding day—which had been the day after she'd turned eighteen. The oval diamond wasn't small, but it looked that way on Sadie's big hand. And it was dainty and sparkly and all the things she wasn't and had never been.

She'd laughed at him when he'd given it to her. But she'd loved it—just as much as she'd loved him. A week after their anniversary, he'd died of a heart attack, and maybe Sadie had died then, too, of a broken heart. She'd never taken off the ring, just as Katie still wore hers.

But twelve years had passed since Big Jake died; Katie's husband had only been gone a year. Maybe the girl wasn't ready yet to move on—just as Sadie hadn't been ready all these years either.

Twelve years…

It was a long time to be alone. Except for a date here and there, Jake had also spent the past twelve years alone. Sure, he'd had Dale and Jenny helping him with the ranch. But he'd never had anyone for him and him alone. Nobody to confide in the way Sadie had confided in Big Jake. Nobody to share all his hopes and dreams with…

Katie had once been that person for him, and Sadie had hoped that she could be again. But maybe too much time had passed. Maybe too many things had happened.

Maybe Sadie was only putting off the inevitable—just as she'd put off taking off her rings.

She'd intended to do it someday…when one of the boys found the girl he wanted to marry. She would have given them to Jenny—she'd been such a sweetheart. But Sadie's sweetheart had only been gone a few years when Dale had asked Jenny Miller to be his bride, and Sadie hadn't been ready. Hadn't really felt like Big Jake was even gone yet…

Then, before she'd had the chance to give them to her, Jenny was gone. Life was so unfair sometimes, but it also had its rewards—like all Sadie's boys. And the women that had moved into the house now. She wanted to keep them here, wanted them for her grandsons and great-grandsons, so all of her family would finally be happy again. But so far none of them were cooperating with her plans. Despite their assurances that they would be around more, Ben and Baker were still scarce.

And Dusty…

What was taking him so long to come home?

But Sadie wasn't willing to give up yet. She wasn't letting any of them go without a fight. And Sadie had yet to truly start fighting. So far all she'd been doing was stonewalling poor Katie.

She'd hoped to give her rings to Katie. But the young widow was still wearing her old ones. Yet she and Jake had been spending more time together—taking Caleb and the boys on more rides around the ranch and working together on the ranch books.

Still, she'd brought those résumés to Sadie, pleading with her to call the applicant. Sadie was going to have to let her go, because it was clear that once the little boy finished up the school year, Katie intended for them to leave. Sadie figured they would probably visit from time to time, but it wouldn't be the same as having them here in the house, sharing every meal, every sweet smile of that little boy's. As much as Sadie wished they would stay, Katie was determined to go.

Sadie moved her hands around Feisty's soft, warm body, getting ready to lift her, so that she could walk over to the desk and retrieve that résumé. Before she roused the sleeping dog, someone else did—with a knock at Sadie's door. Feisty jerked awake with a bark and scampered off Sadie's lap.

She sighed. It was probably Katie or maybe Taye, who'd taken to checking on her before she turned in for the night. Taye was a natural nurturer. "Come in," she called out.

The door opened, and Feisty started growling and tugging at Jake's jeans. With a grumble, he scooped up the ball of fluff. "When are you getting rid of this dangerous thing?"

Sadie snorted. "She only goes after you."

Feisty was after his face now, covering it with doggy kisses.

"You shouldn't complain," she advised him. "She's probably the only one you're getting kisses from."

Instead of grumbling or denying it, Jake flushed slightly. And Sadie wondered...

Had he made progress with Katie? They had been spending more time together over the past week. And Katie hadn't brought Sadie a copy of Bob Lemmon's résumé the last few days.

Hmm...

"I'm glad you're here," Sadie said. "I need your help with something."

Jake tensed, probably figuring—rightfully so—that she was up to something. He was just like his grandfather—the original Big Jake. He could see right through her. "You're admitting you need help?"

"Yes," she said. "See—it's not so hard. You should try it sometime."

His lips twitched, but if he'd been about to grin, he managed to suppress it. "What do you want?"

She shrugged. "You're the one who came to

see me, but while you're here, you can make yourself useful." She held out her left hand toward him. "Help me get these rings off."

"Why?" he asked. "Are they bothering you?"

No. It was going to bother her more to remove them than to leave them on. It was going to make her feel naked and vulnerable to not have her rings on anymore. But she'd been a hypocrite when she'd talked to Katie about moving on because she hadn't done it herself. The young woman had been right to point that out to her. And Sadie regretted not taking the rings off sooner, not giving them to Jenny.

She glanced at her hand—at the diamond that didn't look like it belonged. But the gold band was so old it had nearly become part of her skin. "Maybe just the diamond ring. Help me take that off."

"But Grandpa Jake got that for you right before…"

She nodded. "I know. But it's time to pass it on."

He pushed his hat back farther on his head and stared at her with narrowed eyes. "Who are you going to pass it on to? There are only boys in this family."

"Yeah, I'm going to give it to one of them to give to their bride."

"Ian or Miller seeing someone I don't know about?" he asked.

She chortled. "You think they're the only ones who'll get married in this family?"

"I don't think any of the rest of us are about to get hitched," he said. "But I know Ian's really sweet on his teacher. And I think Miller has developed a crush on Melanie, as well."

"Melanie's already taken…" she murmured. Should she save the ring for…?

"She is?" Jake asked.

"Why? Were you interested?"

"I barely know her," Jake said. "She just seems so…"

Lost and lonely. Sadie was going to have to get serious about that part of her plan. But first she had to deal with Jake—before he killed himself trying to do everything on his own. Now that he'd pushed back his hat, she could see the dark circles beneath his eyes. He was barely sleeping, barely eating, although Taye woke up early to fix him breakfast and pack him a lunch before he left for the barn.

She was such an incredible young woman.

"I don't know who should get this," she mused aloud. But she remembered thinking, when Big Jake had first given it to her, that it would've looked better on little Katie

O'Brien's hand than hers. That had been about the time Katie had graduated and headed off to the same college where Jake had already been going for a couple of years.

It should have been Katie's ring then, to replace that opal promise ring Jake had already given her.

"What do you mean—you don't know who?" Jake asked.

Sadie tugged on it, but it caught on her knuckle. No. It was just the gold band that stuck, unwilling to come off. She must have grabbed that by accident because she intended to keep it. Miraculously the diamond ring slipped over her knuckle, coming off without any help from Jake. But then even twelve years ago, her knuckles had been swollen from all her hard work, so the diamond band was bigger than the gold one. "I don't know who. Should I give it to Ben? If he wants to get reelected, he's probably going to have to get married. People have been making him out to be some kind of playboy."

"Because he is," Jake said with an exasperated-sounding chuckle. "Ben's not getting married. Not any more than Dusty will ever get married."

A smile tugged at her lips now, but she managed to suppress it. "Maybe Baker then…" she mused.

"Baker's a baby," he said.

She snorted. "Baker's twenty-eight. He's not a baby any longer." And it was past time that his big brothers realized that.

"He's still too young to get married."

"I was a decade younger than he is when I married your grandfather," Sadie reminded him.

Jake shrugged. "Those were different times."

"Dale and Jenny were just a little older than I was," she pointed out. "And there's no denying how happy they were."

Jake sighed shakily. "No, there isn't. They were incredibly happy."

"You would have been if you hadn't blown it with Katie all those years ago," she said.

"She wouldn't have been…" he murmured. "She would have had to give up too much."

Instead he'd made her give up him. And maybe that had been too much, although Sadie doubted Jake would ever see it that way. He couldn't see how much he had to offer someone beyond all the burdens he tried so hard to shoulder alone.

She ignored his comment as she twirled

the diamond ring around the tip of her finger. "Maybe Baker then…"

"Maybe Baker what?" Jake asked, as if he was having trouble following the conversation.

It was late, so perhaps he was too tired to focus. But he was staring at that diamond as she continued to twirl the ring.

"Maybe I should give this to Baker," she said.

"Why? He's not even seeing anyone," Jake said.

That smile tugged at her lips again, but she resisted. "I'm sure he'll find someone. After that firemen calendar, he has young women—" *and some older shameless ones* "—throwing themselves at him."

Jake quirked a brow. "And you want him to give one of those women the ring that Grandpa Jake picked out for you? The ring that you've worn every day since he's been gone?" He shuddered as if horrified at the thought.

She nearly shuddered herself. But she resisted that urge just as she resisted the urge to smile. She did want to make sure her ring went to someone she loved and respected. And she had loved Katie for years, since that first day Jake had brought her out to the ranch. Because the woman was a wonderful mother and strong widow, now Sadie respected her, as well.

"It's up to your brother who he chooses to give the ring to," she said. But not if she had her way...

Which Jake must have realized because he smirked. "Yeah, right."

"No, really," she insisted—hollowly. "I'm going to give this to Baker, and he can give it to whomever he pleases."

Jake tensed. "I'm the one named after Grandpa. I should have the ring."

She tilted her head. "Really? For what? I thought you were too busy to get involved with anyone."

He glared at her, but he also nabbed the ring off the end of her finger. "Maybe I'll take out the diamond and make an earring for myself."

She chuckled. "Yeah, right..."

He held it up to his lobe. "Wouldn't it look good?"

"I can pierce your ear if you'd like," she offered with a smile. "I think I have a knitting needle around here somewhere..."

Jake snorted. "Like you knit..."

Another chuckle slipped out. She'd never had the patience for fine work like that. She preferred riding and working with the animals to doing anything inside the house—though she had slowed down in recent years. She couldn't ride as long or as hard as she used to, or she would have stepped up to help out Jake more with the ranch work.

"I'm surprised you're not in bed already," she said. "What did you want?"

She suspected she knew—Katie. He just had to work up the nerve to ask her. At least now he had the ring to give her.

He stared at it now—maybe imagining it on Katie's finger. She hoped...

He sighed. "I don't know... Like you said, I should be in bed already." He turned around then and left her suite, left without even telling her what he'd wanted to see her about.

The résumé?

Had he wanted to find out if she'd called Bob Lemmon yet?

The fact that he hadn't asked meant that maybe he wasn't ready to give up on him and Katie yet.

Maybe he was going to use that ring as Sadie had intended...for the woman he'd always loved.

CHAPTER TWENTY-ONE

THE CONVERSATION JAKE had had with Sadie the night before kept running through his mind while he worked the ranch the next day. He'd known all along that she was up to something, but he hadn't had any idea exactly how determined she was to marry him off. He wasn't the only one, though, so he'd called his brothers.

Later that morning they found him in the barn, standing near the bronco's stall. Midnight reared up at their approach, kicking his front hooves against the stall door.

"Step away from there!" Baker warned. "That beast is going to hit you."

Jake shook his head. "No, Midnight and I have come to an understanding." Midnight tolerated his presence just as he'd begun to tolerate Caleb's—because the little boy brought him carrots every day.

Baker shook his head. "Yeah, Midnight understands that he's going to trample you the first chance he gets."

"He already had that chance, and he didn't take it," Jake said, thinking of how he'd flung himself over Caleb's body to avoid disaster just a few short weeks ago.

Sometimes it felt like Katie and her son had been at the ranch forever and sometimes like they'd just arrived. They would be leaving soon, though. Unless…

"You gave that horse the chance to trample you?" Ben asked with shock. "Are you that overwhelmed with everything? I thought Grandma was just trying to make us feel guilty about not helping out more with the ranch and the kids."

"No, you were right," Jake said. "Grandma really is just trying to manipulate you." Not that he couldn't use more help around the ranch, but as much as he loved Ben and Baker, neither of them was Dale. Not even Dusty was Dale…although they looked exactly alike. "But I don't think her intention is helping me out."

"What do you mean?" Ben asked, his dark eyes narrowed with suspicion.

Jake pulled the ring from his pocket and flashed the diamond at his brothers.

Ben grinned. "You're finally going to propose to Katie?"

"About time," Baker added.

Jake shook his head. "No..." It wasn't about time. It was too soon. She was still wearing her late husband's ring. She had no room for Jake's ring on her hand and no room for Jake in her heart. She'd sent that opal ring back to him—twelve years ago—after he'd broken up with her. He had that stashed in the back of a dresser drawer, but he never looked at it. It just reminded him of how he'd upset her.

"Grandma took off her ring to give to one of you," Jake warned them. "I think she kind of had her heart set on Baker getting it."

"Baker?" Ben snorted. "He's the baby."

"That's what I said," Jake added.

Baker glared at both of them. "You make me sound like Little Jake."

Jake just wished Little Jake sounded like Little Jake—like the happy, babbling baby he'd once been. Since Caleb and Katie had moved in, the toddler did laugh again. Ian laughed again. Sometimes even Miller laughed despite his growing frustration with his cast.

That would be off soon, though—just not soon enough for the seven-year-old.

"And what would she be giving it to me for anyway?" Baker asked. "I'm not even dating anyone."

"I think you would be if you were falling in

with her plans," Jake said. Which woman had she intended for Baker? Emily or Taye?

Ben laughed now.

"She mentioned you too," Jake warned the mayor. "That you're not likely to get reelected if you don't have a wife soon."

Ben laughed again, but it sounded hollow now. Maybe there was some merit to what Grandma had said then. The politician shrugged. "Then I guess I won't stay in Willow Creek if the voters can't see that someone's marital status has nothing to do with their ability to do their job."

"So you'd leave?" Jake asked.

Ben shrugged again. "If I don't get reelected, maybe."

Jake's stomach sank at the thought. Even though Ben didn't come by the ranch as often as Grandma liked, he wasn't that far away in town. Not that Jake ever got to town very much...

Baker was staring at Jake. "Grandma was right."

"What? You are seeing someone?" Ben asked.

Instead of handing over the ring, Jake found himself clasping it in his fist and shoving it inside his jean's pocket. "You are?"

Baker laughed. "No. Not about that, and I really doubt that she intended to give that ring to anyone but you. She was just jerking your chain."

Heat rushed to Jake's face. Had he fallen for her manipulation that easily? He didn't regret it, though, because if he'd called her bluff, she might have given it to one of his brothers instead. And he couldn't imagine anyone else having Grandpa Jake's ring. Except...

"I agree with that," Ben said. "It's not like she seriously was going to give it to me or Baker. She must not have mentioned Dusty or you would have known she was playing. There's no way he's ever getting married."

Jake chuckled. "Sometimes I'm not sure which of you is the pot and which is the kettle..." They were the two heartbreakers in his family. But knowing he'd probably never get that answer, since neither was likely to get married, he turned back to his youngest brother. Maybe Grandma had been right; maybe the baby would be the quickest of them to settle down.

Unless...

But he couldn't even bring himself to think it. Would Katie consider giving him a second chance? Would she consider staying on the ranch? No. She already had that house in town picked out for her and Caleb.

He shook off the thought and focused on Baker. "So what do you think Grandma was right about?"

"You."

"Yeah, Jake's the one who should have that ring," Ben agreed. "He's the one with someone to give it to—the person who should have had it twelve years ago."

Jake flinched at the thought of how different his life would have been if he had not forced himself to make the sacrifices he had. But that was the past. And he couldn't undo it.

And if he could, there would be no Caleb, and right now he couldn't imagine his life without the little boy. How could Jake just let him and his mother leave?

"Yeah, yeah, we all know that." Baker agreed with Ben now. "But I mean Grandma was right about Jake being overworked. About us not doing enough…" He turned back to Jake. "You look exhausted, man. What can we do to help out more? What do you need?"

"Dale." The name just slipped out, his heart hollow and aching over the loss he usually tried to avoid thinking about…just as he'd tried to avoid thinking about Katie the past twelve years.

Ben released a shaky breath, and tears glistened in Baker's eyes before he blinked them away. "Don't we all…" Ben murmured.

"The kids most of all," Baker said, and he closed his eyes now, probably to hide those tears or hold them back. "I… I hate that…" His voice cracked and he shook his head. "It just sucks."

Jake nodded. "It does." He hadn't realized until now how hard it must have been on his baby brother to be first on the scene of that accident.

He'd been thinking about Dale and Jenny and the boys. He hadn't thought, until now, of how that must have affected Baker. But he was handling it, just as he'd handled his years in the service. Grandma was right. Baker wasn't a baby. He was a man, a hero.

"We'll be around more," Ben said.

Jake cocked his head. "Seems like I've heard that once or twice already. Is that like one of your political promises? One you make to get the votes but don't ever intend to really carry out?"

Ben glared at him. "No. I will. I'll have Mayor Lemmon—Deputy Mayor Lemmon—step in and handle more. I'll spend more time with the boys."

"And I'll help you with the ranch," Baker said. "I'll try to step in to fill the void that Dale…"

Nobody was going to fill that void, and they all knew it. But Katie had found a suitable candidate to take over the books. Maybe if Jake looked, he could find a suitable candidate to take over as ranch foreman.

They wouldn't be Dale, but they'd help him out enough that he might actually have more time for a personal life.

Burying his pride, for maybe the first time ever, Jake said, "I could really use the help around here."

"Done," Ben said. "Really. I'll make sure I'm here every day."

"I can't promise every day," Baker said. "Not with my shifts at the firehouse, but I'll be here as often as I can."

Jake nodded. "Thanks, guys."

His brothers had turned away from him to the entrance of the barn and the woman who'd walked into it. Jake's pulse quickened at just the sight of her. Katie's hair glowed even in the dim light of the barn, as if the sunlight outside had gotten trapped in the auburn tresses. And her eyes glowed, as well, that beautiful green…even from a distance.

Even if Katie didn't stay, at least she'd been here. At least Jake had gotten to know Caleb…

But there was something else he needed to do before they left. Something Katie deserved to know.

Would it make a difference, though?

Would it make her stay?

KATIE COULD ONLY see shadows at first. Three tall shadows standing in the barn at the stall of the bronco Caleb was so fascinated with. So much so that he'd had to run back to the house to get the carrots he'd forgotten for the horse.

Even without being able to see their faces, Katie knew which shadow was Jake's. He was just a little taller. A little broader…and a little more…

Everything.

He was everything.

Despite not seeing them clearly, she felt that they were all staring at her. And she suddenly felt self-conscious, like the new kid in class who everyone turns and stares at when they walk in.

Caleb must have felt like that when they'd first moved back to Willow Creek. But he'd managed at five. So she forced herself to start moving forward again to where they stood, even though she didn't have the fascination for the bronco that her son and Jake had.

No. Her fascination was with Jake.

"Hey, Katie," Ben said. "You finally going to give me the chance to take you out?"

"I'll take *you* out," Jake warned his brother.

As unrepentant as ever, Ben, the flirt, chuckled. "On that note, I think I'll take myself out—to the house to check in with the boys."

"Miller and Melanie are in the playroom doing some physical therapy," she said. "Emily is finishing up an extra lesson with Ian, and Little Jake is in the kitchen with Taye." For all her talk of Emily being the kid whisperer, the cook also had a special knack with the boys.

"Did she bake?" Ben asked, hopefully.

Katie chuckled. "When doesn't she bake…?" But Jake's brothers wouldn't know how Taye Cooper was spoiling all of them with her special treats since they didn't come around very often—as Emily often lamented.

"I'll go to the house with you," Baker said, but the reluctance was clear in his deep voice and in the slowness with which he followed his brother out of the barn.

"Emily's right," Katie remarked. "They really don't want to help out."

"It's not easy for them," Jake said, coming to the defense of his brothers as he often had when they were growing up. She remembered the times he'd stopped Ben from getting beat up from—usually—some girl's jealous boyfriend. And the times he'd defended the twins when they were pulling some prank.

"It's not easy for *you*," she said. "You're handling everything on your own."

He shook his head. "No. I have Grandma." He sighed. "As manipulative as she can be, at least she's hired the right people to help out around here."

"She hired people to help with the boys," she said. "You need help on the ranch." And instead of helping him, his brothers had gone into the house.

"She hired you to help me on the ranch," Jake reminded her.

She doubted that had been Sadie's true intention, but she wasn't eager to point that out either. "I can't help you with the livestock."

"You're getting better at riding," he told her.

She was actually enjoying it more too. But it wasn't because she was any more comfortable on horseback than she'd ever been. It was because she loved seeing the ranch with Caleb and Jake.

Through Caleb's excitement and Jake's love of it, she was beginning to fall for it too. But that wasn't all she was falling for…

And she couldn't…

Even if she could trust Jake with her heart again, she couldn't betray Matt that way. But she struggled to remember that, especially now with Jake looking so pensive from his brothers' visit.

"Is it just you and me for this ride?" Jake asked.

Heat rushed to her face, and she shook her head. "Caleb forgot his carrots."

"Midnight's carrots…" Jake chuckled, but it sounded hollow.

"Are you all right?" she asked. She knew how much he missed Dale. Maybe being with his other brothers reminded him more of the absence of the brother with whom he'd been the closest.

He nodded. "Yeah…" But he sounded lost to her, lonely, as she so often felt lonely now.

Except when she was with Caleb.

Or with Jake.

She found herself reaching out for him, offering him a quick hug. But when her arms slid around his waist and he leaned his head toward hers, she kissed him. Instead of kissing just his cheek like she had last night, her lips brushed across his. Then again and again. She couldn't stop kissing him, didn't want to stop kissing him.

"I got the carrots!"

She jerked out of Jake's arms and whirled toward her son. He stood just a few feet from them, a bunch of carrots held aloft in his hand. But his blue eyes, so like his father's, were wide. With shock? Or horror?

She glanced at Jake, whose chest moved as if he was breathing hard. She was, too, from their kisses, but now she was struggling to breathe for another reason—panic.

"Caleb," she said, and she closed the few feet between them to crouch down in front of her son. "Are you okay?"

"Yeah…" he said, as if he had no idea why she was asking.

"But…what you just saw…"

"You and Mr. Big Jake kissing," he said matter-of-factly.

As if it was a matter of fact. As if it was no big deal.

But he'd acted that way about moving to Willow Creek, about starting a new school. And she knew now he hadn't been completely honest about how hard that had been for him. How hard was this? To see his mother kissing another man?

She needed to know. She turned back toward Jake, but she couldn't look at him—not with her face flushing with embarrassment and guilt. She was the one who'd kissed him. This was her mess to clean up. "Can you give us a little bit of privacy?"

Which was something she should have made sure they'd had before she'd kissed him. Not that she wanted to be alone with Jake. Not that she'd intended to kiss him…

But once she'd hugged him, it had seemed natural. Inevitable even…

And irresistible.

"Of course," Jake said. "I'll be waiting outside by the corral fence. I already have the horses saddled."

"I have carrots for Midnight," Caleb said.

Jake nodded. "You can give them to him."

Usually Jake supervised all her son's interactions with the bronco, but obviously he wanted to give them the privacy she'd requested.

Caleb only wanted to give the horse the carrots.

Midnight must have seen what was in the boy's hand because he arched his neck over the stall door and reached out for them.

Panic fluttered in Katie's heart when her baby held out the carrots and the horse took them, his big teeth so close to Caleb's little fingers.

The boy giggled. "He really likes carrots, Mommy."

"Yes, he does," she agreed.

He clapped his hands together after Midnight chomped up the last of the bunch. Then he whirled around and headed toward the open doors of the barn. "Let's go!"

"Wait," she said, and she caught his shoulder in her hand to stop him.

"Jake's waiting for us," he said.

"I want to talk to you," she said. "About what you just saw…"

"You kissing Mr. Big Jake?" he asked. "You must really like him—like Midnight likes carrots and I like cookies."

She wanted to deny it. She didn't like Jake. Not like that. Not that much.

But she also didn't want to confuse her son any more than she probably already had. "How do you feel about that?" she asked him instead.

"I like Mr. Big Jake too," he said.

She knew that.

"But what about your daddy?" Didn't he feel—like she did—like she was betraying Matt? Betraying his memory?

"Daddy would've liked Mr. Big Jake too," he said.

She wasn't so sure about that. Even though the men had never met, Matt had been furious with Jake—over how he'd treated Katie, over how he'd broken her heart.

But had Jake done that for her? Had he been making sacrifices for her happiness, like Sadie had suggested? Because he hadn't wanted Katie to give up college and her dreams of traveling?

Katie wanted to know, yet she was afraid to

ask Jake, afraid that then she might not have any excuses left not to fall for him again. But even if she was falling for him again, that didn't mean he was falling for her.

Or that he wouldn't sacrifice his happiness all over again because of all his responsibilities at the ranch and with his nephews.

She couldn't risk her heart on Jake. Not again…

It had already been broken too many times.

CHAPTER TWENTY-TWO

JAKE HAD MADE two trips to town over the last week. The first had been the afternoon that Caleb had caught him and Katie kissing.

The second trip had been a few days later to pick up what he'd dropped off that day. That had been two days ago...and every day he waited, expecting Katie to tell him that she was leaving.

He knew that she'd hired Bob Lemmon herself. Jake had seen him working at her little office on Main Street because the jeweler he'd had resize and redesign Grandma's ring was next door to her space. What did that mean?

That Katie was going to let him handle her clients in town while she dealt with the ranch? Or did she intend for him to eventually take over the ranch books? And what about that house she'd had pictures of on her computer? Had she already purchased or rented it?

She hadn't said anything to Jake about it, and he'd been too afraid to ask, not wanting confirmation that she'd planned out her new life. A life that had no place in it for him.

From how happy Caleb had been, she must not have brought anything up with her son either.

Jake doubted Caleb would be happy about leaving. And he was happy, especially since school had officially ended for him on Monday. He'd had more time for riding lessons the last few days since then.

And Jake had had a little more time to give him since Ben and Baker had kept their promises. They were around the ranch more, helping him and helping out with the kids too. He didn't know how long they could manage it, though, when they both had full-time jobs in town.

Their help made Jake realize how much of it he needed. Dale wasn't coming back, and while he could never be replaced, someone could shoulder some of Jake's load. He'd placed an ad for a ranch foreman. But that wasn't the only position he wanted to fill.

He'd had that ring resized and redesigned especially for Katie, and it was burning a hole in his pocket now. When he'd gone to town to pick it up, he could have stopped at the blue Victorian house just down from the jeweler's on Main Street. He could have knocked on the bright purple door and asked Katie's father's permission for what he was about to do. But her dad wasn't the most important male in Katie's life now.

Caleb was.

So Jake had taken advantage of their extra time together and invited him out for a riding lesson that didn't include his nephews or the little boy's mother. Because he wanted to talk about her.

Caleb, as usual, did not come into the barn empty-handed. He held a bunch of carrots for Midnight in one hand and some smushed cookies in his other hand.

"Don't get those mixed up," Jake advised him with a chuckle. "Midnight might like cookies, but I'm not sure how much you like carrots."

Caleb's little nose wrinkled with distaste. "Mommy says they're good for me. That they'll help me see better. But I don't eat them unless I'm trying to lose a tooth." He smiled then, showing a couple of gaps in his mouth.

Jake chuckled again, his heart warm with all his affection for this funny and sweet little kid.

"And the cookies are for you," Caleb told him as he held out the handful of dough and chips.

Jake shook his head. His stomach churned with nerves, and he doubted he could hold down cookies right now. Or anything else...

"I washed my hands," Caleb promised.

Jake held out his hands and let the little boy dump the gooey cookie mess into them. Then he watched as the kid's attention turned to the bronco, who greedily but gently took the bunch of carrots from him.

As usual Caleb giggled over his brush with the horse's big mouth. "He must have the bestest eyesight ever."

Jake smiled. "He probably does now, thanks to you." That wasn't the only thing for which Jake could thank the little boy. He could thank him for brightening the darkness of the days since Dale and Jenny's loss—for his nephews and for himself. And yet Caleb wasn't the only one responsible for making Jake's loss a little more bearable.

Having Katie here again...

Being near her...

It had reminded him of how much he'd once loved her. How much he still loved her. Watching her with her son and the other boys, he'd fallen for her even harder.

He wasn't certain of her feelings, but he was hopeful—since she'd been the one who'd kissed him the last couple of times. But before he talked to Katie, he wanted to talk to Caleb. To make sure that her little boy would be fine with another man in his mother's life.

As if Caleb had read his mind, he glanced around the barn. "Where's Mommy?"

"I didn't tell her about this lesson," Jake admitted. "I wanted to talk to you alone—just man-to-man."

Caleb grinned. "I'm a man?"

"You're the man of your house now that your daddy's gone," Jake pointed out.

"But me and Mommy don't have a house anymore," Caleb said. "We live here—in yours and Miss Sadie's house."

And Jake wanted more than anything for them to stay here—with him. "Do you like that?" Jake asked.

Caleb nodded. "I love living here."

"That's good," Jake said. "You love the ranch?"

The little boy nodded again—vigorously—and that lock of blond hair fell into his eyes. "I love all the animals. And Feisty."

Jake chuckled that the little dog got her own category, but she deserved it. She was more family than any of the other animals.

"What about the people?" Jake asked.

Caleb giggled. "I love Ian and Miss Trent and Miss Sadie and Miss Cooper and Miss Melanie and Miller and Little Jake…"

"What about me?" Jake asked, and he held his breath, waiting for the answer to the question that mattered most to him. He had to have Caleb's answer before he could ask Katie the next-most-important question. Because if Caleb didn't love him, then there was no hope that his mother would.

Caleb flashed him a big smile. "I love you most of all, Mr. Big Jake."

Humbled and overwhelmed, Jake swept the little boy up into his arms. "And I love you," Jake told him.

"And Mommy?" Caleb asked. "Do you love Mommy?"

Jake nodded.

"I figured that with all the kissing…"

Was he talking about just that time he'd caught them in the barn, or had he spied them another time? There hadn't been enough kissing for Jake. He wanted more. He wanted Katie.

"Would it be okay with you if I asked her to marry me?" Jake asked.

The little boy eagerly nodded. "Yeah, yeah.

Then we can be a real family! Me and Mommy can stay on the ranch—"

"Whoa!" Jake said. "You have to slow down. It's up to your mommy—not us. And she might not be ready." Now or ever. Maybe Jake shouldn't have talked to Caleb first... Maybe he shouldn't have gotten the little boy's hopes up, like he was getting his own hopes up for the future.

"Mommy likes it here too," Caleb said.

"She does?" Jake asked skeptically. She did seem to enjoy their rides more than she had twelve years ago. But he wasn't entirely convinced.

"She hasn't made us leave yet," Caleb pointed out. "Like she said we would when school was over."

That was what had compelled Jake to get Grandma's ring resized for her in the same size as the opal ring he'd bought her so long ago. The size wasn't all he'd taken from that ring.

"She hasta say yes," Caleb continued. "Then we can stay here on the ranch forever. I can work on it with you and..." He trailed off and wriggled down from Jake's arms.

Jake let him go but he crouched down in front of the suddenly quiet and shy boy. "What?" Jake asked. "What is it, Caleb?"

The little boy peered at him through that lock of blond hair. "Will I call you Daddy?"

Jake felt a pang in his chest as sharp as if Midnight had kicked him. But it wasn't his gasp that broke the silence in the barn.

It was Katie's. "No! No, Caleb!" she shouted.

No.

No. No...

And at that word from her mouth, his heart felt like it had been kicked again—even harder.

KATIE'S SHOUT ECHOED in the barn. She'd shouted so loud that she'd scared the horse. The bronco reared up and kicked his stall door. But the little boy and the man standing in front of it didn't even move. It was as if they were frozen.

Katie couldn't look at Jake. She was too embarrassed that her son had asked him such a question. And she was too upset that he had.

Panic pressed heavily on her chest. She'd screwed up so badly. She'd let Caleb get too attached to Jake. She'd let him use the man as a replacement for his father. Her stomach churned with guilt over the betrayal.

She'd betrayed Matt on so many levels. But this was probably the worst. And it was all her fault.

She'd started dragging her feet about leaving—even though she had everything in place. She'd hired Bob Lemmon. She'd even signed a lease to rent the man's house in town—a house where Caleb wouldn't have to be quiet or careful. Even though the house had a big backyard, it couldn't compare to the ranch.

And so she'd hesitated…over the upset she knew she'd cause her son again. But it would have been better if she'd stopped this sooner, if she'd cut the tie that had formed between her son and Jake.

"No," she said, and while she forced her voice to be quieter, it was still sharp with the panic gripping her over how attached her son had gotten to her old boyfriend. "You cannot call Jake Daddy. He is not your daddy."

Tears stung her eyes, but she blinked them away. She needed to focus—focus on what was right for all of them. That had never been Jake for her.

"But you can marry him," Caleb said. "And we can stay here. We can be a family."

She sucked in a breath of shock at Caleb's suggestion. She dared not look at Jake—ever again. How had she not seen that her little boy was getting his hopes up this much about staying here? About being part of a family again?

She shook her head. "No. We can't, Caleb.

I already found a house for us in town. I was going to tell you that today." She'd intended to tell him every day over the past week, but she'd never quite brought herself to break the news to him.

He'd been so happy—celebrating no more school with Miller. Ian would still have some more lessons, still need some help to finish up the school year so he could go on to first grade.

And Caleb had increased his riding lessons with Jake. She hadn't known about this one; she'd just noticed her son heading toward the barn. She'd been on a call at the time with Bob Lemmon, but once they'd wrapped up she'd come out to check on him.

Too late…

She'd been too late with so many things.

"I don't want to go back to town!" Caleb said. And he was the one shouting now. "I don't want to leave!"

He never raised his voice like this—never in anger. And he sounded so angry now. But better he be angry than heartbroken.

"This isn't your decision to make," Katie said, and she focused solely on him, too embarrassed to look at Jake. "You're the child and I'm the parent. I make the decisions about where we live."

Tears trailed down Caleb's face. "But Mommy—"

"You need to go into the house and pack," she said. "We're leaving today. Now."

Caleb shook his head. "No! I don't wanna! I don't wanna…"

"Caleb!" Her heart was breaking now over how upset he was. That was why she'd hesitated, why she hadn't told him, but she should have known it was going to hurt him no matter when they left. "We have to go!"

"But we don't," he insisted. "We can stay here. We can stay forever! Mr. Big Jake just—"

"You need to listen to your mother," Jake cut in. "She's the boss, Caleb."

She didn't feel like the boss of anything right now. How had her life gotten so out of control?

Jake.

She'd always lost herself around Jake.

"We need to leave, Caleb," she insisted. Before she got as attached as he was. Before her heart got broken again.

But she suspected it was already too late for that. That she'd already lost her heart again— as well as her head. "You go inside and start packing and I'll be inside to help you in just a little while."

For the first time ever, her little boy gave

her a look that chilled Katie. He looked at her
like he hated her. She couldn't blame him—
at the moment she hated herself. Then he ran
out of the barn.

She waited a moment and drew in a deep
breath before she headed out after him.

"Katie," Jake called to her. "Wait…"

She shook her head. "No…"

"We need to talk."

She shook her head again. "I can't…"

She couldn't speak through the guilt choking
her. Matt's son had asked to call Jake Haven
Daddy.

And that wasn't the little boy's fault. That
was hers. She'd brought him here. She'd agreed
to the riding lessons. Then she'd started riding
with them—making it seem like they were the
family that Caleb obviously missed so much.

But they weren't a family. They wouldn't
even be here if Matt hadn't died. She would
have never left the man who'd made her and
her son so happy, who'd made them laugh
every time they'd been together, and that had
been most of the time.

Despite Matt's love and devotion, though,
a piece of her heart had always stayed with
Jake. She'd thought that was the ultimate betrayal until now.

Overcome with emotion, with guilt, Katie ran out of the barn like her son had. But she couldn't go to the house yet. She couldn't let anyone—especially Caleb—see her this upset. So she ran into the office. And once she closed the door, she sank to the floor and sobbed.

CHAPTER TWENTY-THREE

WHAT HAD HE been thinking?

He'd made such a mess of everything. This was what he got for being selfish—for thinking he could have it all. The ranch and Katie and Caleb.

How much of his conversation with her son had she overheard? All of it? Or just the little boy asking if he could call Jake Daddy?

He felt a twinge of guilt over that. He didn't want to replace Matt Morris—not with his son. Not even with his widow. He just wanted them to love Jake and let Jake love them.

He just wanted to make them happy, like Matt had made them happy. Jake had already failed miserably—making them all miserable. He could have been a coward and stayed out in the barn until they were gone. But he had to do what he could to fix it.

To apologize fully and explain.

His explanation to Katie was long overdue anyway. Twelve years overdue. He suspected she'd stopped in the office, that she'd needed a moment to compose herself before she talked to her son again. When he pushed open the door, it bumped into her—where she sat on the floor, her head in her hands.

Her sobs—her pain—reached inside him, wrenching his heart around his chest. "Oh, Katie…" he murmured. And he dropped to the floor next to her, wrapping his arms around her. "I'm so sorry…"

Her body tensed, and her sobs hushed. But she didn't pull away from him. Instead she buried her damp face against his shoulder. "I knew it was a mistake coming here, letting him get attached."

"It's not your fault," he assured her. "And it's not Caleb's."

She shook her head. "I shouldn't have brought him here. I was just setting him up for more heartache."

Jake's heart was breaking now, breaking with her pain and the little boy's. "I'm so sorry," he said again. "So sorry you're hurting."

"I'll be fine," she said. "If he ever forgives me for making him leave…"

"I won't be fine," Jake admitted. "If you leave…"

She pulled her head up from his shoulder then and stared at him through eyes damp and swollen from her tears. Her face was blotchy from crying too. But she was still so beautiful to him.

So beautiful that his heart ached with longing. With love...

"What are you saying?" she asked him.

"That I made a mistake. I asked him for his permission to marry you."

"What?" she asked with obvious shock.

"But that wasn't my first mistake," he continued. "My first mistake was letting you go twelve years ago."

"You didn't let me go," she said. "You pushed me away. You dumped me."

"That was my biggest mistake." Maybe until now. The last thing he'd ever wanted to do was cause a problem between her and her child. They had such a close and loving relationship, and he would never forgive himself if he ruined that for them.

"Why?" she asked.

"Because you were everything to me," he admitted.

"Then why did you dump me?" she asked.

"Because I didn't want you to make the sacrifices I had to make—"

"You didn't have to make those sacrifices either," she said. "Your grandmother told you to stay in college."

He shook his head. "I couldn't risk losing her like I lost Grandpa. Maybe if I hadn't gone away to college he'd still be alive…"

She gasped. "Oh, Jake, you've been carrying around guilt all these years too."

"More than you know," he said. More than he'd ever really admitted to himself. His heart felt a little lighter for sharing that now. But he still hadn't given the explanation she deserved. "I didn't want to hurt you, but I didn't want you giving up your education and all your dreams. Or winding up like my dad or my grandpa…" He shook his head. "God, what was I thinking? I shouldn't ask you now to take those risks, to make those sacrifices."

"Jake, it wasn't your fault anybody died," she assured him. "It wasn't your fault. You've done more than you needed to. Made more sacrifices than you needed to…"

He realized that now. Realized how much he'd given up when he'd given up her. She was still everything to him. But it wasn't just her alone anymore; it was her son too. They'd both stolen his heart. And when they left the ranch—*if* they left the ranch—they'd be taking it with them.

Jake hadn't fought for her twelve years ago, but he wanted to fight for her now. Then he'd thought he was doing the right thing by letting her go. And maybe he had because she'd realized the dreams she'd had—with Matt. But Matt was gone now.

Had he left any room in her heart for another man? For Jake? He wouldn't know unless he asked. Since he was already on his knees beside her, he reached into his pocket for the ring he'd been carrying with him. He held it out toward her. "Will you marry me, Katie?"

And he held his breath until his lungs ached with it, waiting for her answer.

Was it going to be what she'd shouted in the barn?

Was it going to be a resounding no?

KATIE HAD NEVER been so confused. She stared at the ring that looked so small in Jake's big hand. There were two stones in the band; one a big diamond, the other a familiar-looking opal. Then she glanced up at his face—his handsome, earnest face—and her head pounded with confusion.

Was this real?

Was this happening?

"I... I don't understand," she said again.

"You're still everything to me, Katie," he said, "and that's why I added the opal to Grandma's diamond ring. I wanted to keep that promise I made you so long ago. I want to be your husband. I want to be a father to Caleb. I know that I can never replace Matt, but I would like to be there for your son—for you..."

"Why?" she asked. Did he feel sorry for her? For the widow? For her fatherless son?

"Because I love you," he said. "I've always loved you."

"Then why did you break my heart?" she asked because now she remembered that pain, how broken she'd been until Matt had helped her heal. "Matt wouldn't have done that. He wouldn't have hurt me for any reason." She had to remind herself of that, remind herself of the man who'd only ever treated her with love and respect.

Jake released a shaky sigh, as if he'd been holding his breath for a long time. "I know. I knew that twelve years ago when I went back for you, to beg you to take me back, and I saw the two of you beside the fountain. He was making you laugh in a way I never could. In a way I wouldn't be able to with all the responsibilities I'd inherited when Grandpa died."

"You saw me with Matt?" she asked, her confusion growing.

He nodded, and a muscle twitched in his cheek, as if he was clenching his jaw. He uttered another sigh and admitted, "When I saw you two, I figured that I'd done the right thing then. You'd already sent back the ring, so I realized you'd moved on. I knew that you would be happier with someone else."

She sucked in a breath, shocked over his assumption that she'd been so fickle. "You broke my heart, Jake. You said such terrible things to me."

"I didn't mean any of them," he said. "But I knew you wouldn't let me go otherwise."

Heat rushed into her face that she had been so in love with him that she would have willingly made all those sacrifices. But now she realized that Jake had loved her. He'd loved her enough to let her go.

Tears pooled in her eyes again, momentarily blurring her vision of him. She blinked them back and focused on his face. "You did that for me?" she asked.

He nodded. "I should do it now too. I have more responsibilities and less time and attention to give you and Caleb. But I'm going to hire a new foreman—maybe some additional hands. I'm going to make the time. Will you make the room, Katie? Will you let me into your heart again?" He glanced down at her hand, where she still wore her rings from Matt.

To accept Jake's ring, she would have to take them off. She probably would have already, if she hadn't felt as much guilt as she had pain over his loss. That guilt overwhelmed her now. Matt Morris had been such a good man.

He'd deserved so much more. And maybe if Jake hadn't walked away that day when he'd seen them, maybe Matt would have found the love he'd deserved with someone else. But her heart ached with loss at the thought, because then she wouldn't have Caleb, who was the very best of Matt.

She opened her mouth, not to give him an answer yet but to try to explain, when the door burst open behind them. Ian stood on the old schoolhouse porch. "Miss Katie, Miss Katie! You have to come now!"

"What's happened?" At the urgency in the little boy's voice, she jumped up from the floor.

Jake did too. "What's going on, Ian?" he asked.

And the little boy looked confused.

"Uncle Jake!" Miller yelled. He stood below the porch, leaning heavily on his crutches while Little Jake leaned against his big brother's cast. "Caleb's trying to run away. He said he's going to take Midnight and hide out somewhere on the ranch!"

"Oh, no!" Katie cried.

Jake uttered something that might have been a curse beneath his breath before he rushed past Ian and down the steps.

She hurried out the door too. But when she moved to pass Miller, he swayed and would have fallen. She caught him and held him against her for a moment. "Thank you! Thank you for coming to get me."

Jake was moving fast. He'd already reached the barn. She could only hope he got there in time to rescue Caleb like he had before, like he had when the bronco had nearly trampled the little boy the first time.

But when she and Jake's nephews approached the barn, she heard the big cowboy calling out, his voice gruff with emotion. "Caleb? Caleb, are you all right?"

She stepped inside the barn, but she couldn't see anything until her eyes adjusted to the dim light and shadows. Then she noticed Jake on his knees, like he'd been moments ago before her, but he leaned over her little boy in the open door to the bronco's stall. Her heart slammed against her ribs with shock, with fear and dread…

He hadn't gotten there in time. He hadn't stopped Caleb from getting hurt. She rushed forward and dropped to her knees beside Jake.

Caleb lay so still, his eyes closed. There were bits of hay on his clothes, but she could see no bruises. No cuts.

"What's the matter? Is he all right?" she asked breathlessly. "Is he breathing?"

Jake reached out, his big hand shaking, to touch the little boy's neck. "His pulse is strong. But he won't open his eyes."

"Make him open his eyes!" Ian shouted. "Make my friend come back!" The panic in his voice echoed the panic gripping Katie.

Chubby little fingers caught Katie's hair as Little Jake pushed closer, leaning over her shoulder to stare down at Caleb. "Cab!" he called out. "Cab!"

It was first word she'd heard the toddler speak.

Miller's breath escaped in a gasp. "That must be how he thinks you say Caleb."

"Cab!" Little Jake repeated.

"Wake up!" Ian yelled.

"Yeah," Miller said, and tears streamed down his face. "Wake up!"

Caleb's blue eyes opened, and he stared up at all of them. "What happened? Where am I?"

"You don't remember?" Katie asked. "Did you get hit in the head?" He started to move, but she touched his shoulder, holding him down. "You might have internal injuries." He could be bleeding inside in his body or his skull. The horror of that gripped her, made her shake with fear.

"Does anything hurt?" Jake asked, his deep voice gruff with concern. "Your head or anything else?"

"No, Daddy," Caleb said. "I'm fine."

Katie gasped. How confused was he? "Oh, no! No..." And the tears she'd been holding back rushed over her, streaming down her face.

"Mommy!" Caleb exclaimed, and he pushed against her hand, pushed up and threw his arms around her neck. "I'm sorry. Don't cry! Please, don't cry! I was faking. I didn't hit my head. I didn't even fall. I just wanted you to..." His voice cracked now with his own tears. "I wanted you to think we were a family. You, me and Jake. I wanted you to be happy—like you used to be..."

"Caleb…" Tears choked her so much that all she could say was his name.

"Please, Mommy, don't cry. Daddy hated when you cried. He wanted you to be happy. That was all he wanted."

She gasped and nearly choked on her tears because she knew he was right. Her little boy was wise far beyond his years.

"Daddy would be happy if you married Jake," Caleb continued. "He would be happy because you'll be happy. He said that was all he ever wanted for us—to be happy."

She'd heard Matt say it herself so many times, but she hadn't listened as intently as their son had. She hadn't understood that Matt was that kind of person. He was never jealous or negative—all he'd ever wanted for those he'd cared about was happiness.

He wouldn't care if she found that with Jake. Matt would have understood more than anyone why Jake had broken up with her—because he hadn't wanted her to make the sacrifices he'd had to make when his grandfather had died. He'd wanted her to live out all those crazy teenage dreams she'd shared with him.

"You're right," she told Caleb. And she hugged him closely and kissed his little head before she lifted him up from the ground and stood up herself. "Now go back to the house and unpack your bags."

His gaze slipped away from hers and she laughed as she realized, "You didn't pack."

He shook his head. "I don't want to leave."

"Neither do I," she admitted. "Now give me a minute alone with Mr. Big Jake."

"So you can say yes?" Caleb asked hopefully.

"Yes to what?" Ian asked.

"Yes to Mr. Big Jake being my new daddy," Caleb replied.

She opened her mouth to protest but then she remembered what Caleb had just told her. Matt wanted them to be happy—both of them.

Jake was the one to protest, "I don't think you should call me—"

Katie gripped his arm to stop him. "If it makes Caleb happy to call you that, it would have made Matt happy too," she assured him.

Jake blinked as if he was fighting back tears of his own. Before he could compose himself, Caleb hugged him, and one of those tears won and trailed down his cheek. He dashed it away with one hand while he clutched Caleb against him with his other. "Don't pretend like that again," he told him. "I think you gave me a heart attack. I don't want anything to happen to you. Ever."

Katie's heart filled with warmth that Jake clearly loved her son so much.

"Me neither," Ian told his friend.

"Yeah, that wasn't funny," Miller chimed in.

Little Jake spoke again. "Cab…" he murmured. And when Caleb pulled back from Big Jake, the little version hugged him too.

"Let's leave 'em alone so they can kiss," Caleb said, and he took Little Jake's hand and led him out of the barn. Ian trotted beside them while Miller trailed behind, hobbling on his crutches.

And Katie's heart swelled with love for them all. They'd been so sweet to come and get her, to be so worried about Caleb. She didn't need to worry any longer about her son being an only child like her; he had cousins now.

Or he would have if Jake hadn't changed his mind…

He had yet to say anything, and the boys had disappeared out the open barn doors seconds ago. She turned away from those doors to focus on him. He looked like he'd been struck with one of Midnight's hooves.

"Are you okay?" she asked with concern.

He nodded. "I just…" He cleared his throat. "I knew Matt must have been a good man because that little boy is so amazing and you clearly still love him…" He cleared his throat again. "But I had no idea…"

Tears stung her eyes and she blinked them back. "He was a great guy."

"No wonder you fell for him so fast," Jake said.

She shook her head. "I didn't, you know. We were just friends for the longest time. He was really sweet to me when I was heartbroken. He was such a good friend for so long. I was lucky to have him in my life. Lucky to love him. But I didn't fall in love with him until years later, just before he proposed after we graduated from college." Then she admitted her most shameful secret, the reason she felt such guilt, "But even with as much as I loved him, I wasn't completely over you."

"Katie…" he murmured.

Her breath hitched, and she steadied it. "I didn't ever get over you, Jake." The tears threatened again as guilt overwhelmed her. "I felt so badly about that. Matt was the kindest man, but he never had my whole heart. A piece of it still belonged to you."

He touched his heart now. "You always had my whole heart, Katie. That's why I pushed you away. I didn't want you to give up anything for me."

"I would have," she admitted. "I would have given up everything."

He drew in a shaky breath and nodded. "Then I definitely did the right thing. Because if you hadn't married Matt, we wouldn't have Caleb." His voice cracked. "And I can't imagine a world without that kid in it now. I can't imagine my world without you and your son. Katie, you didn't answer me earlier. Will you let me keep that promise I made so long ago? Will you marry me?"

She didn't hesitate this time. She knew this was what everybody she loved wanted for her—even Matt. Maybe especially Matt. "Yes, Jake. I will marry you."

He released a shaky breath of relief and he pulled out the ring he must have shoved back in his pocket earlier.

Before she held out her hand to accept it, she pulled off Matt's ring. And she didn't feel even a flicker of guilt now. She felt only happiness. "I'll save these for Caleb and someday he will put them on the finger of the woman he marries."

"I think Grandma saved the diamond ring for you," he admitted as he slid the band on her finger.

"This was Sadie's?" she asked with surprise, as the ring fit her perfectly.

"Yes, she gave it to me a week ago, and I had it resized, and I redesigned it to add the opal to it. Or is that too terrible a reminder of how I hurt you?"

She shook her head. "No, not now that I know why you broke your promise. I can't believe you kept it all these years..."

"I never got over you, Katie," he admitted. "And Caleb wasn't the only one who wanted you to stay."

"No, he's not," she said with a smile. "Sadie's going to be thrilled."

He groaned. "She's going to be insufferable."

"But when she's right, she's right," she said. "You did need me, and I need you."

"I'll see if the mayor can pull some strings and get us a marriage license right away," he said. "I've already waited too long to make you my wife."

"Better late than never," she said, and she linked her arms around his neck to pull his head down for a kiss.

SOMETHING WAS GOING ON. Sadie knew it even before the little boys burst into the kitchen.

She'd felt it in the air and had seen it in Feisty's agitation. Doors had been opening and closing.

And now four little boys rushed into the kitchen, bursting with excitement.

"What's going on?" she asked the ring-leader—the little blond one who wore the biggest smile she'd ever seen on his face.

"You're going to be my grandma now," he said.

"What?" Taye asked the question before she could.

Caleb had taken Sadie's breath away with what he'd said, with the realization of her most fervent wish. She had to stop and steady herself for a moment, so she reached out and grasped the little boy's shoulders.

"What?"

"Mommy's going to marry Mr. Big Jake," he replied. "He asked me first and then he asked her…"

"And then Caleb pretended to get hit in the head by a horse," Miller said. "And Little Jake spoke…"

Sadie's head reeled with all these revelations. "What?" she said again.

"Cab," Little Jake said. "Cab…"

Tears rushed to her eyes as so many emotions overwhelmed her. Happiness and hope.

She hadn't felt them in so long. She moved her hands from Caleb's shoulders to below his arms, and she lifted him into hers, hugging him close.

Jake clearly suspected she'd been up to something when she'd brought Katie and her son to the ranch. But he had to see now that she'd had the very best of intentions…for everyone.

His brothers would come to see the same thing…once they stopped fighting it. They would realize that she was right, that she knew what was best for them.

For all of them…

"Yes," she told Caleb. "You can call me Grandma."

"Grandma," Little Jake repeated, and the tears rolled freely down her face. She shifted Caleb to one arm and reached for the littlest one. And she clasped him close to her heart.

They were all her heart—every one of these sweet boys. The little ones and the big ones.

* * * * *

If you loved A Rancher's Promise,
be sure to check out the next book in
Lisa Childs's Bachelor Cowboys series,
The Cowboy's Unlikely Match*!*

Coming soon from
Harlequin Heartwarming.

Get 4 FREE REWARDS!

We'll send you 2 FREE Books plus 2 FREE Mystery Gifts.

Love Inspired books feature uplifting stories where faith helps guide you through life's challenges and discover the promise of a new beginning.

FREE Value Over $20

YES! Please send me 2 FREE Love Inspired Romance novels and my 2 FREE mystery gifts (gifts are worth about $10 retail). After receiving them, if I don't wish to receive any more books, I can return the shipping statement marked "cancel." If I don't cancel, I will receive 6 brand-new novels every month and be billed just $5.24 each for the regular-print edition or $5.99 each for the larger-print edition in the U.S., or $5.74 each for the regular-print edition or $6.24 each for the larger-print edition in Canada. That's a savings of at least 13% off the cover price. It's quite a bargain! Shipping and handling is just 50¢ per book in the U.S. and $1.25 per book in Canada.* I understand that accepting the 2 free books and gifts places me under no obligation to buy anything. I can always return a shipment and cancel at any time. The free books and gifts are mine to keep no matter what I decide.

Choose one: ☐ **Love Inspired Romance Regular-Print** (105/305 IDN GNWC)   ☐ **Love Inspired Romance Larger-Print** (122/322 IDN GNWC)

Name (please print)

Address   Apt. #

City   State/Province   Zip/Postal Code

Email: Please check this box ☐ if you would like to receive newsletters and promotional emails from Harlequin Enterprises ULC and its affiliates. You can unsubscribe anytime.

Mail to the Harlequin Reader Service:
IN U.S.A.: P.O. Box 1341, Buffalo, NY 14240-8531
IN CANADA: P.O. Box 603, Fort Erie, Ontario L2A 5X3

Want to try 2 free books from another series! Call 1-800-873-8635 or visit www.ReaderService.com.

---

*Terms and prices subject to change without notice. Prices do not include sales taxes, which will be charged (if applicable) based on your state or country of residence. Canadian residents will be charged applicable taxes. Offer not valid in Quebec. This offer is limited to one order per household. Books received may not be as shown. Not valid for current subscribers to Love Inspired Romance books. All orders subject to approval. Credit or debit balances in a customer's account(s) may be offset by any other outstanding balance owed by or to the customer. Please allow 4 to 6 weeks for delivery. Offer available while quantities last.

Your Privacy—Your information is being collected by Harlequin Enterprises ULC, operating as Harlequin Reader Service. For a complete summary of the information we collect, how we use this information and to whom it is disclosed, please visit our privacy notice located at corporate.harlequin.com/privacy-notice. From time to time we may also exchange your personal information with reputable third parties. If you wish to opt out of this sharing of your personal information, please visit readerservice.com/consumerschoice or call 1-800-873-8635. Notice to California Residents—Under California law, you have specific rights to control and access your data. For more information on these rights and how to exercise them, visit corporate.harlequin.com/california-privacy.   LIR21R2

HARLEQUIN SELECTS COLLECTION

19 FREE BOOKS IN ALL!

From Robyn Carr to RaeAnne Thayne to Linda Lael Miller and Sherryl Woods we promise (actually, GUARANTEE!) each author in the Harlequin Selects collection has seen their name on the *New York Times* or *USA TODAY* bestseller lists!

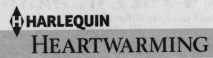
#407 HER HOMETOWN HERO
Polk Island • by Jacquelin Thomas

Trey Rothchild returns home to Polk Island a marine veteran
and an amputee. He barely recognizes the life he lives now—
and he certainly can't make room in it for old friend Gia Harris,
his beautiful physical therapist.

#408 THE SHERIFF'S VALENTINE
Stop the Wedding! • by Amy Vastine

Nothing can tear Sheriff Ben Harper away from his duties.
Except perhaps thrill-seeking Shelby Young, who rolls back into
town before his brother's wedding—bringing all kinds of trouble
in her wake!

#409 MONTANA REUNION
by Jen Gilroy

When Beth Flanagan becomes guardian to her late friend's
daughter, she heads back to the Montana camp where she
spent her summers. Her teenage crush is now the rancher next
door—a complication or a blessing in disguise?

#410 HOME FOR THE HOLIDAYS
Return to Christmas Island • by Amie Denman

Camille Peterson can handle running her family's candy
business—she can't handle running into her ex and his
adorable son. Maddox betrayed her years ago...but idyllic
Christmas Island might just weave the magic of a second
chance.

HWCNM0122A

Visit
ReaderService.com
Today!

As a valued member of the Harlequin Reader Service, you'll find these benefits and more at ReaderService.com:

- Try 2 free books from any series
- Access risk-free special offers
- View your account history & manage payments
- Browse the latest Bonus Bucks catalog

Don't miss out!

If you want to stay up-to-date on the latest at the Harlequin Reader Service and enjoy more content, make sure you've signed up for our monthly News & Notes email newsletter. Sign up online at ReaderService.com or by calling Customer Service at 1-800-873-8635.